LEGACY OF
LIGHT
AND
SHADOW

RYAN KIRK

OLIVERHEBERBOOKS

Cover design by Covers by JV Arts

Published by Oliver-Heber Books

0 9 8 7 6 5 4 3 2 1

The emissary held tightly to the void as he appeared on the surface of the world that had caused his master so much suffering. Spheres of perfect darkness surrounded him, ready to be unleashed at the first sign of trouble, the first hint of resistance against the world's rightful rulers.

He sighed when none of the world's rebels greeted his arrival.

He'd been expecting a fight. Hoping for one, really. How long had it been since he'd fought an opponent that had the slightest chance of defeating him? He searched his memories, but to find an answer to that question, he would have had to go to a time before, an era long lost to the passage of countless years, a time when he had been a mere mortal.

He was often surprised that he still remembered those days as well as he did. Before his ascension to emissary, if a stranger had asked, he would have guessed his most recent memories would always hold sway, that time would have erased his past like a rising tide sweeping a sandy beach of footprints. Instead, it was his yesterdays he struggled to remember, whereas his distant past lived on, as vivid in his memories now as they had been two hundred years ago.

Before his ascension, he would have been disappointed to learn the truth of his future memories. He'd been shaped by a lifetime of war, and though he'd been gifted at it, the gift carried a steep price. He dreamed only in nightmares, forced to lose those he'd loved every time he closed his eyes. Wine and women kept the darkness at bay for a time, but eventually even they had failed him.

His fame had risen as his bitterness grew. In a world of constant warfare, those who were best at killing were elevated. He'd been told to lead, and to teach others how to kill. In the eyes of his followers, there was a number, never defined, but believed in with the same belief that they looked to the sun rising in the east every morning, that if they killed, they would finally have peace. Sometimes, a general would claim the number was just one more, that if an enemy leader was to fall, the war would be over for good. Sometimes the number was a few dozen, an elite enemy unit that had harassed his own warriors to no end. Most often, though, the number was much larger. A city, a nation, or sometimes even a people.

When he'd first developed his theory about the number, he'd called his followers fools to their faces. Killing could bring peace for a time, and in their brutal world it was often necessary for survival, but the only harvest that grew out of fields fertilized with blood was revenge.

After enough years, though, he started to wonder if his followers weren't on to something. They weren't right, of course, but perhaps they pointed in the right direction. What made them wrong wasn't that they believed enough killing would bring them peace. They were wrong because they never realized how many actually needed to die.

Once the thought first entered his mind, there was no pulling it out again.

If everyone died, then he'd finally have his peace.

That was when he discovered Void, sitting there as though it had always been waiting for him, waiting to see if he was ready to wield the power it offered. It promised him peace and a respite from his memories turned nightmares.

Now that he understood his master better, he understood he hadn't been wrong in thinking that Void had been waiting for him. It had a way of always being where it was needed when it was most needed. It *had* been waiting for him, recognizing a disciple on sight.

He'd embraced the power, almost without question, and why wouldn't he? He rose through the ranks and passed through the rite which made him an emissary, and he had his peace, destroying the world that had caused him so much suffering with little more than a thought. His nightmares faded, and no new ones replaced them, as there was no one left for him to love. He'd wiped the world clean, and in so doing, ended his troubles.

Which led to the question that troubled him today. Why didn't his master simply destroy this world and be done with it? These rebels had already caused Void to lose more servants than any other world in recent memory, and the loss was all the worse because it came at the hands of such a weak people.

He understood the reasons the previous emissary had given. The red hearts were, without doubt, the greatest source of strength their master had found in decades. He didn't need to be a strategic wonder to see the potential. Back when he'd been a general, more of his victories came from his ability to feed his warriors over vast distances than any martial skill he might have possessed. Today he fought on a battlefield far more vast, harnessing powers he'd only fantasized about as a young man. And yet Void needed sustenance, the same as the warriors he'd once commanded across the plains of his home world. The red hearts provided that sustenance, the same way the wheat of his home world had fed his own troops so many years ago.

As a matter of fact, this world reminded him of his homeland. Adani was what they called light here, and he sensed it running beneath his feet, a rich web that the humans here had only developed since learning more about the power that they'd taken for granted for so long. He breathed in deep, the smell of grass reminding him of the long hours he'd spent on his horse as a boy. He held out his hand and let the stalks waving in the breeze brush across his palm.

This was an old world with a young people, courtesy of the dragons that had so long held them back. A unique situation, and not one found often across the many worlds he'd spread his master's message of peace.

It was a world that could sustain Void. A world that could, possibly, turn the tide of the endless war. Master clearly believed as much, because otherwise these grasslands would be as dead as the emissary that had last called this world his. Was it worth the risk, though? These humans were young, but clever, and at least one had ascended to the point where they were a threat even to emissaries. Another feat rarely accomplished across the worlds.

The world that might turn the war in their favor might very well be the one that doomed them. It was a deadly spear, thrown high into the midst of a battlefield, where it was equally likely to strike either the allied or enemy commanders.

The emissary shook his head. No, this world was not worth the risk it posed. It would be better if the people were simply eliminated, and the world wiped clean. Unfortunately, the decision was not his to make.

He had been chosen by the master and given specific orders, the first of which was to resume the harvesting of the red hearts. It wouldn't be an easy task, now that the humans had experienced the sweet taste of a rebellious, victorious strike. He would need servants, but how many?

He extended his awareness through the world, surprised at just how strongly adani flowed through this planet. For all the conflict the world had seen in the past hundred years, he would have expected something weaker, but it was strong. He sensed the wandering clans, burning bright even against the bright back-drop of adani, as well as the cities, which shone with a wider, more diffuse light. The gardens his predecessor had begun still existed, the ability to repair them probably still beyond the healers of this world. That, at least, was a good sign.

He didn't sense the ascended one, which was a complication he hadn't expected. His predecessor had said nothing about the humans being able to travel between the worlds, but it was possible light had finally realized what a treasure it had in this world and had sought to contact them directly.

He searched the world with his senses again, more carefully this time, like a concerned parent running a comb through their child's hair to look for ticks. He sensed not just the clans and the cities, but the individual adanists wandering through the land. The dragons, too, stood out as beacons, and he figured that for his answer. If the ascended one rode atop a dragon, disconnected from the web of adani that ran through the land, the emissary wouldn't be able to sense him.

The emissary looked to the cloudless sky as his heart beat with sudden fervor, but its deep blue was unbroken by any approaching shadows. The ascended one may be on a dragon, and he may even be approaching, but he wasn't close. By the time he arrived, if he arrived at all, the emissary would be ready.

He wasn't sure why the ascended one would travel by dragon when he could appear anywhere at a thought, but there was still much the emissary didn't know. Was the ascended one even aware of the full extent of his powers? What little the emissaries knew came from the survivor, the traitor the master welcomed with open arms, and she hadn't seen most of the battle. As the first and only transformed, it seemed likely he wouldn't know his full strength.

The emissary wouldn't underestimate the humans, though. His predecessor had made that mistake and was no more.

He kept one eye on the sky as he turned his focus once more

to the world. How many servants would he need? Master had promised as many, within reason, as he desired, and he feared they would be needed. The wandering clans couldn't launch another surprise attack. That tragedy could only have happened once, when the overconfident emissaries and their servants believed themselves untouchable.

Even so, the wandering clans had proven they didn't intend to accept the peace the emissaries offered, and their taste of success would make them even more unmanageable. If he hit them hard to start, diminished their numbers and broke apart their precious clans, then maybe he could establish a tenuous peace. He'd used the strategy when he'd been a mere mortal, and it had worked well. Constant vigilance would be required after, but that was acceptable, given the benefits of occupation. Never again would this world know a day without an emissary.

So busy was he with his preparations, he didn't notice he had company until the man stood beside him. He was tall and broad-shouldered, with long hair that hung loosely down to his shoulders. The invader stood like he'd been there all day keeping the emissary company.

There was only one being on the planet that could have appeared so suddenly, and the golden light shining behind his eyes was even more unnecessary proof. The emissary turned, only to find that he couldn't. He looked down and was surprised to find a pair of bound, golden swords piercing his torso and holding him in place. The swords moved and cut through his core, and all his power slipped from his fingers like water.

His death was unexpected, but the real surprise was his absolute lack of desire to struggle. All living beings fought to stay alive, but he found he had no interest. He didn't attempt one last attack, nor did he snarl and spit at his murderer.

Perhaps it wasn't even murder. If he wasn't fighting to stay alive, maybe he had already been dead, and you can't murder what's already dead.

He missed the thrills of his earliest years, when he'd risked everything to see the next sunrise. When had he gone wrong? When he'd started to prize peace over the chaos of daily living?

He didn't know and would never know.

He said a silent thanks to the ascended one, who'd freed him from a burden he hadn't even realized he'd been carrying, and then there was only the true peace that nature provided, an endless rest at the end of one's labors.

BAEL WATCHED the emissary as its body dissipated into shadow and vanished, leaving no trace that it had ever threatened his world.

"You're not welcome here," he said, as though someone, or something, might be listening.

Then he, too, vanished, to return to the Great Heart of adani from whence he'd come, and to prepare for the war that was coming.

2

Elyn hadn't been conscious when the emissary, *her emissary*, had died, and so she didn't know how Void had reacted to the loss. Those who served Void, who had given their spirits and their futures to its keeping, were connected across vast distances, more parts of a whole than separate beings. The loss of any, even a mere servant, was a loss felt by all. When Bael and Father had launched the attack that killed so many servants, Elyn had sensed it as clearly as though she'd been standing beside the victims.

Today she learned how Void reacted to the loss of another one of its emissaries. She sat alone in her cave, barely more than a crack in a mountain upon a desolate world, warding off loneliness and any questions about her future by listening to Void. If she listened for long enough, she might even find the answers to questions she was too scared to ask herself.

Instead, the emptiness between the stars thrummed and screamed, like a string instrument plucked loudly by an angry child. It was the same as when the servants had been lost, only multiplied over and over again. She recoiled from the sound and almost disconnected completely, but the thought of another long, empty day alone in her cave held her in place. Instead of retreating from the sound, she traced it to its origin, and found, to her horror but not to her surprise, that it had come from the world of her birth.

Bael, she was certain, had struck again. No one else was capable.

It would have been easy to hate Bael for that, because every attack against the emissaries did nothing but doom their planet further, but hate was too strong an emotion for her spirit to hold. The fight for the world of her birth had left her feeling hollow and thin, as though her skin might shred in a strong breeze. She'd barely eaten anything since her return, which was just as well, as no one had come to deliver her food. Maybe they never would. Maybe the punishment for her failure to protect her master wasn't to perish at the hands of the wandering clans, but to suffer here alone until she died. She cursed Bael, but there was no strength behind her curse, her voice barely more than a whisper.

She didn't want to think about Bael, the wandering clans, or her failure, and so she broke apart from Void, finding herself alone in the cave, the fire flickering low. She brought her knees to her chest and wrapped her arms around them, thinking of nothing and everything.

Time here was as much a mystery as her future. Day and night didn't exist here, leaving instead a permanent dusk that brightened and dimmed in a pattern she'd never been able to discern. Hours might have passed, or maybe the better part of a day. She sipped sparingly from a half-empty water skin, more from habit than from thirst. Food held no appeal, nor did movement.

She wasn't so disconnected that she missed the arrival, though. Her visitor was an emissary, that much being obvious from the lack of a portal and the awesome sense of the void that spread through Elyn's body like an autumn chill. This emissary's strength was much greater than her emissary's had been, enough that Elyn was halfway convinced that if the emissary so wished it, they could destroy this world.

The figure who stepped into the cave took the form of a young woman with long hair as dark as a moonless night. She'd visited once before, when her own emissary had been summoned before Void for judgment. Elyn hadn't liked her then and the feeling had only grown stronger since. Even though she knew emissaries could take whatever form they chose, the mismatch between what her eyes told her and what her other senses revealed left her uneasy.

Too late, she realized she was staring, and she came to her senses and shifted to her knees so she could bow, pressing her forehead all the way to the cold stone floor of her cave. She welcomed the chill, belatedly realizing she'd started to sweat in the emissary's presence.

"Rise, child," the young woman said, her voice surprisingly soft.

Once again, the distance between what her physical senses reported and the void she felt unsettled her, made her doubt what was real. She rose as commanded and allowed herself a full look at her visitor.

Old eyes watched her from behind a young visage, as still as a pond on a windless day. Her irises were ringed in black, but her skin was nearly as pale as bleached bones.

"How may I serve?" Elyn asked.

"The very question I've been sent to ask you, as it so happens."

Elyn noted the word choice. Other emissaries had visited before, but always of their own volition. Only their shared master had the ability to order them about, and given her strength, Elyn wondered how close to Void she was. If she had to guess, it was close. Closer than the emissary who'd recruited her, at least.

Her mind raced for an answer, but settled on nothing. She was only a servant, and a failed one at that. What could she do? She hadn't even been able to protect her emissary when he needed her most. Lacking anything specific, she settled instead for the general. "I would be honored to help in any way that I can."

A look of disgust flickered across the young woman's face, so quickly Elyn wasn't sure she hadn't imagined it. Then her gaze went distant. When she spoke again, her voice was deep, throaty, and raw, as though the words were being scraped from her throat. "Kneel."

Elyn instinctively obeyed. As she pressed her forehead once again to the stone, she understood. Void filled her cave, not emanating from the emissary, but from everywhere at once. She'd only ever felt this power from a distance, only dared to brush against it in her own explorations. This close, it felt as though the weight of an entire world held her down.

And yet, at the same time, some part of her understood that what she sensed was only a part, a small fraction of this inde-scribable force. Like a spider with a hundred eyes, it only focused one on her, but she trembled before it all the same. She tried to speak, but words couldn't escape her throat, and what was the point? Void was already a part of her, and she a part of it. It knew her more intimately than any of her family ever had.

Void invaded her memories and picked them apart; from the moment she and the emissary had set foot on the world until the moment she'd formed a portal and asked to be taken home. She relived her assault on her father, and if there was something inside of her that churned at the sight, she pushed it as far down as it would go.

The young woman spoke with the voice of an ancient. "Why did you not simply kill him?"

Sweat beaded from Elyn's forehead. She would have been grateful that she pressed her face to the ground, if not for the certainty Void didn't need to see her face to accurately judge the state of her spirit.

Half a dozen lies came to mind, but she dismissed them all. Void already knew, the question was only asked to see if she understood herself well enough to answer truthfully. "He didn't deserve to die. I only wanted him to be punished for what he did to me."

The emissary spoke in what Elyn considered her "normal" voice, that of a young woman. "She isn't ready."

The emissary's words weren't to Elyn, but there was no need to speak to Void, and so the emissary intended for Elyn to hear her.

Void's presence within the cave moved about, the pressure of its existence sometimes stronger and sometimes weaker, but such terms were relative, as it always felt like she was being crushed. Its movements carried meaning, but Elyn wasn't versed enough in the mysteries of the void to decipher those meanings.

The emissary's voice became ancient again as she became the mouthpiece of Void. "You will continue to serve," she said.

Then the presence was gone, leaving only Elyn and the emissary within the walls of the cave. Elyn sucked in a deep breath, filling her lungs completely for what felt like the first time in half a day.

"Rise, child," the emissary commanded, in her own voice.

Elyn did, her knees feeling old, like they had back when she'd worked such long hours on her farm. She met the emissary's cold gaze, devoid of any of the sympathy she'd come to expect from her previous master.

"I don't know if recruiting you from that world was a work of inspired genius or sheer idiocy. There is no doubt you have the ability to become an emissary someday, but your spirit is weak, and you misunderstand Master's purpose. Our strength is not for judgment, but for destruction."

Elyn's knees trembled, and she almost reached out to the cave wall to steady herself. She kept herself upright, though it was more stubborn pride than any strength of will.

The emissary continued driving her verbal knives into Elyn's spirit. "The only reason your world remains is because those red hearts may give our master the strength necessary to carry its work to its conclusion, at which point, it will be destroyed like any other. Do you understand? There is no judgment, no weighing of worthiness. If our master is successful, our last service will be to end ourselves. That is how complete our mission must be."

"I understand."

"You are to return to the world of your birth. We've lost our eyes and ears on the world. You are to observe and disrupt the wandering clans. Destroy as much as you can. You are to have unlimited use of portals across the world as you see fit. In time, one or more emissaries will arrive with their servants, at which time you will report to them for further orders."

Elyn bowed. "Yes, ma'am."

"You are an intelligent woman. You understand, of course, the consequences of your failure?"

"Yes, ma'am." She put her life on the line with her service, and very possibly the future of her world.

"Then there is no more to be said. The next time we meet, it will be either because you are ready to learn more of the mysteries, or because our master has found your weakness of spirit irredeemable."

The young woman's form melted into shadow and vanished, leaving Elyn well and alone, her fate determined.

Elyn sat with the emissary's final words for some time. They were like a persistent flame, burning through layers of her spirit to reach whatever she'd buried deep within. The only way to quench the flame was to stop giving it attention, and so she looked around her cave to consider what she should pack for her return, but there was nothing.

The void waited for her and there would be no more putting it off. Fortunately, obedience meant freedom from doubts, and so she stepped out of her cave without a look back and created a portal. The void connected her with the world of her birth, and she walked through the portal to whatever future awaited her.

3

For as long as Elian had been alive, he'd always looked forward to the dawning of the new day. In good times, the new day was an opportunity to explore the world and learn its ways, to get stronger, and to celebrate with the family and friends that made the world as special as it was. In bad times, a new day was a new start, a new opportunity to make a difference in the lives of those he cared most about.

Elyn had taken that joy away. His own daughter, with her violence and her hate, had stripped something from him he didn't realize it had even been possible to take.

The sun had already risen and started cooking the inside of the tent, making him feel as though he was a piece of old meat tossed into a stew to slowly boil. The inside of his mouth felt dry and parched, but water would do no good. Ever since Elyn had punched a hole through his jaw with void, he'd suffered. Samora healed the area again and again, pouring enough adani into it to fill a dragon to bursting, but nothing returned it to the way it had been.

Much like his leg and his stomach. Healed as well as Samora could, but she'd found her limit just as he'd found his.

Elian groaned and threw the covers from the bed, regretting the sudden movement a moment later. He cursed through gritted teeth as needles of pain shot from his side and up his back. He breathed in and out and willed his muscles to relax. Before, he would have simply filled his body with adani, but that option brought only pain now.

In time, the pain eased, but Elian remained uninspired. The sounds of the camp already busy with the chores and training of the day filtered through the thick canvas of the tent, but Elian had no desire to observe any of it. Bael had invited him to take part in any way he could, and Elian had thanked him, but hadn't yet taken him up on the offer. Maybe he never would.

He stared up at the ceiling of the tent, even when he heard the commotion near the center of the camp. The thudding impacts of training faded, as did the chatter of the families as they performed their daily chores. No instructors shouted at their students.

He cared less about what was happening in the camp than he did about answering what had happened with Elyn. Even now, he couldn't find it in his heart to hate her. She was his daughter, and more precious to him than any heart.

He knew she'd been hurt by her failed ascension, hurt in ways that he'd never fully understand. If she'd stayed among the clans, he would have helped her find a path forward, no matter how long it took. Instead, she'd left, and that had been a cut that sliced him deep. It wasn't just that she'd left him, it was that she'd left her family, left everything that he, Capricia, Samora, and so many more had built. He'd tried to understand, promised that he would give her the space she demanded, certain that with enough time she'd eventually return.

Eighthdays had turned into months, and months into seasons, and seasons into years, and though it was clear to his reasoning mind that she wasn't coming back, he refused to believe. And yet, at the same time, he'd gotten used to having her gone. As much as he wanted her back, he grew more comfortable with the hole she'd left in his spirit.

Was that why she was so mad at him?

Maybe, but that didn't sit right with him. That didn't explain what she had done to him, nor the emotion which had pushed her to it. Capricia believed that Elyn had been under the influence of Void, which was certainly true, but that didn't seem like enough, either.

He had no answers. Strange, but even though she was the one who had put him here, he would have given almost anything for her to be in his tent right now. Anything to know what had twisted her against him so.

A cheer from the center of the camp broke his wandering thoughts, and he wondered what news could evoke such joy. The entire camp labored under the knowledge that their war was far from over, and that the next series of battles might be the ones that ended humanity for good. The daily commotion of the camp returned even louder than before, people's excitement leaking through their muffled conversations.

The tent flap opened without warning, letting in the late morning sun. He winced from the sudden brightness and tears streamed from the corners of his eyes. A familiar shadow was silhouetted in the light. "I wasn't sure you'd even be up," Capricia said.

From anyone else, Elian would have expected a hint of bitterness, but from his wife of so many years, there was none. She was a far better woman than he deserved, and that knowledge ate at him the same way the mystery of Elyn's hate did.

He forced a smile onto his face, not to fool her, but to let her know he was trying. "It wasn't that long ago that I woke up. What happened?"

She came into the tent, kicking off her boots with an ease that sparked a hint of jealousy. For as long as they'd been together, he'd prided himself on being the one who could protect her. Now he relied on her for next to everything. It was a burden she shouldn't have to bear.

Capricia squatted down beside him. "Bael returned after vanishing mysteriously this morning. Samora tracked him into the core of the world, then lost him. But we had an emissary appear."

The words twisted Elian's stomach, but he understood the cheer better. "He killed it?"

"Decisively. In one move, though he credits luck more than skill. The emissary couldn't sense him when he was hiding within the Great Heart, and he struck when the emissary was distracted."

"Not something that will work again, then."

"Probably not. He'll still be able to hide, but they'll be more careful next time."

"So, a victory, but not one that will matter."

A shadow crossed Capricia's face, and Elian feared he'd unleashed a storm in the confines of his tent, but she breathed out her frustrations and closed her eyes. She slowly and deliberately breathed in and out once again, and when her eyes opened Elian saw nothing but care.

The lack of censure was worse than if she'd yelled at him. He didn't deserve this patience, this grace. It did nothing but make him feel worse about himself.

Capricia's care didn't take the form of permissiveness, though. "Time to get up," she said, an implied promise lurking behind her words.

"Why?"

"You've had enough time to lay around in the tent feeling sorry for yourself. It's time you get back on your feet."

He almost argued, almost made the claim that he'd been on his feet plenty the last few days. Contrary to her implication, he spent most of the previous day up, hadn't he? Now that he thought about it, he wasn't so sure. It felt like he had, but his memory wasn't as sharp as it had been. Regardless, the glare Capricia gave him served as warning enough. Often, he'd discovered, true wisdom could be found in silence.

He worked his way to his feet, first by bracing his body with a hand, then placing one foot carefully. He pushed off both his good limbs, then placed his other foot flat. Pain, his now-constant companion, flared in his calf, but he gritted his teeth and breathed deep through his nose. Once the pain had faded to an ache, he stood up straight, a motion that sent another wave of needles down his spine, but then he was standing, and standing wasn't too bad.

Capricia watched, unable to hide her concern, but she made no move to help. Not because she didn't want to, and not because she wouldn't have been useful, but because Elian refused it. He had to be able to stand on his own. On that, there would be no compromise.

Once he was certain of his feet, he looked to his wife and asked, "Where to?"

Her answering smile was mysterious and melted more than forty years from her face. He was reminded of when they'd been younger, and she'd been the one dragging him farther into the wilderness than he'd ever intended to go. At that look, it didn't matter how much suffering the journey was going to cause. He'd follow her wherever she led and thank her later.

She offered him the walking stick propped up near the entrance of the tent, and he snatched it from her. She wouldn't offer without reason, so it was best to swallow what little of his pride remained and accept. They left the tent and stepped into the bright light of day. Elian blinked, shielded his eyes with his free hand, and waited for his eyes to adjust.

Once they did, he took a look around the camp, expecting curious stares. Instead, his departure earned only a handful of quick glances up from whatever work was ongoing. Then gazes and attention fell back to the work.

He grunted softly to himself. "I'm not sure if it's worse being an object of constant speculation or if it's worse to be ignored."

"It's probably the worst if you're worried about what they think of you at all," Capricia answered.

Her words landed like a slap across the face, and Elian winced. It only stung because she had the right of it, though. Still, what else was he supposed to do? He was stuck near his tent most days with nothing to accomplish but to sit and think. It was only natural, given everything that had happened to him, that he would wonder what others thought of him.

Capricia led him outside the camp and headed north. Bael had parked them in the foothills of the great mountain range that ran close to the western edge of the continent, and Capricia's trail led them up a moderate hillside. A month ago Elian would have bounded up the hillside and stared out over whatever vistas it offered, but today he stumbled forward slowly, more reliant on his walking stick than he cared to admit.

If their slow pace bothered Capricia at all, it didn't show on her face. When he snuck a glance at her, he saw no discontent at all. There was a slight hint of a smile on her face, and he swore she radiated an inner light that wasn't just his sense of her adani. "You're enjoying this, aren't you?" he asked.

Her smile fell, but only for a moment, and she looked like she was about to use the question to leap into a long monologue, but then her smile returned. "I am."

She didn't need to speak for Elian to know what she was going to say. They'd been bonded long enough now that they'd developed an understanding that was far richer than mere language. Even Elian's bond with Samora, which provided a window into her thoughts, lacked this intimacy. He'd sometimes wondered at that. He suspected it had to do with the fact he didn't need to see into Capricia's thoughts the way he did Samora's. His understanding of his wife went deeper, was written in the marrow of his bones. Today, she wanted to ask why he *wasn't* enjoying the walk.

He gripped his walking stick tight enough that his knuckles turned white. How could she even think about asking him such a question? Day in and day out his life was nothing but various blends of pain. It wasn't even that the pain was often that sharp. While moving could sometimes hurt enough to bring a tear to his eye, at any given moment, it was little more than an annoyance. But it never faded. It was always there, nibbling at the edges of his awareness, never leaving him alone. Even now, his jaw ached as though he'd been punched earlier this morning, and his calf complained every time he didn't place his foot just so. Of course he wasn't enjoying himself, and if it wasn't for her, he wouldn't be hurting as bad as he was!

Before he could spew the bile that collected in his thoughts, they reached the summit of the hill and were greeted by a warm breeze from the south. A small group of songbirds twittered as they were disturbed by the new arrivals, and they took off from a row of bushes, their wings catching the southern breeze and sending them spinning and twirling away from the couple. The sight tugged the corners of his lips up into a smile, which was followed a moment later by another understanding.

He should be enjoying himself. Walking alone with Capricia had always been one of his favorite activities, and had always been precious. Between the demands of raising children and leading the clans, time alone was difficult to come by, and when such opportunities had arisen, this was what they'd always done. It didn't matter how far adani took them, any high place was worth exploring.

He stopped shuffling forward and forced himself to stand straight. His broken body complained, but only for a moment, and then he was fine. He closed his eyes and let the breeze play with his hair, which had gotten too long the last month and needed a cut. He reached out for Capricia's hand, and it was warm in his own. His fingers traced the callouses on her palm, a reflection of the ones he carried. He breathed in deep, then let the air out slowly.

"I'm sorry, and thank you," he said.

She squeezed his hand. "Come on."

He'd thought the hike was all she'd planned, but as they crested the hill and started wandering down the other side, he saw a collection of children from the clan had gathered. When Bael had first sent out his invitation for warriors, they'd come without their children, but now that it had become apparent that Bael's gathering of warriors would be a new wandering clan, unwelcome back among their home clans, the children had come in droves.

"What's this?" Elian asked.

There was a hint of mischievousness in Capricia's answering grin. "Training. I promised them that if they came, you'd teach them some of your techniques."

Once more he gripped his walking stick, and he gritted his teeth together to stop from lashing out at her. A dozen objections sprang to mind, and had it been anyone other than Capricia, he would have unleashed a tirade that would have caused the mountains to tremble.

But it was Capricia, and he'd never been able to deny her. They'd argue tonight, but he was already out here, and the eagerness in the children's eyes couldn't be poisoned by his bitterness. He nodded once, sharply, and reminded her with a glare that their argument was far from over. His stare did nothing to wipe the self-satisfied grin from her face, though, and in the end, he turned his back on her so he could give his full attention to the gathered children.

They were conveniently gathered next to a stone with a relatively smooth, flat top, and Elian walked over and sat down. "I hear you're interested in some training."

The response was enthusiastic, and Elian had them stand in

lines, then begin cycling their adani. As befitted the children of ascended warriors, adani ran strongly through their bodies, but their skill in wielding it varied widely. He had Capricia stand before the group, leading them through a series of punches and kicks. More weaknesses became apparent, and the children soon started to struggle. Some responded by trying less, while others plowed through with reckless abandon, making up for a lack of coordination with an abundance of volume.

Elian snorted softly to himself. The problem was hardly a new one among the wandering clans, and had only grown worse as their ability with adani had grown. Though few would express the sentiment so baldly, most warriors had stopped seeing the point of training the body's fighting skills. Why bother, when one could form shields to defend and throw darts powerful enough to bring down dragons?

Fortunately, Elian was no stranger to addressing the problem. He'd done it for this generation's parents and could do it again. He gathered them close so he wouldn't have to shout. "Did you know that when I was young, I couldn't use adani to form spears or shields?"

Most of the children, and particularly the older ones, were aware, having heard the stories often enough around the campfires. Some of the younger ones looked at him as though he were a monster. Everyone in their lives could form a spear.

"It's true. But I knew I wanted to fight, so I had no choice but to learn how to use adani in my body. In time, that was how I discovered the secret to ascending. I assume most of you want to ascend?"

Every head in the group nodded, and Elian was reminded of Elyn, who'd once answered the question just as these children did. The thought closed his throat, and for a moment, he couldn't speak. He swallowed hard and took a sip of water while he composed himself. "That's good. But it means we'll need to work on how we use adani within our bodies, so that's what we'll do today."

A boy who appeared to be about seven said, "But it's so much harder than forming a spear."

"Perhaps. But almost everything that's good is on the other side of a struggle. If you work with me, just for today, you'll see how strong you can be. Can you give me one day?"

The boy nodded, and they began. Elian and Capricia had run training sessions like these time and time again, and they fell into familiar rhythms, adapted to Elian's limited abilities. Capricia worked the group while Elian observed, pulling one child and then another out and offering them a personalized suggestion. In a group this close, he could sense the adani moving through their limbs. Some students just needed a small nudge. Others needed an example, and he looped adani through his good arm so they could sense what success would feel like.

By the end of the day, they'd all improved, and many of them considerably. They ended with a group exercise not that different from the one they'd started with, and Elian grinned at the wide eyes as their jumps took them higher and their robes snapped as they delivered their punches. The students returned to the camp as a group so they'd be back in time for supper.

Elian and Capricia remained and watched them go. "They're all so gifted," Elian observed. "I would have given next to everything to possess a fraction of their natural ability. They'll surpass us someday soon."

"As children should," Capricia said.

She didn't say anything else, but she didn't need to. Elian sighed dramatically. "You were right."

She was humble in her victory, answering with only a smile.

"I'm still not sure what I should do, though. Training a group of inexperienced children is one thing, but I won't even be able to do that for long. I can't demonstrate any advanced techniques, which a few of them will need soon."

"I don't know what you should do, either, but you need to *do* something, even if it's just stumbling about, trying new things while you look for an answer. Bael needs you. I get the sense that he has ideas and notions, but he's never led a clan, and that lack of experience will destroy us. You couldn't have led the Bears without help back then, either."

Elian held up his hands in surrender. "I'll try. It won't be easy, but I'll try."

"You were the one who was just saying that everything good is on the other side of struggle."

Elian shook his head, but surrendered the point. He squeezed Capricia's hand. "And thank you," he said.

"You're welcome. I'll remind you again, if you forget."

"I'm sure you will."

They stood from the rock and made their way back to the summit of the hill, where they could watch the sun slowly fall toward the horizon, the hills casting the camp below in early shadows.

4

Adani surged through Samora as she laid down the bundle of wood she'd carried from the grove north of the camp. It started in her core, where the heart she'd ascended with felt as though it had lit on fire. She ground her teeth together as she let out a silent groan. Her family was close by, and she would rather take an arrow to the knee than let them see her suffering. They worried too much about her as it was.

Adani wasn't content with her core, though, and despite her frantic efforts to contain it, it sped through her limbs, granting her the strength and speed to fight a wolf and the endurance to outrun a horse. Normally she would have welcomed adani into her body, but she was all too familiar with the suffering she would endure tonight as a result. Still, the suffering was better than the alternative, which was closing in more rapidly than she thought possible.

Experience had taught her not to fight the surge, for it would only last longer if it encountered resistance. She let it flow through her body, and in time, it disappeared, returning to the heart which was the source of the problem. She imagined adani lying in wait, hidden by the mysteries of the heart, ready to pounce the moment she gave it the opportunity. Soon there'd be nothing she could do to stop it.

As was her practice after all such attacks, she closed herself off from the heart, severing the new connections the surge of adani had stitched throughout her body. She felt the blood draining from her face as she worked, and her knees came close to buckling, but they held her weight long enough for her to finish. Once it was done, she searched her body for any wayward adani and found little. She couldn't ever cut herself completely off. Life and adani were inextricably linked, and to push it entirely away was to commit suicide.

She turned and came face to face with her husband, Aldrick, who'd approached during the attack. He took one look at her face and knew. Instead of commenting, he offered her his arm, which she was more than happy to take. He led her in the direction of their tent.

"I was meaning to help with the cooking," she said.

"Let Kerina take charge tonight. She's been wanting to show off a new dish she learned."

"I love my granddaughter, but not so much I'm willing to risk tonight's meal like the last one."

Aldrick chuckled. "It was only the once, and if we don't make mistakes, there's no way for us to learn. She'll be fine."

Samora wasn't so sure. The last time Kerina had cooked alone for the family it had taken days for the taste to flee from Samora's tongue. She didn't have the strength to argue, though, and she let herself be guided to the tent. Aldrick held the flap open for her and she stepped in. As soon as the flap closed behind her, she felt some of the weight lift from her shoulders. Here, in the space that only she and Aldrick shared, there was no need to be anything more than what she was.

She slumped over and lay on their bed, positioned near the center of the small tent. Back when they'd been raising all their children, they'd had a much larger tent, filled with small toys, chests of clothes, and bedding for all. They'd kept the tent for a while even after the last of their children had bonded and started their own families, then had decided they didn't want to travel with so much. They'd given the tent to one of the younger families who'd just birthed twins and accepted in return this one, barely large enough for the two of them. They shared one small chest of clothes between them, and Samora also had a cabinet filled with healing herbs she'd collected over the course of her travels. She'd joked once, maybe an eighthday or so ago, that at least when she died Aldrick wouldn't have to worry about getting rid of too many possessions, but he'd been in no mood for the humor, and so she'd let the matter drop. Even so, she was glad they'd deliberately chosen to travel lightly these past years. It had made much of their lives easier, and it was one less problem to worry about as the end neared.

Aldrick lay down beside her, and she turned over onto her side and wiggled closer to him. She rested her head on his shoulder, still strong even as he entered his twilight years.

The thought of not having him around struck with unexpected force, and she felt the tears welling up in the corners of her eyes. She wiped it off and flung it away, but she had no doubt Aldrick had noticed.

"Care to share?" he asked.

"Thinking about what life would be like without you."

He wrapped his arms around her and held her tightly. Neither of them was a stranger to death, especially now. Most everyone they'd grown up with had either passed away or was on the verge of dying, and though Samora knew their adani had returned to the world, she missed them still. Grief was a familiar companion, but whenever she contemplated her inevitable separation from Aldrick, it struck with unfamiliar force, as though it had ascended and become something more.

He sought her hand with his own and their fingers inter-twined. "I'll miss you, too, you know."

"I know."

They lay together for a time, their breaths coming as one, and slowly the strength returned to Samora's body. Her avoidance of adani meant slow recovery, but it kept her as she was, and that had to be enough. She had to hold on for just a while longer, but the end was inevitable. She'd seen it once already with Bael, and now she'd taken the first step on the same journey.

The next time adani struck, it was at least kind enough to give her some warning. Even though she was disconnected from the heart in her core, she felt it growing warm, the power within it no longer content with being contained. She swore softly, but of course Aldrick heard her. His body tensed and he propped himself up on one elbow. "What is it?"

"Another attack."

"So soon?"

She had no better answer for him. Suffering two attacks in a single day was rare, but suffering two attacks in the same evening was unheard of. All she had time to do was nod, though, before adani once more burst free of the impromptu cage she'd used to contain it.

Thanks to the warning, she had all her senses trained on the heart when adani began its escape. Its first moves were subtle, so slight she didn't think she would have noticed them if she wasn't paying attention. It extended small tendrils of power, thin threads that snuck from the heart like worms coming to the surface after a summer rain. Once they'd reached past the barrier she'd built, slipping through the cracks like water, they hooked themselves into her body's adani channels. Even the hooks were gentle, but the result was anything but.

The heart shoved an enormous amount of adani, all at once, into all the small threads. Since they'd already found the cracks in her defense, the flood of adani encountered little resistance. Like using a lever to lift a stone, adani simply shoved aside her defenses and rushed to fill the emptiness in her channels.

For the briefest of moments, all was well. Even though she fought against adani, her body welcomed the energy. It had been a significant part of her life since she was a child, and she'd spent almost every day of her life training her body to welcome more of it. Only now did she attempt to deny it, and her body suffered as a result. It filled her limbs with strength, allowed her to breathe more easily, and sped her thoughts until she felt as mentally sharp as ever.

Life with adani was glorious, and she'd worked hard to become someone who could enjoy its strength. This was hers, and she'd suffered for countless days to earn the right to this power.

Except adani wasn't content to merely fill her adani channels. Wasn't satisfied with the physical garden she'd prepared for it. It wanted more. Demanded more, but she wasn't ready to give it what it wanted. It nibbled at the edges of her adani channels, devouring the boundary between what was Samora and what was adani. She'd sensed the same process happening in Bael, but to feel it happening inside her own skin was terrifying. How he'd maintained his composure was beyond her.

Samora curled into a fetal position and Aldrick held her, his arms around her waist an anchor keeping her spirit attached to her body. She focused of the feeling of his arms on her skin, fought the encroachment of adani both within her body and within her mind. It was a losing battle, but if she could maintain an orderly retreat instead of a complete rout, that would be enough.

She fought it wherever she could, holding it back from expanding her adani channels in her arms, legs, and torso. Adani assaulted her spirit, too, pulling it deeper into the web of life that surrounded them. She fought against the pull, focused harder on Aldrick's arms, but adani had become a persistent enemy, and she lost her grip on her spirit as it fell into the web of life.

How many times had she willingly thrust her spirit into the web? How many times had she relied on it to bring her news from beyond the horizon? Thousands, at least, and never once had she felt her spirit pulled the way it was now. Adani yanked her around as though she'd gotten caught in a maelstrom, turned and twisted and thrown in different directions. She knew better than to fight. No matter how capable she became, the adani in the world would always be greater, and when it chose to exert what passed for its will, resistance was about as useful as spitting at a wind blowing hard into your face.

The vicious pull on her spirit was meant to sever the link between her spirit and body, and it nearly succeeded. Adani yanked her deeper, toward the center of the world, and the sense of her body's place, which she'd maintained through every violent tug, faded, not because she lost her focus, but because the sheer amount of adani that surrounded her blinded her to anything distant.

That was enough to frighten her. She wasn't ready and there was so much more she needed to do. Samora fought against adani even as she knew the effort was ridiculous. She scrambled and clawed her way closer to the surface, but all she succeeded in doing was slowing her fall into the great heart of adani.

Her descent ended suddenly, and all sense of movement ceased. She tried to climb, but couldn't direct her spirit anymore. Something held her in place, not yet lost to the Great Heart of adani, but nowhere near the camp and her family. The sense of her surroundings was familiar, though she'd never dared venture anywhere near here before. If she would have had a body she would have smiled, but the other presence sensed her spirit here as clearly as Elian did when they opened their connection to one another.

"You saved me," she said to Bael, whose spirit surrounded her and protected her from adani's pull. Not with words, for she had no lips to speak, but with her spirit, emotion and intention communicated as one.

She hoped the statement was true, but if he was here to save her, why hadn't he sent her back to the surface? Why was she still here, separated from the others?

"It shouldn't be like this. Why do you fight, Grandmother?"

Most answers would have sounded better, but there was no place for lies here, where all was laid bare. "It would destroy Elian, and I'm not ready to leave my family."

"I wasn't ready to leave mine, either." The words came out too quickly, and she understood that she had struck at his spirit with her reasons.

Her first instinct was to argue, to remind him that he'd come back, and that as far as she could tell, it was *him*. He'd even come to ask her if she thought it was possible he might someday father children, and she'd examined the physical form he'd taken and sensed no reason why he couldn't. She didn't know, for too much of adani remained a mystery to her, but she suspected that if the world survived, and if the wandering clans survived, he'd someday be the patriarch of a large family.

Even if all that was true, though, it didn't change what mattered. Bael had left, and though he'd returned, something about him would always be *different*. How could it not? He had *died*.

That was the change she feared. She believed, though she couldn't be certain, that she would return as Bael had returned, and though the body she would inhabit would appear the same as the one she called her own now, she would still be something different. Would she still even be herself? Bael claimed he felt like himself, but it didn't serve as compelling evidence. She wanted to *know*, but the only way to know was to die, to let go of everything she loved. Despite everything, she wasn't ready to take the risk of losing everything, of losing herself. All her years and all her battles, and she still wasn't ready to die.

"What if Elian needs me and I'm not there?"

"He's stronger than you think. He'll find his way, in time."

"Are you sure? I've known him since he was a child, and I've never seen him like this before. I don't doubt his strength, but even the strongest sword breaks under the right amount of pressure."

Reassurance emanated from Bael's spirit. "I'm sure of it. I cannot see into the future, but I understand adani better now. It isn't done with him."

Despite herself, she believed her grandson. "And me?"

"You've felt its pull, so there's no need to ask. It has wanted you for ages."

Agitation faded, and her spirit felt as still as a pond on a quiet winter morning. "Can you bargain with it? Strike a deal?"

"We don't bargain with adani. We surrender to it."

"I know, but all the same, I'm not ready. I want to say my farewells again, and I want to spend some time with Aldrick. Just a couple of days, please."

Bael didn't answer for what felt like a long time, but she sensed the changes in his spirit, and she wondered if she was sensing some sort of communication between him and adani. When his spirit settled again, he said, "A few more days will be granted to you. So long as you make no connection with adani, you should remain untroubled. It will be better, if, once you are ready, you connect once again with your heart and welcome the transformation. Otherwise, as soon as the sun completely dips below the horizon two days from today, adani will fulfill its purpose within you, regardless of your readiness."

"Thank you, Bael. It means the world to me."

"Trust me, Grandmother. I understand."

She knew he did, and she thanked him again as his spirit escorted her back to the surface, back to her body, where she suddenly gasped and felt once again Aldrick's arms around her waist. Her breath came fast and shallow through open lips, but in time, her heart stopped racing and her breaths slowed.

"I thought I'd lost you," Aldrick said.

She clutched tighter at him, encouraging him to hold her even closer. "You will soon, but not today."

❧ 5 ❧

E lyn wasn't sure what it was, exactly, that hit her senses like a slap across the face. Perhaps it was the sight, witnessed through a crack in the trees, of a field full of ripening wheat, reminding her of the home she had left behind. Maybe it was the sound of two children playing in the woods to her left, cracking downed branches as they built a shelter together. Maybe it was something else entirely, a scent or sight that bypassed her awareness and struck straight at her spirit.

Whatever it was, her return brought her to her knees, her legs too weak to support her weight. Breathing was hard, as though the air was too rich and too full to be forced into her lungs. The adani within her that had been so quiet on the other world stirred to life, bringing her memories forcibly back to her childhood, when it had last flowed freely within her body.

The attack, if that was the proper term for it, only lasted for the duration of two deep breaths, and then her body and breathing calmed and she was herself again, one of Void's treasured servants. Thankfully, her sudden arrival and collapse had happened far enough away from the oblivious children that they hadn't heard her, and for the moment she was alone.

When she'd opened the doorway on the other planet, she'd requested that the void bring her back to her home. From there, she planned on finding her way. Instead, it had left her here, though she didn't know exactly where *here* was. She turned slowly. The void had deposited her in the middle of a small clearing in a fairly young grove. The oak trees hadn't yet grown tall, and when the children stopped shouting at one another, she heard the soft tinkling sounds of a stream somewhere behind her. Ahead, the trees gradually ended and gave way to an unremarkable plain. The farm closest to her was hardly the only one she could see, with other small homes dotting the horizon.

Not enough to be sure of her location, but if she'd been forced to guess, she would have said that she was somewhere close to the ancestral lands of the wandering clans. Back in Father's day, the clans had guarded the farmland with their lives from the encroaching Debru, understanding how precious fertile land was to humanity's survival.

After the Debru had been defeated, larger farms, like the one before her, had become more common. Now that farmers no longer feared for their safety like they had before, they spread out so they could live on the land they worked. The surviving clan members had guarded the land even as they explored new-to-them territories, and the ancestral lands, no longer spoiled by blood and warfare, became the breadbasket of a rapidly expanding population. There were other places on the continent with large farms and rolling farmland, but her guess felt right. Void had brought her here, no doubt for a reason.

But why? The wandering clans were no longer common in the area, and if her duty was to scout and weaken their defenses, the choice of location hardly made sense. Was she supposed to destroy the farms? Doing so would certainly reveal one glaring weakness in the clans' distribution.

Even before the arrival of the emissary, her emissary, the clans had moved to protect the edges of human territory and to the areas surrounding the cities. Their reasoning had been understandable. The cities housed far more people, and as the self-proclaimed protectors of the people, that was where the clans would most likely be needed. Likewise, the borders of human expansion were where the most dangerous predators on the continent roamed. Mostly wolves and bears and the like, but sometimes a rogue otsoa that had somehow found a way to survive for generations without the protection of their Debru masters. Even if a farm was hit, it wouldn't be long before adanists on dragons arrived to put an end to any problems.

If her only aim was destruction, though, she could put a field and farmhouse to the flame with little more than a thought, then, with the help of the void's doorways, be long gone before help arrived. The loss of any single farm was nothing more than a pinprick for the clans, but a hundred pinpricks added up to a nearly fatal blow.

She was still on her knees, but she lifted up her hand and wove adani into a spark of flame that danced across her palm. She watched it, mesmerized by the movement, and old familiar feelings pulled into her present moment. The last time she'd summoned fire she'd been what, fourteen? And it had been nothing at the time, but how often had she wished for the ability since?

She looked up again at the crack in the trees and studied the farm. She wouldn't even have to move. From here she could just sketch a line of fire from her hand to the home. The soil was dry beneath her knees, and she guessed that once the flame started, it would spread on the western breeze with no need of further encouragement. As easy as picking your own nose, as one of her childhood friends had used to say.

The children off to her left, too far away to be seen through the grove, laughed as if they'd heard her last thought, and she closed her fist on the flame, snuffing it out. What had that child's name been? Kleon? She hadn't thought of him in decades, but now she wondered where he was and what he was doing. He hadn't been able to take any part of his training seriously, but he'd never wanted to ascend, and he'd been fun to play with. He was one of the few who didn't care that her father was Elian, savior of the clans. To him, she'd just been Elyn and nothing more.

She looked at the farm again, then stood and shook her head. She was here for the clans, not a family of farmers.

Encouraged by her success with the flame, Elyn thrust her adani into the ground and let it spread. A dull ache bloomed above her right eye, but she ignored it, remembering now what it was like to bring in so much information at once. The growth of the grove was no accident, she realized, as she sensed a heart beating on the other side of the stream.

She pushed her adani further away, ignoring the headache that grew more intense. It didn't take her long to find a small camp filled with adanists. A hunting camp, unless she missed her guess. Seven warriors, and none of them seemed aware of her. *That* had to be why she was here. She pushed a bit further to make sure there was nothing she was missing, then started through the trees, giving the children a wide berth. Far better for them to never know that she'd been here.

ONCE AGAIN, the grove provided adequate protection for her approach. She didn't know if she'd become so weak that the adanists couldn't sense her, or if void protected her from detection in another way, but the warriors didn't take any notice of her as she came closer. She took up a position behind a tree and observed the camp's daily routines.

Her guess of it being a hunting camp was quickly proven accurate. The seven adanists were on the young side, most likely only a few years beyond their full initiation into the wandering clans. Five young men, two young women, and at the moment, they were gathered in the center of the camp skinning and cutting the meat from the deer they'd recently killed. They used steel knives for the work, and their quick, confident cuts told Elyn they'd performed this duty many times before. They talked as they worked, their voices carrying on the wind but not quite loudly enough for her to make out their words. At least one of them made the group laugh often.

Elyn dug her nails into her palm and ground her teeth together. Joining a hunting party was yet another rite of passage she'd never experienced. It was one of the first duties given to newer warriors, an opportunity for them to complete meaningful work on their own without the supervision of more experienced adanists. When Elyn had been younger, the clans had even cooperated in the creation of hunting parties, allowing half to come from one clan and half from another. Father had argued it built a tighter-knit community among all the wandering clans, and Elyn's friends had looked forward to joining their first hunting party so they could meet potential partners.

She'd looked forward to joining a hunting party, too, only Father had stolen the opportunity from her when he'd pushed her to ascend too quickly.

She turned away from the sight and pressed her back to the tree she'd been peeking out from.

Was this what Void wanted? She held out her hand and summoned the strength, forming void into seven small spheres that floated above her palm. The technique came to her with surprising ease. It wasn't that much different than the attack Samora had taught her with adani when she'd been a child. The spheres were darker than a moonless night, and even if the adanists were ascended, a surprise attack would be an almost guaranteed victory.

But she didn't have any desire to kill a hunting party. They were hardly a threat to the emissary, and therefore didn't deserve death. She almost let go of the spheres.

The head emissary's words came back to her then. Her place, as a servant, wasn't to ask why. And with the void, there was no why. It was the force of destruction, the answer to the problem of all of life's suffering. She raised her hand, and the spheres jumped faster, eager to consume the enormous amount of adani before them.

Another round of laughter reached her ears and the spheres faded. What was she thinking? It was just a hunting party, barely of any importance at all. She'd also been asked to scout, and perhaps she'd learn more from observing them than killing them. She poked her head slowly out from behind the tree and watched them again.

One of the young men was sitting on a downed log close to one of the women, his arm around her and an easy smile on his face. The others ignored the outward display of affection, but they'd also stopped working on the harvest, too distracted by their conversations to continue. They held their bloody knives loosely in their hands and grinned at one another, so self-satisfied it made Elyn's stomach churn.

The spheres had been dancing in her palm for a while before she noticed they were there, and when she noticed, she stared at them for a while. She lost herself in a trance, slipping into the void where she took comfort.

In time, though, she sensed another presence within the void, watching her even as she observed the void. It shouldn't have come as any surprise, yet it was. She was being judged, and the intent behind the observation was clear as day. These adanists were to die, doomed by their mere proximity to her.

Elyn still didn't want to kill them, but now she weighed their deaths differently. If she didn't kill them, and perished herself, she'd lose any say in the future of this world. She'd be no more useful than she had been as a farmer. She closed her eyes and pressed her forehead against the rough bark of the tree. They were just youths.

She slipped out from behind the tree and raised her hand before doubt could overwhelm her, the spheres still dancing above her palm. She steadied them with her will, assigned them their targets, and shot them on their way.

Released from her grip, the spheres moved almost too fast to be seen. They left thin trails of shadow behind them which faded in the blink of an eye.

She hadn't put much void into the spheres, worried that if her techniques were too powerful, she'd draw Bael's attention, but her aim was true. The first sphere struck in two beats of the heart, slamming into the back of the head of the young man who had his arm around the woman. He pitched forward, and Elyn felt the moment adani fled his body. The woman followed her young lover into death before she realized anything was wrong, and only then did the fools realize the danger they were in.

They started to turn as the rest of the spheres struck their targets. In three cases, their movement meant nothing. She'd aimed for their heads and it didn't matter if she struck in the front or the back. Either way her spheres would dig straight into the mind before adani could protect its host, and once part of the mind was gone, so too went the spirit.

One of the adanists was plain lucky. Instead of turning, his reaction was to duck, and it served him well. Her sphere passed over his head, grazing him across the very top of his skull. The impact stunned him, but he kept moving, refusing to grant Elyn an easy target.

The final adanist's survival had nothing to do with luck. A bound sword of adani flashed in her hand, and her reaction was so quick she had time to find the sphere and cut at it with her blade. Adani and void met, and although the adanist struggled, her adani proved the victor, slicing the void in two.

Her gaze tracked the attack back the way it had come and she tugged the other adanist after her. Their speed was that of ascended adanists, but Elyn had suspected nothing less. She sent another spread of void spheres their way, but as she expected, they dodged with little difficulty.

Elyn noted that their tactics were the same ones Bael and the others had used so effectively against the emissary's last assault. She didn't think this hunting party had come from Bael's camp, as they were a little too young to be part of his circle of friends, which meant that word had spread to all the wandering clans.

That, finally, was a useful piece of information the emissaries would welcome.

She let them get close, then threw up a wall of void. They cut at it, but it served its purpose and slowed them down. By the time they reached the other side, she'd prepared more than a dozen spheres, and she launched them in a pattern they had no hope of avoiding.

Their bodies fell at her feet, riddled with holes from the spheres, and she was reminded briefly of Father, falling before her assault before Bael came to kill the emissary and turn the tide of the battle. She spit on the corpses, then reached down and collected the hearts from the two of them. Each one glowed with a dark red light as she pulled them out, and the feeling that washed over her when she absorbed them into her being was far more powerful than any surge of adani.

The red hearts went to Void, and it roared with pleasure. Her limbs grew stronger and her mind sharper, and she wondered if this gift was given just to her or if Void distributed its gifts more evenly.

She made her way to the camp and repeated the technique, harvesting another five hearts and offering them to her master.

Elyn formed a portal, but before she could step through, she sensed him. He'd arrived where the five had fallen, where he'd no doubt felt so much adani being lost at once.

She turned and studied him. He looked the same as he always

had, right down to the look of disbelief on his face when he saw her. For all his strength, in so many ways, he was still just a child.

"Elyn?" Bael asked.

She dipped her head toward him, knowing that even if she spent days trying to explain, he'd never understand, then stepped through the portal and vanished, leaving him alone with the dead.

6

When Bael appeared on the hilltop outside his clan's camp it was close to evening already. The longest days of summer had passed them by in relative peace, but he feared they would be fighting for their lives again before the first snows fell. Elian was below, in the same place he'd been training the children for the last few days, and they surrounded him now.

Bael watched with his new eyes that saw both the physical world and adani. In the past, Elian had always burned against his senses, like standing too close to a bonfire. That was gone now, his adani channels mangled by void, beyond Bael's or Samora's ability to heal. Even so, Elian retained an incredible strength. He'd win no duels against any of the ascended, but he might triumph over an unwary adanist. His lifetime of experience was obvious in the way he manipulated adani through his body, and it was that experience he tried to pass on to the children.

From what Bael could see, the children were devouring the knowledge. Most had joined the clan within the past two months, and the transition had been so chaotic their training had fallen by the wayside. Now it resumed, and under the demanding eye of a clan legend. Bael would have fought for a position in such a lesson when he'd been a child.

He'd appeared, by design, near the end of the lesson, and once it was over, Elian dismissed the children, who ran past Bael with all the eagerness of youth who'd been training all afternoon on empty stomachs. Elian followed after, though his movements were slow and careful. His adani amplified his physical pain, angry it couldn't follow the channels it had grown so used to.

In Bael's eyes, it was needless suffering. Adani invited the old warrior to ascend to a new level. Elian hadn't been too keen to listen to him in the past, though, and so Bael held his thoughts close.

"They're improving considerably," he said to Elian.

His great-uncle had little patience for niceties, but in this case, Bael had spoken about something he cared about, and so let it pass. "They are. Every generation keeps getting stronger, and soon even you're going to look like a weak old fool."

Bael grinned. "I look forward to the day."

Elian grunted. "It's not all that it's made out to be. Now, what do you want?"

Bael held up two fingers, and chose the more difficult of the topics first. "Elyn has returned."

Elian stared hard at him. "You saw her?"

"She killed a group of hunters using void."

A shudder ran through Elian's body, and he swallowed hard. "Can you track her?"

Bael shook his head. "I can sense when she kills an adanist, but until then, no. I don't know her spirit well enough."

Whatever thoughts troubled Elian, and Bael didn't doubt they were legion, didn't reach his expression.

"And the second reason you're here?" Elian asked.

Bael wanted to talk more about Elyn, but Elian's dismissal was absolute. "I could use your advice."

"On what?"

"I'm at a loss for what we do next. We've gathered all those who want to fight, and we passed on what we've learned from our battles to the other wandering clans. We've established training routines and developed new strategies for when the emissaries return, but now it feels like we're sitting around, doing nothing. Urgency brought us together, but I don't know what keeps us going."

"Has there been any word from the cities?"

"Nothing new. They don't want us anywhere near."

Elian thought for a moment, then said, "Let's consider our enemy more carefully, then. If you were in their position, what are you thinking about? Why have they sent Elyn?"

"We're fairly certain at this point that the emissaries are interested in our world because of those red hearts. As best we can tell, the red hearts can only be created in the dead zones the first emissary made within the cities, and requires the active assistance of adanists."

"Which is the only reason we're all still alive," Elian agreed.

"Assuming all that is true, the only people standing in their way are below us right now, which makes us the likely target for an attack."

"That feels right to me. So why haven't they attacked? Assuming Elyn is here at their behest, why isn't she leading an army?"

"To that, I don't know. It's the question I've been asking myself for a while now, and I don't have an answer. Perhaps we hurt them worse than we think. Maybe there's something about my transformation that worries them. Or, for all we know, they're having a feast that lasts several months, and they can't be bothered."

Elian's grin was bitter. "It's probably not the last one."

"Probably not, but we can't say for sure."

"True. But it also means we're probably doing about as much as we can. So long as we stay away from other clans and cities, we're keeping them safe, and so long as we're training and preparing, we'll be as ready as we can be."

Bael shook his head. "That's not enough. When they attack again, it'll be with a much larger force. That's what I'd do, and we're not nearly strong enough to fight them off. An ascended adanist is no real match against an emissary." He cast a meaningful glance at Elian. "We need more transformations. We're weak so long as I'm the only one who can meaningfully stand against them. You can become strong enough to make a difference. I'm sure of it."

Elian shook his head. "No."

The older adanist meant it as the final word, but Bael couldn't let him escape without an argument. They'd been lucky to have as much time as they'd had, but now that Elyn was back, he suspected the deciding battles were closer than ever.

"Why not? You're broken and next to useless as a warrior. Why remain that way, when you can become stronger than you ever have before? I don't understand."

He'd halfway expected Elian to snap at him, but his response was so soft Bael had to lean forward to hear. "Broken as my body is, I'm not ready to let go."

"There's nothing to be afraid of. I'd like to think I'm evidence enough of that."

"But are you? You sound like Bael and look like Bael, and your adani feels like his, but Bael died. You claim to be Bael, and I'm sure you believe it, but how would you know?"

"I still have all my memories. I remember sitting on your lap as a child, feeling the way you manipulated adani in your body."

"But what does that matter? Samora has dragon memories in her head, but that doesn't make her a dragon! How can any of us know that you're you?"

"Does it matter? I believe that I'm Bael, and if what happened to me happens to you, you'll be Elian."

"Of course it matters! You're asking me to surrender everything that has ever mattered to me. My life, my family, even my scars, they're all part of *this* body. I won't just give it up."

"Some of us didn't have a choice," Bael said.

That silenced Elian quickly. He breathed out sharply and stared at the clouds in the sky. "I know, and I'm sorry. But it also means that you know, better than anyone else, why I'm terrified. If I was at the end of my life, perhaps it would be a different story, but I've still got years and years ahead of me. I've still got grandchildren to meet."

"From where I'm standing, you would. You would meet your grandchildren, and their children, and their children. You'd live to see your family spread across the land, and you'd be strong enough to fight off the emissaries when they return."

"But would it be me? Or something else?"

Bael's patience ended, for there was no way to answer Elian's question, and Elian knew it as well as he did. The only way to know was to experience, and the only way to experience any of it was to surrender to adani, and Bael didn't think Elian had ever surrendered to anything in his life. It was the quality that made him the leader and the fighter he was. It also made him a pain when they disagreed.

Elian sighed. "I'm sorry. It's not an easy place to be in, as you well know. I'm afraid I'm not handling it as well as you."

"You have a choice. That makes it harder."

Elian tapped the side of his bad leg with his hand. "It's not that much of a choice, though, is it? Not if I want to have any say in what's coming. Not if I want to protect my family, same as I've done since I was a child."

"Not really, no."

They looked out over the camp together. The campfires were roaring as the families prepared their evening meal, and soft laughter sometimes floated through the air, so soft Bael feared that it would vanish if he were to speak over it. A lump formed in

Bael's throat as he watched the camp, burning bright both in the physical world and with adani.

That wasn't a normal clan below. Every single adult had chosen to be there, because they'd been Bael's friends, and when he'd called them to battle, they'd come running. He'd considered the matter plenty since the clan had formed and still wasn't sure he understood. Why should they be so willing to risk everything for him?

"Elian?" he asked.

"Yes?"

"Why do they follow me, knowing what the cost will be?"

"Bothers you too, does it? I can't tell you how many nights of sleep I lost to that question."

"Did you ever answer it?"

"Not completely, but well enough." He paused for a moment to gather his thoughts. "Perhaps the most important part, I think, is understanding that there is no one answer. People are a mess of emotions and reasons and passions, and what compels one person to follow you probably isn't the same as what persuades the next. There's no one answer. Our world isn't that simple, and trying to make it that simple is a mistake."

Bael nodded.

"I think that for most of your clan, their decision to follow you is based on a careful consideration of the facts. They know well enough what the emissaries plan, and they know you're the only leader, *the only one*, who will stand and fight against it. There are some who just want a fight, and you're the only leader who will give them one. Others see something in you, and what that is might be different for everyone, that they think is worth following."

"Worth losing their lives over?" Bael said.

"Perhaps. If it means enough, and for all those down in that camp, it means enough."

"I don't know that I deserve that amount of respect."

Elian grunted. "I once thought that, too, and better to have that humility than to take too much pride in your accomplishments. But you are the only person in any of the clans to defeat an emissary, and you've done it twice. That's worth following."

Bael bowed his head to Elian. "Thank you. I'm not convinced, not yet, but this has helped."

"I'm always happy to help in whatever ways I can."

"So you'd surrender your body to adani?"

Whatever goodwill the conversation had built between them vanished in a moment. Elian's half-smile fell. "I'm going to start heading down before it gets too late. I'd prefer to walk it alone."

Bael didn't bother arguing. He bowed again, then watched as Elian made his slow way down the hill, wondering all the time how long his great-uncle would hold onto his broken form.

7

News of Elyn's reappearance burned its way through the camp like a brushfire in a dry, windy grassland, chilling the normally optimistic mood of the camp. Even the younger children, who didn't know what the news meant, seemed to understand its import, and they joined the adults in a quiet evening meal. Samora stared down at her own hearty stew, but didn't eat much.

She blamed adani. The more it took over her body, the more it expanded her channels against her will, the more she felt herself pulled away from the daily needs of her flesh. A cup of water and half a slice of bread was all she needed, and even that sometimes seemed like too much.

She still ate, partly out of habit and partly because she feared adani made her hunger a liar, that her body actually needed food and adani was trying to trick her out of it. Food rooted her and connected her with her family. No matter how far they wandered, everyone had always returned for all the meals they could.

Even today, the mood muted by Elyn's return, the conversation jumped from topic to topic, and Samora listened to it with interest. Kerina was constantly blushing. Her meal attempt a couple of nights ago had gone well, and this was now her third attempt at feeding the entire family. The compliments were effusive, and if poor Kerina's cheeks turned any redder, Samora feared her hair may catch on fire.

She stirred at her bowl absently as she let the waves of conversation crash over her. Once, she'd had dreams of learning all there was to know about adani and seeing every piece of their enormous world. Now all she wanted was here, around this campfire.

Aldrick leaned over and whispered in her ear. "Are you afraid they didn't stir the stew well enough?"

She stopped the idle spinning of her spoon in the bowl. "Sorry, is it annoying?"

"I don't mind, but did you want to talk about it?"

She let her spoon rest against the side of the bowl. "Maybe, but there are some questions I need to get answered first. Did you want my stew? I'm not hungry."

"I don't need it, but I think I can find someone who does." He eyed Killan and Kaeda's youngest, Minetta. Bael's younger sister seemed to have hit a late growth spurt, and she devoured as much food as people would hand her.

Samora handed Aldrick her bowl, thanked him, then stood and dismissed herself from her family circle. It was hard to leave them, harder, too, because she guessed well enough what the ultimate destination of her trip would be.

Finding Bael was never hard. Even surrounded by ascended adanists, his spirit shone the brightest. He was at a campfire with Shayna and some of their closest friends, and though they seemed the same as they always did, Samora thought she heard an edge to their laughter that hadn't been there yesterday.

Bael's eyes locked on her across the campfire. She knew he always saw adani now and couldn't be surprised, but the effect was still disconcerting. His new ability to know everything happening around him made him seem inhuman.

Samora tilted her head away from the fire and Bael nodded. He had no bowl in his hands, for he didn't eat anymore. His body, if it could properly be called a body, was nourished directly from adani. Samora would soon be the same. He stood from his place, asked to be excused, then joined her. He followed her as she meandered slowly around the tents, choosing paths that would be unoccupied as most of the clan ate their supper.

"How, exactly, did you know Elyn had returned?" Samora asked.

"I didn't notice her return. What I first noticed was several adanists dying at once. When I focused my attention on the area, I felt some of the passing effects of void, and so I traveled there. I didn't know it was her until I appeared before her."

"Why did you not sense her right away? Was she masking herself the way the servants were before?"

"No, I didn't sense her because she blended in. She has control of void. That's abundantly clear, but I sensed her the same as I would any other adanist."

Samora's face fell, and Bael asked, "Why did you want to know?"

"I'd hoped you would say she was masking herself, in which case, almost anyone in this clan could have eventually found her. But if she's presenting as just another adanist, it means only I can find her."

Bael's eyes narrowed for a moment, but he understood quickly enough. "You know her spirit well enough to pick it out?"

"She trained with me an enormous amount when she was younger. She was so sensitive I was sure I'd found a successor to my techniques. Assuming that her spirit is still the same and that void hasn't twisted it in some way I wouldn't recognize, I could find her."

"Even if she's not ascended? That's quite a search."

Samora agreed, wondering if he would guess her next request on his own. She wasn't disappointed.

"Pushing that much adani is going to send you over the edge, almost without a doubt," he said.

"Which is why I'm hoping that you'll pull me back."

Bael rubbed his eyes, then dragged his hand down, pulling at his cheeks. "Between you and Elian, I'm not sure who's worse. Neither of you should be delaying, not when we know I'm going to need support against the emissaries."

"I know, but I'm not ready. Not yet. Can you give me this, please?"

Bael looked to the sky, as though the constellations might hold the answers to the problems his elders gave him. "I can't promise anything, but I'll try. Is that good enough?"

"It's all I could ask for," Samora answered.

THEY WAITED that night until most everyone had gone to bed, and then they left the camp. Only Aldrick and Bael joined Samora, as every additional observer would make the hunt more difficult. She hadn't said much to the rest of her family, putting her faith in Bael, that he would keep her safe from adani's grip. She'd made sure to hug each of her children and grandchildren tightly and tell them she loved them, but she'd made that a nightly practice since the last battle with the emissary, so she didn't think they sensed anything unusual.

Aldrick kept his hand in hers, supporting her over the uneven terrain, her silent support, the same as he'd been almost every day since they'd met. He'd been displeased when she'd returned from speaking with Bael, but only for understandably selfish reasons. He didn't want to risk her departure any more than she did, but all he did when she told him was grimace and nod and ask how he could help. She'd asked if he might stay in the camp, but he'd refused. If her search was what sent her fully into adani's grip, he intended to be there, and she didn't press the matter. Though his presence would make the search harder, she wanted him by her side, too.

They walked into the foothills only because it was the emptiest direction. The dragons camped to the east of the tents, and the farther away from any large sources of adani, the easier the search would be. When Samora thought they were far enough away, she stopped and found a place to sit. She placed her hands against the ground, just as she had when she was a child. It was a good place, thick with adani. She sat and crossed her legs.

"Is there anything else you need from me?" Bael asked.

"Accompany me at a distance. If I stop next to a spirit, that will be her. Commit her spirit to your memory, and you should be able to find her no matter where she tries to hide. Other than that, just bring me back."

Aldrick squatted next to her for a kiss. "How far?"

Samora shrugged. "Five paces?"

He stepped away and found his own seat, a nice-sized stone that would keep his influence on the local adani small. "Love you."

"Love you, too."

Bael took one last look at the pair of them, then vanished, his adani diving deep into the ground.

"I'm not sure I'll ever get used to that," Aldrick said.

"I know how you feel," Samora answered. She took out four hearts from her pocket and buried them up to her first knuckle around her, creating a gathering ground that would help her stretch her adani farther than she would be able to otherwise. Adani surged around her, and it was all she could do to keep her spirit disconnected from the heart in her core. "I'll be back soon," she said.

With that, she closed her eyes, pressed her hands firmly into the ground, and opened herself up to adani.

She'd never experienced it as she did now, so wild and uncontrolled, like a small child that hadn't gotten her way. It fought and crawled for more space within her body, a surge of strength as powerful as she could remember. With a single effort of will, she wrapped it up and sent it into the web of life that stretched from one end of the continent to the other. It shot out in all directions, but she focused her attention on a handful of strands, jumping miles at a time from one heart to another.

Elyn could be hiding anywhere, but that didn't mean every place was equally likely. She'd just struck and been discovered, so she'd either retreat someplace she associated with safety, or she'd hurry to find a new battle. Samora went first to Elyn's abandoned farmstead. Yes, it had been one of the first places Bael had checked, but better to be sure.

The farmstead was empty, but Samora checked for miles in all directions, including the nearby towns in her search. Elian said she'd only gotten along a little with her nearest neighbors, but even that might be enough to be considered a place to hide. The towns were active enough, but she found no trace of Elyn.

Throughout the search she sensed Bael trailing well behind her, connected and aware of her search but far enough away that his overwhelming presence didn't blind her senses. This version of Bael was more patient than the young man she'd helped raise, as though he had more than enough time for everything.

Which was true enough, she supposed.

She pushed the thought away and searched next around the wandering clans, worried that she'd find her niece preparing for her next attack. The clans were easy enough to find, and she searched both within them and around them for any sign, but there was none. She breathed out a small sigh of relief, then continued her search.

Next were the lands they'd spent time in as she'd been an older girl, when she'd been preparing for her ascension. Those lands had been north of the Bears' ancestral lands, and Samora remembered Elyn getting lost for countless afternoons in the woods. She'd loved those woods as much as anyplace they'd visited, and they'd been a source of comfort to her during the final, stressful stages of her training. Both Samora and Elian had been terrified of something going wrong, and so they'd pushed her so hard in those final eighthdays.

Not that it had mattered, in the end. Everything had gone wrong anyway.

She found Elyn in the woods, apparently at ease, as her spirit was calm and even. Her sense of Elyn brought Samora to a standstill. She hadn't sensed Elyn like this since she was a child, her adani flowing smooth and even through her body. Despite everything that had stemmed from Elyn's healing, Samora was still glad she'd been restored. The poor girl had always deserved better than what life had given her.

That was Samora's last thought before adani took control of her little expedition. While she'd been on the move it had obeyed her will, carrying her spirit across vast distances, but now that she stopped and focused on her niece, it seized the opportunity to take her body as its own. Adani surrounded her spirit and pulled her farther from her body, cutting at the thread that connected her. She pulled hard on the thread, fighting against adani, but her strength was nothing compared to the powers she'd harnessed to find Elyn. She might as well as fought off a Vada with a twig.

The rapidity of her failure caught her by surprise. Even though she'd expected something of this nature, she'd completely underestimated its strength. The thread connecting to her body was almost shredded when Bael fought his way through the tempest. A wave of will rolled over her, sending adani fleeing. Bael held the life-giving force at bay, but even he didn't have the strength to fight it for long. He couldn't send a thought her way, but she caught a hint as well as the next person. She pulled herself back along the thread, gasping as she returned to her body.

Samora wrapped her arms around herself, but she was so cold she wasn't sure she'd ever be warm again. A shiver ran up and down her body and then Aldrick was there, wrapping his arms around her and holding her close. She leaned into his warmth.

"Did you find her?" he asked.

All she could do was nod.

Bael appeared a moment later, his eyes narrowed. He looked—diminished somehow—as though he'd become less solid. She blinked and the impression faded, but she couldn't help but think she'd seen something true. "I can find her now. There's no place in this world she can hide."

He looked as though he was about to disappear, but Samora found her voice. "Bael, don't."

"I don't like it any more than you, but it needs to be done, and better it happens now."

"Take Elian."

"Why would I make him endure that?"

"Because he is her father. Let them talk, please. Is she any threat to you?"

"No, but there's no telling what powers she can call. She's asleep now. I promise I'll make it quick and painless."

Samora shook her head and tried to stand, but her legs wouldn't support her weight.

"Get some rest, Grandmother. You need it. The next time you touch adani, there's nothing that even I'll be able to do."

Which was another question, and one she wanted the answer to. Anything that she could use to keep him here, to keep him from killing his cousin. "What did you do? I've never sensed anyone manipulate adani like that."

He looked off into the distance, then said. "I'm not entirely sure. So much of what I do is just a feeling, a sense of what's right and what's wrong."

"But what did you *do*?"

"When I understand it, I'll be sure to let you know, but I think you'll figure it out for yourself soon enough."

Once again, he looked as though he was about to leave.

"Bael, you need to take Elian, even if you don't think it's wise. He'll never forgive you if you don't."

That, at least, was enough to catch his attention. "Why? It ends the same whether he's there or not, and no parent should have to watch their child die."

"Because he deserves a chance to save his child, no matter how hopeless it might look."

Bael ran his hand through his hair, then said, "Fine."

He disappeared before Samora could thank him.

8

Elian held tight to Capricia as she commanded the dragon to bank toward the west. The grove in the distance grew larger, mirroring the doubts in Elian's mind. When Bael had appeared outside their tent, Elian had expected trouble, and he hadn't been wrong. Bael had told them both that he had found Elyn, that he could likely find her no matter where she hid. Thankfully, he'd given them a chance to speak to her first.

He should be thinking about what he could say to Elyn, but the subject was too painful, so instead his thoughts turned to his great-nephew. To look at him was to think he was alive and well, but the changes the transformation had wrought in him were deep. His mastery of adani went beyond even Samora's understanding, and it made Elian feel as though a stranger lived within Bael's skin. When he spoke about finding Elyn wherever she wandered, he spoke as one who had mastered the world and its secrets. Not just a leader of a clan, but a protector of every mile of rock, stream, and tree. To stand in his presence was unsettling, and to think that was the future Bael imagined for him was even more so.

A shiver ran down his spine that had nothing to do with the cold air that rushed past him. His family kept diving deeper into the mysteries of adani, but the costs kept growing. The sacrifices wouldn't have bothered a younger Elian, but now he lacked the blind certainty of his youth. The life they'd built for themselves in between the years of the Debru and the emissaries had been a struggle, but it had been a good one. Now Bael was charting a new course, and Elian wondered if he was too old to follow. Changing the world felt like a mission for the young men and women of the clans.

The dragon slowly descended, and Elian missed Arok, his companion of several decades, who'd sacrificed himself to protect the wandering clans from the emissary. He kept leaning over to speak to Arok, only to realize he was riding a much younger dragon.

The world kept changing and his friends kept dying, and he started to understand why elders looked forward to returning their adani to the world. But now he had to save his daughter, though he didn't have the slightest clue how he might do so. He was grateful that Capricia had joined him, for her wisdom regarding matters of their daughter was far greater than his.

They landed in a clearing of the grove that immediately brought long-buried memories back to the surface. The clan had camped near here as Elyn made her final preparations for her historic ascension. Samora and Aldrick had been with them, then, balancing the energy of a young Killan with Samora's self-assigned duty to grow hearts across the land. Had Samora been pregnant with Deva, then, too? The timing seemed about right, but he couldn't remember. He'd been so focused on preparing Elyn for her ascension that all other memories had faded. They'd used this clearing for landing dragons then, too. The trees had gotten taller, and the undergrowth was thicker, but it was the same clearing.

Elian worked his way off the dragon first, a process that took at least three times as long as it should have. He had to position himself carefully and plant each foot precisely, but he made it to the ground without falling over, so their mission was so far a success. Capricia scrambled down beside him and dismissed the dragon. If they were about to fight their daughter, they didn't want to risk the dragon's life. Its massive adani would make no difference if it came to a battle.

"Brings back the memories, doesn't it?" Capricia asked.

"It does. I wish they were more pleasant."

"Maybe we can make a pleasant memory today." She didn't believe her own words, but Elian appreciated her effort. He grabbed hold of her optimism and kept it close.

"Do you sense Bael anywhere near?" Elian didn't, but that didn't mean all that much.

Capricia closed her eyes, then shook her head. "I don't doubt that he's keeping an eye on us, but he's subtle enough I can't sense it."

Though the news didn't come as any surprise, it didn't make Elian feel any better about what they were about to try. Bael had claimed it made little sense for him to ride the dragon, nor would he be physically present during their conversation. It was for the best, he said, and Elian agreed. Bael had made no secret of the fact he believed the best thing they could do for Elyn was to kill her quickly, and he'd told them he was willing to bear the burden of the act.

Despite all the suffering she'd given him, Elian wasn't ready for such drastic action. She was still his daughter, and if he could, he would bring her home. He'd promised, on the day she'd been born, that he'd do anything he could to protect her. He didn't know what that promise meant today, but he planned to uphold it.

They would find Elyn on their own, but if it came to a fight,

Bael promised that he would be there in a moment, once again acting as the master of this world. Elian would have encouraged some more humility, but he wasn't sure the attitude wasn't earned.

He would have felt a little better if Capricia had been able to sense Bael, but if Capricia could, then it was likely Elyn could, too. Elian had no choice but to trust Bael, but that trust came easily.

"Do you think she's in her normal hiding spot?" Elian asked.

"Seems likely, don't you think?"

He nodded, and Capricia offered her arm. He took it and they trekked through the dense grove of trees. They made no particular attempt at stealth, as Elian was nearly incapable, and they expected Elyn would sense them before she saw them. The woods were eerily silent, as though the poison seeping through Elyn's heart had scared the creatures away. The path they followed rose gently and they saw a small fire burning in the gaps between the trees, and they made their way toward it.

They found Elyn sitting on a downed log, holding her hands to the flame to warm them. She looked at them with a flat, expressionless gaze, as though they were of no more interest to her than a passing squirrel. Capricia entered the small clearing first, with Elian shuffling a step behind her.

"So, you can find me, can you?" she asked.

Capricia ignored the rude greeting and bowed. "It's good to see you again."

The look on Elyn's face froze Elian to the bones. It was a blank look, as though she couldn't understand the meaning of Capricia's greeting. Like Bael, she had left them and come back, but as something altogether different from what they had known. Bael, at least, maintained the broad strokes of his old personality, but Elyn had shed them like a set of clothes that had grown too small.

A trace of warmth and feeling flickered across Elyn's face, so quickly Elian wondered if he'd imagined it, or if it was a trick of the firelight. Was she hiding her true feelings behind that terrible mask of indifference?

Elyn said, "It's good to see you, too, Mother," and for the briefest of moments she was their daughter again, and Elian would have done anything to protect her.

He shuffled closer, grimacing against the pain of an injured leg that had seen too much use today. He gripped his walking stick tighter and tried to hide the pain. His movement focused her attention on him, and the emptiness settled over her expression once again.

He forced himself to swallow everything he wanted to say, for if he did, he might lose her for good. She remained attached to them by the thinnest of threads, more fragile than Samora's finest weave of adani, and the wrong word would slice through that thread with ease.

His spirit raged within him, though, and adani responded by threatening to fill his body and drop him to his knees in agony. His channels could no longer handle the strength he possessed, and so he kept it tightly bound to his will. How could she look at him like that? After what she had done to him? At the very least, she could reveal her anger, be bold enough to show him her true feelings. This—vast emptiness, for he could think of no other way to describe what he saw—was worse than his defeat at her hands, for even her victory had won her nothing.

He reined in his anger and bowed to her, as deep as he would have to meeting another clan leader. "It is good to see you, Elyn."

She kept looking at him with that empty stare, then turned back to Capricia, as though he was a ghost she was only imagining. "Why are you here?"

"We came for you. We've been worried sick about you for months now. Both of us want you to come home."

Elyn shook her head slowly. "There is no home for me, not anymore."

Capricia took two steps toward Elyn, until she was standing on the other side of the fire from their daughter. Elian almost held out a hand to stop her, but he suspected their best hope of retrieving Elyn lay with his wife, and so he kept his hands at his side. Elyn made no move to harm Capricia as she took a knee and looked Elyn in the eye. "You will always have a home with us, no matter what you do."

Elyn's expression finally changed, but it was a snarl that made Elian take half a step back before he caught himself. "What *I've done*? How could either of you have any idea what I've done? If not for me, this entire world might very well be dead. You should look instead at what you've done."

Capricia was taken aback, but she didn't move from her spot. "What did we do? All we've ever tried to do is keep this world safe. To keep those we love safe."

Elyn rose to her feet so quickly that Elian raised his walking stick to defend himself, but her only goal was to tower over Capricia. "Is that what you think? You ruined my life! You two pushed me to ascend before I was ready, then judged me for its failure."

Capricia was shaking her head. "We never—"

Elyn stopped her with a sharp gesture. "Please, don't. Perhaps you've never accused me out loud, but I've always seen it, in every look you've given me since."

Her accusations rocked Elian like body blows that Harald would have delivered in his prime. They reached into his spirit, where he'd buried a lifetime's worth of guilt, and unearthed it like a rotting corpse.

She'd never once accused him. He was sure of it, because if she had, especially back then, he might have even agreed with her. He'd wondered, countless times, if he'd pushed her too hard and led her to ascend too early. How many times had he and

Samora discussed it? How many times had he and Capricia? But time and again, they came to the same conclusion: there was nothing they would have done differently. Their discussions as a family had always been that adani was still a mystery, and they didn't know why tragedy had befallen Elyn, but that they'd work together to help her live a meaningful life without adani's gifts.

Elyn had never spoken a word against him, and when she'd left, it had been under the claim that she would find her way better on her own. Elian had hated that she had left, but he'd believed that sometimes love meant letting go, and that was what he'd done.

She was wrong about everything, though. Yes, he'd pushed her to ascend, but only because he'd seen the joy mastery of adani had brought her. And when tragedy had struck, no one had abandoned her. They were clan and they were family, and they would have supported her no matter what. She was the one that had left them, the one that had pushed any offers of help away.

Capricia pressed her forehead to the ground. "I'm sorry, but it was never our intent to hurt you. We only did what we thought was best."

Elyn waved the explanation away, her own frustration building. "Which is nothing more than I'm doing today. There's no point in us going over this now. All that matters is that I'm trying to save you all from the destruction you seem to crave."

"By killing innocent adanists?" Elian said, unable to hold his tongue any longer. The moment he spoke, though, he realized he'd made a terrible mistake. Fire flared within Elyn's eyes, and within the blink of an eye she'd formed five void spheres in the palm of her hand. Elian reached for adani on instinct, then stopped himself. He couldn't control enough strength to pose any threat to Elyn. Capricia would have better luck, but given what Elyn had shown herself capable of, he doubted his wife would be much more successful. They'd come in peace, gambling on a love that was no longer shared.

He wondered how many of these feelings were Elyn's to begin with, and how many had sprouted from a milder complaint thanks to the pull of void. Had Elyn's own thoughts been twisted, or were they finally seeing something which had lain dormant since that terrible day?

She left him no time to answer the question. She flung the spheres of void, not just at him, but at Capricia, too.

Elian acted without thought, flinging himself, despite the sharp pains in his leg, between Capricia and the spheres. He expected to feel them digging into his back, but they never landed. The land filled with adani, and Bael was there, a shield between the spheres and his family. The spheres struck hard, and though they drained several dragons' worth of adani from the shield, they couldn't come close to cracking it. Elian landed hard on his side, sending a wave of needles and agony up his leg and spine that exploded like a burst of adani directly inside his skull.

He rolled over in time to see Elyn form a dark doorway and step through. Bael let her go without pursuit, and as soon as the hole in the air vanished, he turned around and knelt beside Capricia and Elian. "Any new injuries?"

"No," Elian said through gritted teeth. "Thank you."

"You're welcome, though I'm sorry it happened the way it did."

Bael stood to leave.

"Please don't kill her," Elian said.

Bael shook his head. "I'm sorry. I gave you this chance, and I hoped that it would work. Whatever has happened to her, she's not who I remember her to be. There's nothing more to be gained from delaying. She'll only kill again."

Elian objected, but it was too late. Bael vanished into the web of adani to hunt his daughter. Elian stared at the empty space, his hand outstretched, before it finally dropped.

There was nothing he could do. If he'd been like Bael—if he'd accepted the transformation adani offered—he could have followed, but he hadn't, and now it was too late. He felt as helpless as he had when he'd first encountered the Vada's true strength.

He collapsed and stared at the stars, reaching for Capricia's hand. She was crying, and there was no comfort he could offer her.

9

E lyn stepped through the portal and glanced around, certain that no matter where she was, Bael wouldn't be far behind. If Mother and Father had been able to find her, he was certainly able to, too. He'd been waiting the whole time, and she wondered if anything her parents had told her was true.

Probably not. It had all been a trap to get her to lower her defenses, to make her easier for Bael to kill.

She shouldn't have attacked them, though. Her feelings had gotten the best of her, and she'd lashed out.

The void within her, which had brought her such peace as of late, was roiled by emotion. When they'd first come, she'd been able to keep her composure, even when she saw how Father had become a cripple. She wasn't proud of it, but in her darkest moments, she couldn't help but think it was fate balancing a scale. Perhaps he would understand her better now that his strength had been taken from him.

She hated that she thought like that, because of what it said about her, but her emissary had taught her to stare the truth in the face.

Her feelings around Mother's appearance were more difficult

to unravel. Mother's guilt wasn't the guilt of a perpetrator, but of an accomplice who saw terrible deeds being committed and didn't raise her voice. Father had always listened to Mother, and even if he'd been too blind to see how he hurt his daughter, Mother must have seen. If she'd only spoken, none of this would have come to pass.

She looked around. When she'd requested the portal, she'd asked for the void to send her anywhere safe, and it had opened the other side of the portal on a rolling, featureless plain. Here there were no trees, and when Elyn thrust her adani into the ground to search for trouble, she understood why. These lands had once been the deadlands created by the Debru. Though the wandering clans had worked to heal them over the decades since the Debru had been eliminated, they were still scarred from the Debru's dominion.

The void had chosen well. Because the web of adani was weaker here, it would be harder for Bael to find her. So long as she kept her adani tightly within her body, she should have some time.

She needed a plan, and quickly. Knowing that Bael and the others could track her changed her options completely. There would be no hiding, no searching for some hidden weakness. So what was left? How could she make a difference?

She closed her eyes and connected with the void within her spirit. She didn't feel its presence the way she had on the other world, when it had inhabited a space beside her, but it heard her all the same. It was always with her, always watching, always listening, and she opened herself to its guidance.

She knew it heard her, but there was no answer to her pleas, as if she'd done nothing more than beg a wall for help. She waited, standing still, hoping that perhaps it was just a matter of time, but the void didn't answer. No emissary appeared to give her orders.

That had to be the problem. Void was short of emissaries, and those it had were busy. Once one was free, then she'd hear back. If only she was stronger, able to speak with Void directly.

A burst of adani south of her ripped her from her meditations. Bael arrived, and she instinctively raised a shield of void between them.

He was the same boy she'd once known, but her senses screamed that he'd become something much more, too. He'd killed two emissaries, and now he had his sights set on her. She would have run again, but he stood still and there was a shield between them. "There's no point in fighting against us. It only makes your situation worse."

Bael spoke quietly, his voice barely carrying to her ears. "Is that what you told yourself, to become what you are? That you had no choice, that everything is inevitable?"

"I've felt its strength. I've been in its presence. Not even you, for all your gifts, can stand against it."

"Maybe not, but that doesn't mean I'll surrender. If both paths lead to death, why not fight?"

"Because this world is different! It can live on, beyond the age of your children and grandchildren, if only you would stop fighting."

Bael shook his head. "But it's all the same in the end, isn't it? Either way, surrender dooms this world. I won't become a slave to the void like you've become, not if it means turning my back on everyone I love."

"They turned their backs on me first!"

"And is your love so weak that you care?"

Elyn took half a step back and for a second she thought she'd been slapped. She blinked. "What?"

"I wasn't there when your ascension failed, so I don't know who's right or wrong. You might have the truth of it. Maybe Elian pushed you too hard. Or maybe your suffering is your own fault. It doesn't matter. It doesn't change the fact that he loves you."

Bael continued. "I've known how to find you for a while. Do

you know why you're alive? Because Samora, Elian, and Capricia have all pleaded with me not to kill you. Do you understand that? You've killed our friends and family. You've crippled your own father, and the emissary's attack, that you supported, has led Samora to the brink of death. Despite everything, they've *begged* me, over and over, to give you another chance. Capricia and Elian came, unable to hurt you, unable to defend themselves if not for me, just to talk with you, to give you yet another chance. If that's not love, then tell me what is?"

Elyn staggered back, holding up her hands as though warding off an attack. She shook her head. "It's all lies."

"It's not me who's lying. You are, to yourself. Your plan for peace? To surrender the world so that the emissaries can harvest the red hearts? Do you hear yourself? Elyn, I know what the red hearts are. I can feel the way they twist adani, and I know they can only be created out of death. That's why you kill adanists, and why emissaries appear in the middle of our cities to destroy them. Your plan for peace is no peace at all. It's just murder."

"Stop lying!" Elyn shouted. She formed three spheres and threw them, allowing her shield to drop. She curved the spheres so they approached from different directions, cutting off as many of his escapes as she could.

He vanished, and the spheres unleashed their destruction against the healing deadlands. Elyn sought his adani, but couldn't find it. Before she could call for a portal, though, he appeared beside her. His hand moved in a blur as he backhanded her across the face. The force of the blow lifted her from her feet and spun her around. She tried to keep her feet, but her balance failed, and she landed hard.

Bael didn't follow up his attack. "Why? Why betray us this way?"

There could be no reasoning with him, and so she formed another group of spheres and threw them. As before, he vanished, and this time, she wasted none of her opportunity. She formed the weave for a portal and dove through. She landed hard on the other side and groaned as her shoulder struck cold stone. For a brief moment she thought the void had granted her reprieve, had brought her home. A quick glance told her the truth, though. It had only brought her high into the mountains, perhaps somewhere in the Scorpions' ancestral territory, but she couldn't be sure. Once again, adani was weak here, but it wouldn't keep Bael from her long.

"Why won't you take me home?" she cried out loud, but there was no answer.

"There's nothing more I can do here. Not anymore," she muttered. She wrapped her arms around herself, suddenly cold.

Bael's words echoed in her thoughts, and she hated him for that. Why couldn't he see? The emissary had seen and understood, and he hadn't even been human. Why not her own family?

Perhaps because they were too blinded by their own beliefs, they couldn't see the truth.

Although maybe the same could be said of her.

She shook her head. There was no point in thinking that way. She knew better. No one else had experienced what she had.

She tried to summon the same anger that had burned in her just moments before, but the freezing mountain air sapped it from her. She looked for some form of shelter, though she'd likely have to run again before she could settle. Her limbs grew heavy, and she almost wished that Bael would appear behind her and end her doubt once and for all.

As though summoned by her thoughts, he appeared before her. She didn't bother throwing up a shield. If he wanted to kill her, he could.

"There's no place you can hide from me," he said.

She summoned a sphere, but when he didn't react, she let it vanish. "Why haven't you killed me?"

"Because that would destroy Elian. He wants you to live, and so I'll give you the chance, even though I don't think you'll change. You've lied to yourself for too long."

She spit at his feet. "So the only reason I'm worth saving is because my death would hurt Elian's feelings?"

Bael shook his head. "Do you even hear yourself? If it were up to me alone, I'd kill you for the adanists you've murdered and injured. Yet you twist my words to suit your delusions."

She bared her throat. "Spare me. Kill me now and let me pass into oblivion in peace."

Bael hung his head, and for a long moment he didn't move. His shoulders sagged, and for the first time since their fight had begun, he looked like the child she remembered. But then he forced his shoulders back and met her eye. "I know you won't believe me, but I'm truly sorry it came to this."

He formed a bound sword of adani, its golden glow so bright she had to shield her eyes from the light. He stepped forward and raised the blade, then froze.

Before she could call him a coward, she sensed what had brought his sword to a stop. Emissaries had arrived, finally. Four of them, somewhere far to the west, though she couldn't tell any more without focusing adani and sending it to where they were. Wherever it was, Bael was terrified. His eyes went wide, and Elyn understood that her life had been spared yet again. He was about to leave.

In the next moment, she understood what she had to do. She couldn't guess at the relative strengths of Bael and the emissaries, but he'd killed two already and looked ready to take on four more. She couldn't allow him to interfere with Void's plans.

Elyn summoned a portal, and it appeared behind Bael, a darkness blacker than a moonless night. He sensed it, of course, but he was being asked to understand too many things at once. His attention was divided between her, the portal, and whatever was happening hundreds of miles away.

She didn't waste any time with a void sphere, but summoned

all the adani in her body and threw herself forward. Had his attention been less torn, she never would have reached him in time, but she took advantage of his moment of weakness. Her choice of attack, which had no chance at all of hurting him, must have also dulled his reflexes.

Even so, it was close. By the time she drove her shoulder into his stomach, tackling him just like she had when she was a child playing with the others in the clan, he was already somehow insubstantial. She wrapped her arms tight around him, holding him the way she wished Father would have held her, and propelled them both toward the portal.

He tried to vanish, but she wrapped her adani around his spirit even as she squeezed her arms tighter. It wouldn't last for more than a moment, but a moment was all she needed. The portal yawned open behind him, more hungry than it had ever been. She'd requested that it take her home, where Bael could no longer influence the battle.

Let him think himself high and mighty on a world without adani. His terrible mercy would be the end of him and the end of the clans' hopes.

With less than a step to go he tried to fight back, but it was too little, too late. She picked him up off the ground, and with a scream of victory, leaped into the portal with Bael.

10

Samora couldn't sleep well that night. She couldn't decide if showing Bael how to find Elyn had been a wise decision or a terrible mistake, and her mind tossed and turned more than her body as she argued one way and then another. Added on top of that, she'd needed Bael to save her once again, and she couldn't lie to herself any longer. Whether she fought the transition or not, her days in this body were numbered. She'd become so sensitive to adani she worried that a casual slip of control might be enough to spark the transition, a mistake she might make in her sleep.

She eventually gave up the fight, but as she rolled out of their blankets, she woke Aldrick. He came fully awake in an instant. "Is anything wrong?"

"Nothing you need to worry yourself about. I just have too many thoughts to sleep."

Instead of pulling the blankets back up and retreating again to the land of dreams, Aldrick sat up and shifted so they were sitting side by side. "Tell me about it."

"Most of it you already know."

"Tell me anyway."

She did, and though it was true he'd already heard most of it, she felt better after going over all of it again. "Do you think I chose well?" she asked.

"There was no good choice, but I think you chose well. We can only hope Bael listened and went to Elian before hunting Elyn."

"I believe that he did. I don't think he would have lied to us about that. He was a man made for honesty."

Aldrick smiled softly and held her left hand in his, warming it between his palms. "He's a good man. Killan and the clan raised him well."

Samora agreed, but her thoughts were elsewhere. "I'd give anything to throw out adani and learn what's happening. Without it, I feel blind and useless, but I don't dare risk it. I don't think I can hold the transformation back much longer."

He lifted her hand to his lips and kissed the back of it gently. "I'll love you whatever form you take."

Samora tried to swallow the stone that had suddenly appeared in her throat, but it refused to budge, so she settled for nodding. Another few tries forced it down, and she was able to say, "I know you will, but it still feels like I'll be losing you. Say I do transform the way that Bael has. It means that someday, hopefully long in the future, I'll lose you anyway."

He wrapped his hands around hers and she couldn't believe how warm they were to the touch. He rubbed his thumb against the back of her hand, as he often did when he was working up the courage to say something she wasn't going to like. "That may be true, and I hear you. Trust me, I do, and there's nothing I would like more than to spend an eternity with you, but saying farewell for good was always how this was going to end. We can't cheat that, no matter how strong we become."

Except they could, and that was the worst of it. Samora's spirit would go on, possibly as long as adani itself, but Aldrick wouldn't be able to follow. Knowing death would eventually separate them was terrible when it was inevitable, but it was worse when there was even a sliver of possibility of avoiding it. Samora bit her tongue, though.

Aldrick gently took her chin and brought her face closer to his. "I've loved you since I was first assigned to guard you, and I'll carry that love for as long as my spirit allows. That's all I can promise you, but it has to be enough."

Samora nodded again. "I love you, too, and I'll carry that love for as long as my spirit allows."

It was as though they were young again, at their bonding ceremony, except instead of making vows to one another before all their friends and family they were alone in a tent, older than dirt.

Aldrick pulled her face toward his, and when the kiss ended, there was a smile on his face. "Being as we're both up …"

Samora shook her head, then pulled her husband under the blankets.

———

SAMORA WOKE from her dreamless slumber with her heart racing. The night beyond the walls of their tent was quiet, but she couldn't shake the feeling that something was dreadfully wrong. She had halfway risen from her blankets when it felt as though her stomach folded over itself. Acidic bile rose in her throat, but she pushed it down. She didn't dare to reach out with adani, but there was only one force she knew of that had such power. At least one emissary had arrived, and close to the camp.

She swore, and the unfairness of it almost brought a tear to her eye, but there was no time for self-pity. Aldrick sat up, once again fully awake, his face pale as he was pulled by the same forces that had woken her. He looked at her, and in the manner of a couple that had been bonded for so many decades, that look said everything that needed to be said. The emissary, as it was so fond of doing, left her with little choice.

She embraced him and held him tight, feeling the pounding of his heart in his chest. "I love you," she said.

"I love you, too."

Samora opened herself up to adani and gritted her teeth as it flooded through her body and overwhelmed her channels. If her last experience had taught her anything, it was that so long as she used adani, it wouldn't complete the transformation it had started, and so she gripped the adani tight and thrust it into the ground.

She swore at what she sensed. It wasn't a lone emissary that had come to visit their camp, but four at once, surrounding them and cutting them off from any escape.

She turned her search to Bael, but his distinct adani was nowhere to be found. She searched below, in the direction of the Great Heart, but her senses were blinded and useless in the face of so much adani. Instead of searching for a man who might not want to be found, she looked for Elyn's familiar spirit, then frowned when she sensed nothing. Elian and Capricia were still in the forest where she'd initially found Elyn, too far away to do any good. She cursed again. Something had happened, and she didn't know if Bael would ride to their rescue or not. Given that he hadn't yet, she feared that he might never, and if Bael was gone, they had no hope at all against the emissaries.

Samora turned to Aldrick. "I can't find Bael."

He nodded once, tersely. He knew what that meant as well as she did. "I'll organize the camp as well as I can. Do we make a run for it?"

"We're surrounded, but I don't know what else we can do. We focus our attacks on the emissary to the east. If we can get it to move, we send everyone for the dragons."

Samora stood to leave the tent, but before she could exit, Aldrick held her in another quick, fierce embrace. She returned it, then tore herself away.

Outside their tent, the camp was already in motion. Bael ran an orderly encampment with high expectations, and the adanists on patrol had given warning the moment they felt the arrival of the emissaries. Warriors ran to their posts as healers prepared to treat the wounded. Samora shouted at the top of her lungs. "Adanists to the east!"

The cry was taken up by the warriors nearest her and echoed throughout the camp. Samora hurried east herself, surrounded by a flood of other adanists. They let her through as she announced herself, accepting her authority in Bael's absence. She appreciated that aspect of Bael's clan. They were too new to be bound to the rigid hierarchies that defined most clans, and Bael had made it clear that in his absence, Elian, Samora, or Aldrick were to be treated as leaders.

She reached the eastern perimeter of the line and looked to the horizon. Clouds covered the moon, so she couldn't see the emissary waiting between them and the dragons, but she could sense it. She kept pushing her adani out, never giving it a chance to settle within her body and tip her over the edge. Adanists formed a loose line behind her, summoning enough adani to destroy almost anything that stood against them.

Anything except an emissary, though hopefully she'd soon be proven wrong.

"Darts!" she called, and dozens of the tightly focused weaves appeared behind her. She allowed adani to rush through her body and into her own weave, creating two, then three of the monstrous weapons. Once, these had caught even the attention of the Vada. Today she hoped they killed an emissary.

"Attack!"

She threw her darts first, one after the other, and for a moment the eastern sky was filled with golden light. A handful of darts arced high while others raced low, but all converged on the point of darkness the adanists sensed as belonging to the emissary. The emissary stood perfectly still, remaining undefended, and for a moment, she dared to hope. Bael had taught them that if the spiritual core of the emissary was pierced, it would die just as any mortal. Any of the darts were powerful enough, they only needed one to strike the target.

The emissary threw up a shield of void, and the darts boomed against it, wasting their incredible strength for no gain. Samora braced herself for the inevitable answering assault, but the emissary simply dropped the shield and remained still.

Why didn't it attack? Why didn't any of them attack? Bael still wasn't here, and so they could have destroyed the camp twice over by now. They could have won the battle before the adanists had even had a chance to organize.

She didn't understand, but she knew better than to waste the opportunity. She formed another group of darts and all the adanists behind her followed her lead. They numbered more now than before, the last of the stragglers finally joining the fight. Once again, they launched their darts as one, and once again they lit up the eastern sky. They were even joined by the dragons nesting behind the emissary, who weaved their own darts and threw them at the invader.

The additional adani crashed and broke against the void shield, the emptiness swallowing up the incredible energies and leaving only more emptiness behind. Once the last of the darts vanished into nothingness, the emissary dropped its shield and resumed its silent vigil. Samora got the sense that it was doing the bare minimum to survive and nothing else, but she couldn't begin to guess at why.

Did they try to make a run for it? Try to sprint past the immobile emissary? It seemed a foolish plan, but no more so than any other she considered.

The emissary saved her from having to decide. It moved suddenly, as though it had been held in place by invisible ropes that had been cut. It raced toward them, and a single sphere of void floated above it.

"Layer shields!" Samora called.

It was a technique they'd developed since the last battle with the emissary, in which each adanist weaved their most powerful shield a few paces in front of the previous one. No single adanist could hope to stand against an emissary's attack, but perhaps together they could.

The emissary was all too eager to put their technique to the test. It hurled the sphere of void at the shields. Two more adanists flung up new layers before the sphere struck, and Samora channeled all the adani that was trying to consume her body into the shield closest to the line.

The sphere ate through the first shields as though they didn't even exist, and the adanists who held the weaves collapsed like boneless dolls as the void made short work of their adani. Four, five, and then six shields vanished as the sphere made contact, but then it slowed as it hit the seventh and eighth. Finally, by the time it hit the ninth, it vanished along with the shield.

Those who had pitted their adani against the emissary's void didn't look like they would be rising anytime soon. Two were so pale she feared they'd never rise again, but she had no time to worry. The emissary was close enough to see now, and it threw another sphere at the adanists. Adanists fell as quickly as their shields. They needed a few brave spirits to leave the meager protection of the shields and attack the emissaries directly, but the emissary wasn't interested in giving them a chance to organize.

Then the other emissaries joined in the attack, and with all the adanists focused in the east, there was no one left to protect the camp. Dark spheres landed among the tents and expanded, consuming tent, soil, and flesh with equal ease. A few adanists tried to protect themselves with personal shields, but they winked out as soon as the void made contact.

What remained of the eastern line started to break. Many warriors had families back in the camp, and their discipline broke as they understood they had no chance of defeating the emissaries. They rushed into the chaos of the falling spheres, dancing around the destruction as they searched for partners, parents, and children. Several vanished as the spheres sought them out, swallowing bone and adani whole.

It couldn't end. Not like this. But what else was there to do? She'd come to rely too much on Bael, come to trust that his mere presence would be deterrence enough. Without him, they were unbelievably weak against the emissaries.

She sensed Aldrick's adani flare, a bright candle among raging bonfires, as familiar to her as the lines on her palm. A sphere landed close to him, and like the rest, his adani vanished from her senses, either because he was gone or because he'd been hurt too gravely for her to sense among the ascended adanists.

Not him.

She called on adani, pulled it into her body, promising that she would give it all it asked for, just so long as this time, it helped her. The boundaries between self and adani ripped until only shreds remained, but she formed the strength into a bound sword and ran toward the nearest emissary. She swung the sword, but the emissary simply stepped to the side, too quick for her to follow. It thrust an open palm into her stomach, then formed a sphere of void and released it directly into her core.

Samora screamed in agony and dropped to her knees as adani wrestled within the void attempting to dig its way through her stomach and to her spine.

11

Bael was the leader of all fools. The fool all others looked to and aspired to be like as they grew in their folly. When he wasn't cursing himself, he was busy cursing Elian and his soft heart. Daughter or not, there was no doubt what Elyn had become, and now she would cost them everything. All that Elian cared for would die because he couldn't let go of the daughter that had already fled from his love.

The darkness of the portal surrounded and attacked him on all sides, and Elyn was but the slightest of shadows in comparison. This, he perceived, was his true enemy.

It was dark and cold, but impossibly malicious, a power of pure hatred, and it finally had what it hated most within its powerful jaws. It tried to snap shut on Bael, but he drew directly from the strength of the Great Heart and resisted. Darkness stabbed into the flesh he'd formed for himself, only to be pushed back by the light within.

Before the portal closed, he thrust a thick rope of adani into the mountains of his home world, spearing it through the stone into the source of adani. The portal snapped shut around the rope, but its light was too strong for the void to overpower, at least for now. Bael tethered himself to that rope, his only lifeline back to the world. If he let go, or if the rope snapped, he'd never see Shayna or Elian or any of his friends again.

So he kept the rope connected to his core and drew more adani into his spirit than he ever had before. Once, his physical body had determined his limits, and some of that body-knowledge lingered, imprinted on his spirit like an animal's tracks in mud that had dried. He'd tested how much he could draw, only increasing the amount incrementally, and still hadn't found his limit, if one even existed.

Something beside the void attacked him, pulling his attention in separate directions, and it took him a moment to realize who it was. Elyn was somehow still holding on to him, and though she didn't seem to be able to use void while stuck in the portal, she helped her new master by pummeling at his face with her fist. Compared to the pain the void shared with him, he'd hardly noticed, but once he did, it became almost all he could think about, and his focused grip on adani lessened.

Bael roared and grabbed her by the throat and squeezed. He imagined how easy it would be to keep squeezing, to crack the bones in the neck and crush the airway. He'd never wanted to more than he did in that moment, but he thought of Elian and relented. Bael had stronger opponents to fight. Elyn punched once more at his face and he flung her away with enough force that had they been upon the surface of his world, she would have broken stone with her skull.

As soon as he let go of her, she vanished, pulled to wherever this portal opened, and no sooner had she vanished than she was out of his mind. He gripped the rope of adani with renewed focus and imagined himself planting his feet. There was nothing solid, not here in the in-between, but the act of imagining it strengthened his grip on adani.

Confident in his hold, he formed a spear and thrust it into the darkness. The golden spear sank deep, disappearing just beyond the reach of his hand, but he had no sense of contact, and the assault against his flesh didn't diminish. He let go of the spear, then weaved a shield around himself.

The void fought against the weave, but so long as he kept the shield close to him, his will proved greater, and thread by thread he blocked the void's attacks with adani, until a small sphere of golden light protected him. Void raged against the sphere but made no progress.

The ineffectual assault gave him time to think, time to gather himself. He could fight the void, but it seemed as though it would do little good. Hurting the void would mean finding its core, and Bael didn't sense it anywhere nearby. He could stab and stab with spears, but would do nothing except burn adani.

Better then, to retreat. He was still in danger here even though he'd successfully shielded himself. It pained him, though. The void's focus on him was a physical weight, distracting it from everything else. So long as he was here, his world was a little safer. But he couldn't stay. He tugged on the rope of adani, which had become the void's focus as soon as it realized it couldn't reach him.

Progress was slow but steady. The void fought every pull, but its strength was too distributed, and so long as adani was close, Bael was stronger. Void gnashed its teeth against the rope, but Bael simply planted his feet against his shield and pulled harder. One tug at a time he came closer to his home world.

There was no gradual transition, no subtle brightening of the void that surrounded him. One moment he was being attacked on all sides, the next he was back on the mountainside. The portal snapped shut as soon as he emerged, and he let his shield go and released his tight grip on the rope. He took one deep breath of the cold mountain air before he felt the twisting of an emissary's presence in his stomach.

He cursed himself again. In the midst of the portal, stuck

between worlds, he'd forgotten the brief sense of the emissaries that he'd felt before Elyn tackled him. Four emissaries had arrived, and they'd just begun an attack on his camp.

Bael's spirit dove deep into the web of adani, pulled toward the Great Heart that he now considered almost as much a home as the camp on the plains. He reached the Great Heart in the blink of an eye, then launched himself up through the web of adani to the surface, directly behind one of the emissaries.

This one was too busy dropping spheres on the camp to pay close attention to its surroundings. A bound dagger flashed to life in Bael's hand, and he stabbed deep into the emissary's core. When the tip of the dagger pierced the core, the emissary shrieked, a high-pitched wail that scratched against any spirit that heard it. Void fled from the broken core, and the emissary misted away.

The assault against the camp stopped as their attention shifted completely to him.

He sensed a portal open behind him and shifted to the side as an emissary emerged and tried to wrap its arms around him. Nails as sharp as claws scraped against his side, but the wounds closed with a thought. Bael bound a sword and cut at the emissary, but it shifted away, readily giving up ground. He shifted next to it, racing the void's servant at the speed of thought.

He was too slow. His transformation had happened too recently, and though he learned quickly, the emissaries had used their bodies for more years than he'd been alive. The gap in experience revealed itself quickly, and only grew worse as the other two emissaries joined the fight. It became all he could do to keep ahead of the swords and spheres that sought his core. Twice they came close, stabbing deep into his stomach with their blades but just missing the center of his spirit.

He fled into the Great Heart, though it pained him to do so. They waited for him to reappear, but as soon as they realized he'd run away, they returned their attention to the camp.

Bael had hoped for more time, but the emissaries were experienced warriors who understood how they could draw him out. For the second time that night he asked the Great Heart for more adani. It focused his spirit, and he appeared before them, bound blade in hand. All three shifted at the same time, too fast for even Bael's eye to track.

He filled the air with adani. Though he couldn't see them, he sensed them as holes that shouldn't exist, and his spirit responded faster than his mind could think. He shifted closer to one, and light met void, each clash of powers vibrating ground, air, and flesh. Bael grit his teeth and kept his focus on the movement of void around him, reacting instinctively to their cuts and attacks.

His sword slipped past the dark blade of one of the emissaries, and he was so surprised he almost missed his opportunity. But the emissary's core was unguarded, and Bael cut straight through it.

The final two emissaries dropped spheres of void at their feet that expanded and swallowed up earth and sky. Bael once again fled beneath the surface, cursing as he felt the adani channels directly beneath the battleground vanish. Their loss wasn't much more than a nuisance, but with the battle as even as it was, even that small difference might be enough.

He darted up along the webs of adani that remained, appearing between the emissaries and the camp. He hurled two spears at them, less to harm them and more to keep them occupied while he closed the distance. To his surprise, his spears were joined by several darts. He risked a glance back and saw Grandmother burning with adani, leading a small group of survivors into the battle.

Grandmother burned brighter than she ever had before, and there was no chance of her going back now. The emissaries had pushed her over the edge, and Bael hoped they would live long enough to regret their error. Adani boomed around them, and

Bael used the cover to advance, shifting between the blasts until he stood before the emissaries. The darts didn't stop falling from the sky, but Bael didn't mind. They affected him less than the emissaries, and any advantage was welcome.

The emissaries retreated, shifting backward as fast as Bael could pursue them. Bael gave up the pursuit, not wanting to run too far away from the protection Grandmother and the others provided. The emissaries halted their own retreat and threw up a shield to protect themselves from the darts that never stopped. Bael extended his senses toward the emissaries, sensitive to any new techniques.

They stood still for several long moments, then Bael felt their presence weakening as they misted back to wherever they'd come from. He shifted toward them, then stopped himself. He'd already run straight into one trap today. There was no need to risk a second.

The darts stopped falling once Grandmother realized the emissaries had disappeared, but Bael held onto all the adani he'd summoned. He listened, expecting the emissaries to appear close by. He waited patiently, then finally released adani. If they were to return, he'd be ready.

The powerful fluctuations of adani behind him tore his attention away from the emissaries' disappearance. Samora's power rose and fell like waves on a stormy sea, and her attempts at control were as ineffectual as a child wrestling a dragon. Bael shifted so that he stood beside her. A quick probe with his adani confirmed that she was too far gone. Adani filled every hidden corner of her body, overflowing the well-worn channels it used to follow. Not even Bael could help her now.

It was nothing short of amazing that she was still here. Adani's pull on her spirit was such that Bael felt it simply standing next to her. Yet she refused to surrender to the pull, holding onto her body with a stubbornness that bordered on foolishness.

He started to remind her that all would be well, but she turned on him and shuffled toward the destroyed camp. Her breathing was labored, but in between gasps, she said, "Aldrick."

Bael sent his adani toward the camp and found Grandfather. Weak and fading fast, but still alive. He picked Samora up in his arms, and though she struggled, her strength was nothing against his own. He sprinted toward the camp, shutting the sights and sounds of the destruction from his mind. Only Grandfather mattered. The rest he would endure later.

Grandfather lay next to several patches of destroyed ground. Void, as was its nature, had simply caused everything it touched to disappear. Tents, grass, lives. All were simply gone.

It was clear what had happened. As the void had fallen all around them, Grandfather had gathered as many families together as he could. He must have had help from others, because he wouldn't have been strong enough alone. They'd raised shields, likely the layered technique they'd been working on, and saved dozens and dozens of lives. He must have been too near the edge of the shields when they finally collapsed.

The effect of his heroism was easy enough to see. A dozen paces behind him was the only intact section of the camp, and though the people still cowered within, Bael sensed many lives.

Grandfather's wounds, though, were grievous. His left arm was almost completely gone, sheared off just short of the shoulder. His left leg was little better, with a section cut away that started below the knee and had taken most of the foot. Small pools of blood surrounded him, and his eyes went in and out of focus.

Bael set Grandmother down next to him, then staggered back. Though the body he'd created was filled with adani, an enormous emptiness opened inside him. He'd never looked up to Grandfather the same way he had Grandmother and Elian, and at times he'd even asked himself what Grandmother saw in him, but now, too late, he understood.

Grandfather had always been there. Always been as dependable as the sunrise. He'd been a strong warrior surrounded by legendary warriors, but he'd never once complained. He was always ready to listen, and Bael had frequently dropped his concerns on him. The idea that he might be gone, that he might not be around, was a blow he hadn't been prepared for, like one of his legs had gotten kicked out from under him without warning.

Grandmother kneeled at his side, holding his right hand in both of her own. Bael couldn't imagine her own pain, but her tears fell freely, and her face as close to his. She was pouring adani into him, trying to heal him and keep herself in her body, but she was doomed to fail. Grandfather was too far gone, the void too destructive to the human body, and no matter how much adani Grandmother sacrificed, it would never be enough.

Grandfather gently pushed Grandmother's adani away, effectively refusing her healing. It had given him some strength, though, and he clasped her hands, and for a moment, he was the same man Bael had always relied on. Though he was a few paces away, he could hear Grandfather's last words clearly, as though they were meant not just for Grandmother, but for them all. "I'll always love you," he said.

Grandmother pressed his hand to her cheek. "And I'll always love you. Thanks, my dear, for the best life I could have asked for."

Grandfather smiled, closed his eyes, and his last breath was an easy one.

Grandmother held his hand for a moment longer, then laid it gently across his chest. She looked up at Bael. "You'll take care of his body?"

Bael nodded once. "Of course."

"Thank you," she said.

Before Bael could respond, Grandmother surrendered the

battle she'd been fighting since her first encounter with the emissaries. Adani consumed her body and her spirit was pulled roughly toward the Great Heart, leaving Bael alone among the destruction and the dead.

12

E lian and Capricia rode the dragon back to Bael's camp, the silence thick between them. Capricia had sensed Bael's travels as he'd reappeared far to the northeast, but then she'd lost him at almost the same time that the emissaries had appeared. Even though Elian couldn't throw out his adani nearly as far as Capricia, he could sense their arrival. It twisted his stomach, the same as it did for all who touched adani. It was even worse this time, because their sudden appearance, combined with Bael's unexpected disappearance, could only bode poorly for the wandering clans.

Capricia had sensed some aspects of the fight, her face pale as she'd listened to adani's whispers. What she knew was precious little. Bael had returned and fought the emissaries, and the battle ended when the emissaries left. She confirmed that Bael was still alive, but that was all she knew.

They didn't know what had happened between Bael and Elyn, and now Elian layered worry for the rest of his family on top of his worry for Elyn. And the worst of it all? There was nothing he could do. For most of his life he'd trusted himself to be the person who could make things happen, but now? Now he was just a cripple being escorted from place to place by his wife, humored by a younger generation that had far surpassed even his greatest strength.

He hated the bitterness that grew in his spirit, but what could he do? No man could endure what he had with a smile on his face.

Capricia's silence proved it well enough. She was the foundation of his life, the one who could always turn his attention to a brighter future when hope dimmed in his own spirit. She was always ready with a kind word, or a piece of encouragement, but when she finished telling him about the battle between Bael and the emissaries, she'd given him a strange look he couldn't decipher, and she'd barely said a word since.

No doubt, she felt the same as him. The emissaries were proving themselves foes that not even the wandering clans could defeat, and there was no denying the truth of the matter.

The dragon flew fast, and Elian sensed the creature's worry for his own family, who had nested outside of Bael's camp. Flying to Elyn had taken nearly half the night, but returning to the camp took only half that. Still, the sun had risen on the eastern horizon by the time they neared, which meant they were forced to observe the destruction of the camp from afar.

Capricia's gasp was audible even over the rush of wind, and Elian felt much the same. The camp reminded him of the destruction the Vada and the Belogs had caused back when they had fought against the wandering clans, but the clean devastation of the void was somehow worse, as it left little to grieve over. When the void struck it simply subtracted, taking everything and leaving nothing behind. A warrior killed by natural causes could be buried or burned, and grief could begin its slow healing process. Void took too much, and without a body the loss remained an open wound. The mind accepted the loss, but the spirit did not.

From a glance, it was clear that much of what he loved, what he'd left behind last night without much thought, was gone. Half the camp, at least, if not more, was bare dirt, without even ashes to mark the destruction. The dragon was kind enough to land them just outside the tents so that Elian wouldn't have to make the long walk to the camp.

Not that it mattered much. Once he'd gotten off the dragon, he couldn't force his feet to move. He should have been here. He wouldn't have contributed that much, but he could have fought, could have done *something*.

Killan was the first to find them. His eyes were red and puffy, and he walked as though he was dragging an enormous burden, but he shuffled up to them. He took the couple in his arms and embraced them both. Great, heaving sobs shook his body, but his grief was quiet. The camp was quiet.

"What happened?" Elian asked.

Killan sniffed, wiped his nose on his filthy tunic, and tried to stand tall as he spoke. "Four emissaries attacked, and for a time, it was just those of us in the camp against them. Mother led the defense, hoping to fight a way to the dragons so that the families might escape. She wasn't successful, and the camp was under fearsome attack. Father had the presence of mind to gather as many families together as he could, and anyone in control of adani was ordered to add layers to a shield. He even added one."

Killan shuddered, then continued. "As the spheres fell, so did our shields. I was one of the last warriors holding one, but I dropped it as soon as the void struck it."

Elian's nephew hung his head. Dropping the shield so quickly might have saved his life, but it had put the rest of the camp in greater danger. "Father shoved me back toward the others and threw up his own little shield to protect us. It wasn't much, but we'd weakened the sphere just enough. It stopped with him, but not before it hit him. He died from his wounds."

The words rang in Elian's ears, but it was as though they

couldn't quite touch him, like his spirit had thrown up a shield around his body that kept him safe from sorrow. Aldrick was dead? It couldn't be possible.

But if he was dead …

Elian's gaze shot up and searched for Killan's, but his nephew couldn't see past the toes of his boots. Elian's knees grew weak, and he feared he might fall, but he leaned harder on his walking stick. He already knew, but he had to ask. "What about my sister?"

Killan shook his head.

Elian's arms trembled, but it was Bael who answered the question from behind Elian. "She gave everything to protect the adanists. Doing so finished the transformation. She's gone, but I believe that she'll return soon."

Killan's shoulders shook, but when Elian went to lay his hand on them, his nephew jerked away. Elian let his hand drop, then backed away and turned to Bael. His great-nephew's arms were crossed, and when he saw he had Elian's attention, he tilted his head to the side. "Come with me."

His tone welcomed no argument, and so Elian did. Capricia stayed behind with Killan, and Elian saw them speak quietly to one another, as though sharing a secret.

Bael led them out of the camp and over a small rise. They didn't go far, but Elian noted that they were out of sight. He didn't care. He had questions.

"What happened?" he asked. "What happened to Elyn, and to Samora?"

Bael's face twisted and he clenched his fists. Elian thought he might strike, but then the moment passed. Bael looked resigned, as though he'd tried to explain a fact to a child a dozen times and found it easier to simply give up. He sighed and said, "I do not know what happened to Elyn. I followed her into the Scorpions' mountains, but then I showed her mercy and gave her one last chance to turn from her path. Instead, she opened one of those doorways behind me and tackled me into it. I let my guard down, and it almost doomed us for good."

Elian started to say that Bael shouldn't be so hard on himself, but a sharp look from Bael silenced him.

"In the portal I encountered what I believe to be the master Elyn claims to serve. A force stronger than the emissaries. I couldn't beat it, but I could escape it. Once I fought my way back to this world I returned to the camp. I killed two emissaries and the other two retreated."

"And Elyn?"

"I don't know what happened to her. She attacked me within the portal, and I threw her off. She vanished, and I assume she returned to wherever the portal originally opened. I cannot say for sure, though. All I can tell you was that she was alive when I last sensed her."

Despite everything she'd done to him, it was the first piece of good news Elian had heard all day. He bowed to Bael. "Thank you for showing her mercy. I know she doesn't deserve it, but she's still my daughter."

Bael's eyes darkened and he shook his head, but he said nothing in response.

"And Samora?" Elian asked.

"Transformed. Or, at least, she's started the process. I don't know if what happened to me will happen to her, but she's with the Great Heart. Only time will tell what happens next."

"You said you thought I'd see her again soon."

"I believe she'll return, though I worry. She was with Aldrick as he died, and that may have destroyed her will to continue on. I worry that she might not finish the transformation."

"What does that mean?"

Bael shrugged. "I'm not sure. I think it just means death, her adani joined again with the cycle of adani that flows through the Great Heart."

Elian looked east, where the rising sun was brightening a brilliant blue sky. He couldn't find a cloud anywhere, and it felt as though the whole world was mocking his loss. It should be raining and overcast, a dreary day that cast long shadows over lethargic spirits.

When Elian looked back to Bael, he saw that anger had returned to his great-nephew's expression, and his fists were once again ready for battle. He kept his voice low, but it seemed to cost him. "You could have stopped this."

Elian frowned and answered with a blank look.

Bael stabbed a finger in the direction of the camp. "They're dead. Dead because I'm the only adanist who made the transformation, the only one who raised himself to a level that can stand against the emissaries. The. Only. One."

He turned his finger on himself, stabbing himself in the chest. "They're dead because I made a mistake. I showed mercy when I shouldn't have, and I was too overconfident in my own strength. I have to live with that. But none of that would have mattered if either of you would have just listened to me!" He was hissing at the end, trying to keep his voice down but starting to fail.

Understanding dawned slowly upon Elian. His thoughts were still battered, tossed about by all the sorrow he'd been forced to absorb. "You think this is my fault?"

"It wouldn't have happened if you'd accepted the transformation. You could have tracked Elyn yourself, spoken to her without me needing to be there. You could have appeared here at the camp the moment the emissaries arrived. We could have fought together. Maybe they never would have even attacked, had they known there were two of us here, ready to fight. I don't know. All I know is that this wouldn't have happened."

"You can't blame me!"

"You might not have been the one who threw the spheres, but it was your inaction that allowed this to happen."

Elian shrank back as Bael seemed to grow taller, towering over him. "We couldn't have known."

The excuse sounded flimsy, even to him, but his tongue moved faster than his mind.

"What did you think was going to happen? That the emissaries were going to simply going to leave us alone after we killed one of them? That they were going to wait until we had all the time to prepare we needed? You're no fool, so don't pretend to be one. No, you couldn't have known they were going to attack last night, but you knew they were going to try, and you didn't prepare."

"I—" Elian had no answer. At least, none worth uttering. He *had* thought they had more time.

Except that wasn't true. He hadn't known how much time they had. All he had were excuses for the action he didn't want to take.

He looked down at the hand that wasn't holding the walking stick and it trembled. He clenched it into a fist and took a deep breath. It was too late to make things right, but not too late to do better.

"I'm afraid I've become a coward," he said.

Bael's expression softened, though he didn't argue Elian's self-condemnation. "It doesn't matter what you say. But you still have a chance to help us, to save humanity again. Are you going to take it, or are you going to keep running?"

Elian looked in the direction of the destroyed camp. "I'm done running, but I'll admit I'm still scared. Letting this happen? It's like taking my own life. Death is death, but I never thought this would end with suicide."

"It's a transformation. Not death."

Elian nodded. "Still terrifying."

Bael came close and laid his hand on Elian's shoulder. It was warm and strong, a human hand, and Elian took comfort in its touch. He kept worrying that if Bael touched him, his hand would pass through him as though he were a ghost. Bael was real, though, and Elian would be, too.

"Give me a day to see my family and speak with them, and to grieve with those who survived this. Then you can guide me through the transformation."

Bael nodded. "Tomorrow, then. I look forward to it."

13

Elyn passed through the portal and skipped across the dim world she now called home. Bael had thrown her with such force that her body bounced twice before skidding to a stop among a barren patch of loose soil. At least the void hadn't opened the other side of the portal among the jagged stone of her cave. Even so, she lay still, coughing up dust and blood. Once she caught her breath she rolled onto her back and stared up at the twilight sky.

A shiver ran through her body and she wrapped her arms around herself, though the cold in her spirit had little to do with the temperature of the air.

When had Bael become a man? More to the point, when had he become a man like that?

He reminded her of a younger Father. When she'd been little, Father had been larger than life. She remembered every one of the stories told about him, every one of the legends passed from adanist to adanist. No one had ever said so explicitly, but they said it to her all the same: Elian was the best of them. They all went silent when he spoke. Giant men who could crush her in their palms whimpered like frightened dogs when he threatened them.

Now Father was nothing better than a cripple, but Bael had stepped forward and become Elian's true successor. Not just in strength, for Bael was stronger than Father had ever dreamed of becoming, but in that moral righteousness.

Elyn snarled and spit in the dirt. Father was so confident that he was always right it never even occurred to him that he might be corrupt, that he might have been the one to make her into what she was. And Bael had the temerity to tell her she was wrong! He was no different, the same arrogance in a younger skin.

Anger gave her the strength to push herself to her feet and she looked around. The mountains that had become her guide for however long she'd been here were nowhere to be found. The barren land surrounding her was perfectly, abnormally flat, and stretched for as far as the eye could see in every direction.

She had no idea where she was, and even less idea how to get from where she was to somewhere she knew. She tried summoning a portal, and the hole in the air opened willingly enough, but she knew, without entering it, that it wouldn't let her pass through. Void wanted her here for now.

A sudden blow doubled her over and it felt as though the entire world was quaking beneath her feet. A moment later, she realized it *was* quaking beneath her feet. She spread her feet out wide for balance, but the shaking ended a moment later. The void within her core trembled, though. It was the same feeling she'd experienced when she was connected to the void, only stronger than before, strong enough that it had shaken the physical world.

Somewhere out there, her cousin had escaped the void's grip, returned to his world, and killed emissaries. She knew it without being told, knew it as though she'd seen it with her own eyes. She raised her fist to the sky and promised that someday, she'd find a way to make Bael suffer the way she'd made Father suffer.

She'd wipe the self-righteousness from their faces and teach them humility.

The world shook again, stronger this time, and she lost her footing. She fell hard into the dead soil, and the impact jarred something loose in her. Not physical, but within her spirit, like for just a moment, adani had burst forth and pushed void into a small corner of her body. The tenor of her thoughts shifted and the thought of Bael no longer sent her into a rage. Adani's warmth, a reminder of the world she'd left behind, almost brought her to tears, and after the shaking subsided once again, she sat up and hugged her knees to her chest.

Why had she ever been glad to be here? She was cold and alone, stranded on a world with Void her only companion.

And why hadn't Bael killed her? She'd given him all the reasons in the world and he had more than enough strength, but he hadn't. He'd tried to talk to her, tried to bring her back to Father, who she'd hurt worse than anyone else.

She couldn't make it make sense, and for the first time since she'd been freed of her curse by her emissary, she experienced a thin sliver of doubt, which on this world felt like a dagger driven through her skull. She'd gone too far to return. Even if she wanted, she had no way of returning home.

She didn't know how long she spent there. This world always messed with her sense of time. All she knew was that at some point, she realized she was no longer alone, and that she'd been watched for some time. She turned her head and saw the head emissary there, staring at her with those dark eyes. There were no footprints in the soil around her. She'd appeared in that place and waited for Elyn to stir.

"You failed," the emissary said.

"They discovered a way to track my movements. My cousin, Bael, has grown stronger than I imagined."

The emissary inclined her head at this, a rare point of agreement between them. "He killed two of the four emissaries sent to your world and threatened to kill two more. Our losses upon your world are unacceptable."

She spoke as though she expected Elyn to have some answer, some insight that Void and its emissaries had overlooked. At the moment, all Elyn possessed were enough doubts to keep her awake for an eighthday. She dropped her eyes so the emissary couldn't see the doubt. There was little chance of hiding it from Void, though. Their connection allowed it to peer within her spirit as though it were an open door.

"What will happen now?" Elyn asked.

"It is still to be decided. The sudden losses have unbalanced us, have revealed to us weaknesses we didn't realize we possessed. Strong as our master is, it is spread across too many worlds. We cannot spare the forces we'd like to subdue your world properly. The cost in other worlds would be too great. Either a new way must be found, or your world must be destroyed. For now, though, we recover, and we argue. There will be no haste in our decision."

Elyn sensed—something—between the emissary's words, a feeling unspoken that she couldn't quite understand. There was more happening than the emissary would say. She wouldn't reveal it anytime soon, either. More immediate problems existed, anyway.

"What about me?"

"It is still to be decided," the emissary repeated.

"And in the meantime?"

The emissary shrugged. "It is none of my concern."

And then she was gone, leaving Elyn stranded in the middle of nowhere on a world she knew next to nothing about.

———

For a time, Elyn sat, surrounded by thoughts and doubts that skipped across the surface of her thoughts like dragonflies skimming across the top of a still pond. She couldn't go deep, couldn't hold on to a thought for more than a moment before her attention was drawn to the next. She wasn't aware of how long she sat, but it must have been for a time, because when she stood, her muscles groaned in protest.

Her throat felt tight, and when she raised her fingertips to it, she could feel the slight swelling from where Bael had grabbed her. Even in that moment, after she'd come close to tearing him away from everything he loved, when he'd had her in his hands and all he'd needed to do was squeeze a little harder, he hadn't killed her.

Had it been another man, she might have called him a coward, but not Bael. He'd proven his courage plenty, and it wasn't fear that held him back.

Elyn pushed thoughts of him away. She had her own problems. Tempting as it was to sit here and wait for something to happen, that wasn't the way she'd been raised. If there was one lesson she'd learned from Father, it was that almost all sins and mistakes could be forgiven, but a lack of effort couldn't. That teaching had become a guiding truth.

She brushed herself off and looked around. The land stretched out, unbroken and the same in every direction, which gave her little to make a decision with. She closed her eyes and sought the void, finding it with ease here. She sank deeper into the feeling, stretching out her senses.

The void was vibrating with activity, far busier than she'd ever noticed it before. Though she couldn't understand what was being passed along, she recognized it as conversation between the emissaries. They were spread out across many different worlds, but were all connected, all held together by the power of the void. They spoke together in pairs and in small groups. At times, emissaries were summoned to speak directly with their master, and at other times the groups would merge and split apart.

It reminded Elyn of when the various clans would get

together back when she'd been younger. The Wolves and the Bears had been frequent companions, but she'd visited all the clans at one point or another. Being Father's daughter had ensured that she would be well traveled. Gatherings had always been memorable. Families were, in some circumstances, reunited with sons and daughters that had joined other clans. New friends were made. Games were held, drawing some groups together for a time before they broke off and went their own way.

The emissaries were much the same, though their conversations lacked any of the joy she expected from clan gatherings. It came as no surprise they'd be talking as much as they were. The emissary had spoken truly. Bael had hit them hard. Knowing there was so much conversation did little to help her, though. She was just looking for a direction she could walk.

Their master, the emptiness at the heart of the dark web, called for another group of emissaries, and Elyn followed their journey through the darkness, wishing she could travel as they did. Soon, when she was an emissary, she would. Then she would travel wherever she pleased.

Something about the emissaries caught her attention, but it wasn't until she focused closely on them that she understood what. As they approached the void, she felt their presence not just through the web of darkness that connected them, but physically, in her body. They were close, but that made no sense at all.

The feeling didn't fade as they drew closer to their master. If anything, the feeling of their physical presence grew stronger. She pulled herself from her meditation on the void and sought their presence in the physical world. Without the deep connection to the void she lost most of her sense of them, but they were here. She turned slowly until she was reasonably certain she was facing them. There were no landmarks with which to fix the point in her mind, but she put her right foot forward and started toward where she thought the presences were.

THE DEAD AND barren plains she'd been left on stretched as far as she feared. The walking was easy enough, for everything had been leveled to a flat plane and the loose soil wasn't as bad as the deadlands had been back when she'd been a child. She thought she was making good time, but as with all things related to time in this place, it was hard to be certain.

She'd walked a mile, or maybe two, when the emissaries she'd been tracking vanished. Her one beacon winked out, and she cried out. Her throat was parched and her legs felt as though they were ready to collapse. She couldn't afford to wander without direction, but the land refused to offer up anything she could use as a landmark. Never in her life had she seen such a swath of destruction.

She reached back out to the void, diving deeper into the darkness. She heard the echo of their master calling for another small group of emissaries from a distant world, and once she had the sense of them, she returned to her body and spread out her awareness.

This group approached just as the other had, and they were even a bit easier to sense. Elyn hurried in that direction, not wanting to lose this next beacon. Her legs complained against the abuse, and she was reminded that she didn't even remember how long it had been since she'd slept or eaten. Her needs were different on this world, but she couldn't ignore them forever.

A growing certainty drove her, though. She was even more sure as she felt this second group of emissaries, clearly pressing against her awareness as she neared wherever they were.

Another mile passed and the second group of emissaries left, but Elyn was no longer worried. She sensed something more, enormous but hidden, nothing more than the softest of pulls upon the void within her core. If she hadn't been looking for it, she didn't think she ever would have found it, and without the void already being a part of her, it would have been too well hidden. She followed it, hurrying for no other reason than the burning desire to know what lay ahead of her.

Her surroundings finally changed. Ahead of her, the ground began to gently slope downward. Her strides lengthened, then came to a stop. It was hard to see in the everlasting twilight of this world, but as she squinted, she was certain. There was a hole in the ground ahead of her, large enough to fit an entire camp with plenty of room to spare, and even from a distance, she was certain it would drop down forever, or at least close enough to forever that it made no difference.

This was where the emissaries went when they were summoned.

Her emissary hadn't brought her to any abandoned world.

He had brought her to the home of Void, where the emptiness at the center of the web lived.

14

Bael sensed its arrival the moment it set foot on his world. The void it possessed wasn't as overwhelming as some of the emissaries he'd fought, but the distinction was meaningless in any way that mattered. It still possessed the strength to destroy enormous swaths of a city with little more than the snap of its fingers.

A fact even more concerning given that it had appeared in a city.

Bael didn't hesitate, despite the prohibition regarding adanists from the wandering clans the cities still insisted upon. Webs of adani carried him to where the emissary stood, waiting for him. He reappeared upon cobblestone streets cast in long moonlit shadows from the buildings that towered higher than most trees.

It was close to the middle of the night here, and though he counted hundreds of human spirits burning gently in the buildings that surrounded him, the street was empty except for him and the emissary. Lights burned in a handful of windows, but most were asleep.

Bael's vision swam as his senses and spirit adapted to the

unique demands of appearing so suddenly within a city. The presence of so many spirits in such a small space overwhelmed him briefly, as though he was asked to stare into the light of a thousand roaring bonfires. Lights and spirits dimmed as he adjusted, but he cursed himself for chasing the emissary so recklessly. Had it been so inclined, an immediate attack could have been devastating.

The emissary had certainly expected his arrival. It took the form of a tall, thin man with pale skin and dark hair. Long dexterous fingers gripped the hilt of a bound blade of void and a protective barrier of void surrounded it. Eyes blacker than night glared coldly at him as it shifted its feet to better defend against Bael's attacks.

The moment of disorientation passed, but the emissary made no move to attack. Adani danced at Bael's command, but unleashing it within the confines of these streets was little better than letting the emissary use void uncontested. "What do you want?"

The emissary pointed its sword at Bael's heart. "Your life."

Bael began to drop back into the web of adani. "Then come get me."

A harsh laugh interrupted his disappearance. "I don't intend to chase you around your world, nor will I let you pull me away from this city."

It formed a sphere of void in its empty hand, then grasped the sphere between thumb and forefinger. It pinched the sphere and held it as though it were a deadly seed to be planted in the street. "Surrender your life to me, or this city becomes the third to experience the cleansing power of my master."

Bael's mind raced. He'd feared an attempt like this since he'd settled into his new transformation. Though he'd imagined a similar scene dozens of times, he'd never solved the problem to his satisfaction. This was why he'd so desperately urged Elian and

Samora to follow his path, to complete the transformation before they ran out of options. Surrendering himself, especially now, when there were no others to take up his mantle, was no different from surrendering the world.

If the question were only a matter of numbers, the answer was simple enough. A hundred, even a thousand civilians were nothing compared to the number of lives across the world. Reason demanded he fight regardless of the immediate consequences.

Only these were lives, not numbers, and he already carried the burden of too many on his shoulders.

He let the flow of adani through his spirit slack, and he stood a little taller, opening himself to more attacks. "You speak true? That if I surrender, you'll spare this city?"

"Void has no need to lie. My word will outlast the mountains of your world."

Bael nodded and spread his arms out wide.

Confusion spread across its face, which lasted only a moment. Then it smiled, vicious and cold. It lifted the hand pinching the sphere of void until it aimed at Bael's core. The sphere shot from between its fingers, a streak of darkness sight alone couldn't track.

Any amount of void was dangerous, but the sphere was smaller than many Bael had fought against. In the heartbeat before it struck, Bael gathered adani to protect his core. The void struck, devoured a lake's worth of adani, then vanished.

Bael shifted the moment the void was finished.

The emissary wasn't a fool, and it had never fully trusted Bael's unspoken surrender, but it had allowed itself to hope, and in that brief moment between when the void had struck Bael's flesh and when it had disappeared, it had believed. Its disorientation only lasted for the blink of an eye, but at the speeds Bael could move, it was time enough to gain a sliver of advantage.

The emissary betrayed something of its past, for its deep-seated instinct was to defend not with spheres of void, but with the bound blade in its hand. The lights in the windows flickered out as Bael pulled adani from the surroundings and the Great Heart. Golden light clashed with void's ink dark edge, both blades seeking the core of the other.

Bael moved slightly faster, but whatever advantage he gained was offset by the emissary's skill with a blade. Time and time again, Bael thought he had an angle on his enemy, but it closed before Bael could cut into the emissary's core. Both Bael and the emissary cut into the other, but the cuts of both healed a moment after they were delivered. Only the fatal cut mattered.

Bael cut too hard, and the emissary pounced on the sudden imbalance. Its void blade drove Bael back toward one of the tall buildings. Bael leaped to avoid a deadly blow, his feet landing upon the vertical wall of the building and holding him there.

If the emissary was flustered by the change in footing, it showed no sign. It pursued Bael up the wall, and Bael suddenly found himself fighting as though the side of the building was as flat and even as the cobbled streets below.

The difference shouldn't have mattered, for the forces that pulled and pushed on physical bodies no longer applied, but his mind and spirit were slow to adapt. The emissary suffered no such problem, and Bael was forced to shift away before the emissary killed him.

Back on the ground of the street, Bael prepared to meet the thrust he was certain was coming for his core, but the emissary didn't pursue, didn't shift to keep itself next to him.

Bael cursed his short-sightedness.

The point of getting so close to the emissary had been to prevent it from using spheres, and now Bael had allowed it the space to do just that. Two formed in its free hand, and it thrust them toward the ground. Both expanded as they fell.

He should have let them strike, but his instincts demanded

otherwise. He shifted so he was beneath the falling spheres. Golden barriers of adani bloomed above him, and the spheres of void struck, once again pulling enormous amounts of adani from the world.

The void disappeared without a trace, but as Bael fought them, the emissary shifted behind him. A blade of void stabbed at Bael's core, and Bael only threw up a shield around his core at the last possible moment.

Unlike the spheres, though, this void was connected directly to the emissary and couldn't be dealt with so easily. The tip of the blade pressed against Bael's shield; the void replenished by the emissary's seemingly endless strength. Adani poured into the void, and Bael had no choice but to pull directly from the Great Heart.

The emissary groaned as it pushed harder, still seeking to overwhelm Bael's defenses. It's focus narrowed to the point of its blade, barely more than a hair's breadth away from accomplishing its master's most fervent desire.

With a growl, Bael reformed his bound sword, risking the division of his focus as he stabbed into the emissary's core.

The emissary's dark eyes went wide as it realized its mistake, but it was too late. A sharp tip of adani slipped into the emissary's core, and the emissary misted out of existence, as though it had never been more than a foggy nightmare blown away by a breeze.

Bael's wounds healed and he slumped against the wall of the nearest building. His heart pounded in his chest and he swore to himself.

In time, his breathing and his heart returned to normal. He hoped that Samora would return soon, that she would complete the transformation that he so desperately wished for. So long as it was him alone, they were vulnerable to attacks like these.

He pushed himself from the wall of the building. More lights were being lit in the windows, but for all the power unleashed in the area, there was surprisingly little damage. That was good. He was tired of the wandering clans suffering for the events that transpired whenever he visited a city.

Bael shook his head, then vanished back into the web of adani before anyone could come and question his presence.

15

She floated in a sea of light and warmth, carried along by gentle currents that soothed a spirit battered by years of struggle. Adani lapped against her spirit like the gentle waves of a lake splashing onto shore. True peace, she found, wasn't a lack of activity, but was instead the full commitment to whatever the moment needed. There was a time to rest, and when she rested, she floated without purpose, just ... being, and nothing else. There was a time to play, and she loved to play, carried along by currents of warmth, she rose and kissed the roots of oaks, dandelions, and thorns, and then she spun around and embraced an adanist, pulled into their body by the force of their spirit, then returned to the world.

There were places in the world she couldn't go, and that was wrong, and when her spirit brushed up against those places it was cold. She didn't linger there long, but she didn't linger many places long.

Except for the places she could not go, there was no discontent. Warmth and peace were good, and she had more of each than she'd ever had before.

Before?

A strange idea. There was no before, and there was no after. There was only the now, the eternal now, as it always should have been. How could it have ever been different?

Samora.

A voice and a name, both familiar and unknown. Her spirit vibrated as the tremendous energies around her rippled, but the disturbance soon passed, like the ripples fading after a child threw a stone into a still pond.

Samora!

Harsher this time, louder, and her spirit ripped, not within, but where it met the energies that surrounded it. For the first time in … forever? … there was separation, a *her* and an *it*, and a part of her was cold, like she'd ended up near that place where adani didn't go. She didn't want to leave the warmth, but something else held her and kept her from returning to the warmth she craved. She was no longer part of a whole, indistinguishable from the rest.

A moment passed and she became something else, similar to what surrounded her yet different. She didn't like it. She reached for what she had been, but knew there was no going back. The coldness in her grew, and she was about to despair when she became warm again. She was embraced by another presence, the feel of its spirit nearly as familiar to her as her own. It was not the warmth of the Great Heart, but it was a worthy reflection, and she wanted to melt into it, but she couldn't do that, either. It held her, as close and as tight as it could for as long as it could, and then it pushed her away, and she went up, up, up, and all was separating, and then …

Samora opened her eyes. She stood in a field, naked as the day she was born. The farmer who'd been working the field stood and stared at her, his mouth hanging wide open. Samora bowed, then looked around. This land was familiar somehow, and yet she didn't immediately recognize it. There was something, though. The shape of the land tickled her memory, and when she realized what it was, she laughed out loud, because of course she'd be here.

The farmer nearly jumped out of his boots at her laugh, and she felt a brief pang of sympathy. She clothed herself with a thought, bowed again to him, then turned east. There was no need to walk anymore, but she walked anyway. It grounded her and gave her time to return to her senses.

She and Bael were going to have plenty to talk about. She understood, now, what he'd wanted to express in their conversations but unable to say. Her hand brushed up against a stalk of growing wheat and she smiled as she sensed both its stalk and its adani.

Before, she'd been human. She still thought she was, though perhaps it was up for debate. She held up her hand and shielded her eyes from the sunlight, though she could have stared at the sun without problem. Now she was both human and adani.

What had once been an effort for her now came to her as naturally as breathing. She'd used to focus all her attention to push adani through the world and learn more about it, but now she simply knew it all. She could sense each of the wandering clans, could surround herself with the noise and bustle of the cities, if she wanted, all as easily as turning her head.

Samora saw how she could, if she wanted, dive into the web of adani and appear somewhere else in the blink of an eye. Movement was no longer a matter of training flesh and bone, but of training the will to move her spirit.

She left the farmer behind, and it was only a little time later when she came upon a small village. There'd been another village here, once, but an angry and afraid Vada had wiped it away with a single blow. Samora thought that if she focused, she could sense the layers of adani here, both the old that had been destroyed by the Vada and the new that had grown in its place. Life always found a way back, no matter how much the Debru had tried to take.

Samora sensed Bael, who appeared a respectful distance away, asking by his position whether or not he could come closer. She turned to him and nodded, and he shifted, appearing beside her in a moment. He bowed deeply. "You're back."

She nodded, not trusting herself to speak quite yet.

He gestured to the village. "I don't recognize this place. Is there a reason you appeared here?"

He didn't ask the question to hurt, but it did anyway, a gentle ache, followed by the quietly dawning realization that time would wipe not just this, but so much more, away. It seemed that she had to have brought him here before, but maybe she hadn't. There'd always been so much to do, and all that was left of what she had known were memories.

"This was the land where Elian and I were born. Our village used to stand here."

Bael knew all their stories by heart, so she didn't need to explain what had happened, nor tell him that these buildings were not the ones she'd known. He looked around, taking it in, and to her surprise, he smiled. "You know, I can almost imagine it. The two of you running through the fields, coming back home for meals."

"Elian was never meant for the farm. He always dreamed of the wandering clans, much to our parents' dismay. He helped how he could, but there were times, when I was mad at him, that I thought he was happy the Debru circle appeared, because it gave him the excuse he'd always been looking for."

"And you?"

"I think I could have stayed. Maybe. I was curious about the world, but I was mostly curious about adani, and I would have thought, back then, at least, that I could have found out all I needed while staying home. Once I left, though, I knew there'd be no going back, at least, not coming back to it as a home."

Bael nodded, and she thought he assigned more meaning to her words than she intended them to have. "I wasn't sure you were going to return. I searched the Great Heart for you and intended to help you, but I couldn't find you."

Samora nodded. "I think ... I think it was complete. There was no coming back and no desire to come back."

The words looked like they'd hurt Bael. "You'd become one with adani, hadn't you?"

Samora shrugged. "Maybe. I don't know. I think, though, that if it had been up to me alone, I would have stayed."

Bael winced, as though she'd pinched him too hard, but the expression only lasted a moment. "It wasn't?"

"I was content."

Again that look of hurt, and Samora felt the need to explain. "I was tired. I've already fought and won one war. Friends have come and gone, and there are more who have returned to adani than I have now. I love my family, and I want to see them well off, but I've always known I would have to say goodbye sometime. We all have to say goodbye sometime."

Bael dug his toe into the soil, twisting it in little half-circles. "I don't understand. We don't have to. Not anymore. That's what this means."

Samora shook her head slowly. "I'm not so sure, but I am glad you feel that way. You're young, and you have more ahead of you than you do behind. That's as it should be. But there comes a time, for me certainly, but I think for most, when we're ready to return, to put our cares down for good. I don't think I want to fight that feeling. Even now, back here, I don't think I want to fight it."

"Then why did you return?"

"It was Aldrick. He gave me the push I needed, and then I was here."

Bael answered with a contemplative grunt, then wiped his eyes with the back of his hand. "I miss him."

"I will, too. More than I can say." She paused, not sure if she should reveal her true feelings, but Bael needed to know. "I—I don't know how long I'll want to stay. I don't even know how much of a say I have, but I'd rather be there, with him, or at least close to him."

Bael nodded, "I understand. But you'll stay with us for a time? We need you."

"For a time, yes. Let's find a way to defeat these emissaries, and then I'll feel like I've earned my rest."

16

Elian shifted his position on the dragon for what felt like the tenth time since they'd taken off earlier that morning. Riding a dragon was never the most comfortable, but over time, one's body adjusted to the rigors.

Except now Elian had lost the adjustments he'd endured years of riding to develop, and that was added to the aches, pains, and lingering wounds that had become his constant companions. He hated complaining, and any single complaint would have made him feel weak. What warrior would complain about a sore calf or an aching shoulder? But the small pains layered themselves one over the other, working together like a well-trained clan to disrupt every routine of his life.

At the moment, he felt the wound in his calf every time he pressed his legs more tightly against the dragon, which was necessary each time it banked and changed directions. He'd relax his legs and grip between the scales tighter with his hands, but then his shoulder would lock up and his forearm would cramp. He bit back a curse, refusing to darken the mood any more than he already had over the past few days.

Visiting Hadena and Harald had been a good decision. They'd

both visited him after the first battle with the emissary, but he'd been in even worse condition then, and the visit hadn't gone well. They'd considered staying with Bael's clan to be close to him, but Capricia had shooed them away. Both had families of their own that needed care, and their lineage made them important voices among the clans. It had been better for them to return.

Now they'd all had a chance to see him again in slightly better spirits, and he had rolled on the ground with his grandchildren, even though it had driven deep needles of pain up his spine. He'd told the children what he intended, and though the announcement was greeted with something less than enthusiasm, they seemed glad that he was at least up and taking action. They'd spoken late through the night and left to tears and heartfelt embraces once morning had come.

Capricia mistook the cause of his constant shifting. She leaned closer and spoke in his ear. "They'll be fine. And so will I."

"I know, but it doesn't mean I want to leave."

She held him close, and continued to do so until they both felt the adani within their dragon shift. The movement was subtle, but they were both connected to it with threads of adani, and so it couldn't escape their attention. Elian recognized the movement, as he'd felt it before. Their dragon had been contacted by another, and they were speaking in the manner of their kind, a rich language of both sense and words that lay beyond the human capacity to understand.

The dragon left itself open to the humans, so if they'd wanted to peek in on the conversation they could have, but Elian didn't feel right doing so. No matter how many times he was assured it wasn't a problem, Elian still felt as though it was no different than pressing one's ear to the side of a tent to hear what was happening within. He waited the conversation out, confident that if the dragon needed to pass anything along, he would.

The conversation ended a few miles of flight later, and the dragon asked permission to speak directly to Elian's mind. His agreement led to a third person joining them on their flight, sitting in an impossible position upon the back of the dragon's head and looking down at Elian and Capricia. The figure had long dark hair that didn't move in the wind, but its eyes glowed with golden light of dawn. He spoke, and though he was gentle, his voice still echoed deep in Elian's head. "Our elders wish to speak to you."

"What about?" Elian asked.

"Adani," was the dragon's cryptic answer.

Elian frowned. "Then wouldn't someone else be a better choice?"

"They were adamant it must be you. They've met together in the center of the continent, an occasion which hasn't happened since you were a youth. It's an honor to be invited."

Elian grunted. "So you're saying that it's not that much of a request?"

The dragon paused as it considered its answer carefully. "Refusing ... would be an unwise choice."

Elian actually laughed. "I've probably made enough of those in my life already." He glanced back at Capricia to confirm his intuition, and she nodded. "Very well. Thank you for carrying us there."

***

THE FLIGHT to their destination wasn't any more comfortable than the miles already behind them, but Elian could at least be distracted by the question of what was waiting for him when he landed. He could think of plenty of reasons why the elders might want to speak to a human, but if it had to do with adani, there were better choices than him. Bael, almost certainly, and even Samora, though it was an open question whether or not she would return. Lacking either of them, there were plenty of ascended more sensitive to adani than he was.

Knowing that the elders had gathered only added to the mystery. Once, there'd been only one elder dragon, but under the Vada's assault, the responsibility had been split between multiple dragons. Samora had been there and seen it done, and since then, the elders, so far as Elian knew, had never all been together. They'd become something like the wandering clans, moving frequently but coming into contact rarely. Whatever had brought them together was important. Plenty of recent events could qualify, but he was at a loss as to which was most likely.

Fortunately, their flight didn't last long. By late afternoon they'd reached the gathering, and Elian asked if they might circle once or twice before landing. Their dragon agreed, and all the pain in Elian's body was pushed from his thoughts as he stared. He'd seen large gatherings of dragons before, but he couldn't think of any that were this well attended.

The elders stood out among the crowd. Not only were they considerably larger, as the transition to elder was physical as well as mental. Their bodies elongated and became more serpentine, and Elian counted five among the dozens of younger dragons.

Capricia stared beside him, and her thoughts ran in a similar direction as his own. "I haven't heard anything about dragons abandoning the clans, have you?"

Elian shook his head. "No. Either there are more dragons than we ever guessed, or they've been having a lot of little dragon babies."

He didn't think it was the first. Samora, in particular, had spent a lot of time with the dragons, and she would have told the clans if there were this many more dragons.

Before he could ask the dragon that carried them, they started losing altitude. So many dragons in one place warmed the air and broke the wind rushing across the rolling plains. They landed closer to the circle of elders than Elian would have guessed, and he couldn't help but feel that it was a gentle accommodation granted to him by the dragons. Regardless of the reason, he thanked the dragon for shortening his walk.

Once they had both climbed off the dragon and thanked him, the dragon took off and joined others who appeared to be his friends. They snapped at one another in what Elian had learned, after many misunderstandings, was a playful way. Elian's spirits lifted at the sight, and then he turned to face the circle of elders.

What had seemed large when seen from above was now enormous. Elian's entire body weighed less than one of the dragon's massive legs, and on the elders, the legs weren't much. The group as a whole had a solemn demeanor, reinforcing Elian's guess that whatever brought him here wasn't news he wanted to hear. Elian bowed as deeply as his body allowed, then took a place in the circle.

He couldn't help but let a sense of awe wash over him. Once the sight of a dragon in the sky would have sent his heart racing. His ascension granted him more adani than the dragons wielded, but his fear of them had never fully faded. Their size was a part of it, and their foreignness another. Arok had been as close to him as a brother, and they'd shared enough trials and adventures to fill an eighthdays' worth of campfire stories, but even so, Elian had never felt as though he completely understood the dragon. Their long lives and different ways of thinking didn't quite translate directly to human perception.

The circle of elders reminded him he shouldn't take their strength lightly, though. Unlike adanists, who burned their strength freely, dragons tended to conserve their adani and use as little as possible. It led him to underestimate their true strength. If they so decided, they had more than enough adani to crush him here, even if he had been healthy.

Elian wished Samora was here, or could at least be in his head, as she had been so often. Her death had cut their connection and left his thoughts feeling empty. She had always been the one skilled at talking to others. He supposed all he could do was his best. "I am honored by your invitation, and it brings me joy to see so many of you gathered here today."

Being as he wasn't connected to any single dragon, he didn't have any insight into the conversation that sprang to life around him, but he'd spent enough time around dragons to catch a sense of what their exchanges of adani meant, and he gathered his introduction had been well received. Even so, none of the dragons extended adani toward him, leaving him uncertain how to best proceed.

"I would guess, both from the invitation and the gathering here, that there is a problem. How may I help?"

How Samora would laugh if she could see him now. From being convinced the dragons meant to destroy humanity to asking politely if there was a way he could serve them. The repeated thoughts of her blurred his vision, and he blinked away the tears before they could fall. He'd known her longer than anyone else in his life, and yet it still wasn't long enough.

He sensed that once again his manners endeared him to the group, but he wasn't prepared for each of the elder dragons to reach out to him at once. Their adani was gentle, but so much at once threatened to overwhelm him. He'd never heard of connecting with more than one dragon at a time, but he opened himself to each of them. They connected, and when he blinked, he stood among a group of their human projections. The human forms they imagined for themselves were wildly different. Some were tall and broad shouldered, one was a shorter and pudgy woman, and another was as muscular as Harald had been. The only quality they shared was their golden eyes, all of which were fixed on Elian. Each form was projected in front of the dragon it belonged to, so Elian could easily understand which dragon was speaking.

The short woman said, "We welcome you and wish to express our sorrow for those you've lost. They were our friends as well."

Elian swallowed down the stone that appeared in his throat as he bowed again. "Thank you."

"Unfortunately, as you've surmised, there is a problem which requires you help. It regards the transformation Bael has undergone, and which Samora might soon complete."

Elian rose from his bow and waited for the elder to continue.

"We fear that this transformation may doom our world as surely as the emissaries' plans will."

Elian fought to keep his expression steady as her words sent him back almost three decades, to an argument much like this. Elian and Samora had already ascended and shown that others could do the same. The first generation of ascended were in the middle of being born, and the second wasn't far behind. It had been a difficult time in human-dragon relations. Elian and Samora had believed it was because dragons could no longer rightfully claim to be humanity's protectors, a role they'd held for untold generations. The dragons argued it was because they were the protectors of adani, which was being abused by all the sudden changes to the world. The hearts, once the dragons' greatest treasure, were now granted to adanist after adanist, each of whom embraced them and ascended.

The dragons had wanted fewer ascended, or even no ascended at all. They'd argued that humanity was altering the balance of adani the dragons had worked so hard to maintain since humanity had been born. Elian and Samora had pushed back. At the time, they'd still been certain the Debru would return stronger than ever, and that ascended would be needed in the wars to come. Samora's efforts to replant hearts across the continent were largely guided by the dragon's fears at that time.

Since then, though, Elian had always expected the dragons to be sensitive about humans becoming stronger. He should have expected this summons, but with everything else happening, he'd forgotten.

"How so?" he asked.

The man whose stature reminded Elian somewhat of Harald said, "The transformation allows your spirits to access the Great Heart which resides in the center of the planet. Bael has used this strength repeatedly already. It is how he's fought the emissaries, but it's also how Samora had enough strength to heal as many of your wounds as she did. The Great Heart is the largest source of adani in the world, and it seems likely Bael believes it to be inexhaustible. Unfortunately, that isn't true, and the more he and all of you pull on it, the more severe the consequences will be."

"What sorts of consequences are you describing?"

"They range in severity, depending upon the purposes the heart is used for. The best future that seems reasonable is one in which the deadlands return, but this time extend far beyond their previous boundaries. The darker futures destroy all life."

Doubt seeped through his connection and the dragons noticed. The woman interjected and said, "Perhaps it would be best if we show you what we've seen. Would you permit us?"

"Of course."

The connection with the dragons deepened, and more of their adani poured into him. He ground his teeth together as the adani pressed against the wounds Elyn's void had left in his body, but the pain passed as his sight was consumed by a vision from the dragons' past.

He was flying over snow-capped mountain peaks which looked like they belonged to the far northern edge of the continent. The view entranced him for a moment, until his attention was drawn to the dragon's sense of adani. The sense was about as different from his personal sense of adani as could be. He fought to notice anything more than a few hundred paces away, and even that required a focused push and concentrated effort. This was more of an effortless awareness that spread across the land, supported by the other elder dragons.

Was that part of why they'd spread out?

The vision didn't give Elian time to ask. He could sense the battle unfolding between the emissaries and Bael. The emissaries were points of darkness that spread their corrupting influence like a heavily-dipped quill spreading ink across a page. Bael was light itself. His great-nephew drew his attention, and he witnessed the battle for the first time, even if it was only through adani.

The dragons allowed him to focus for a moment, then pulled his awareness wider, until he could sense almost the whole web of adani that spread across the land. Only then did Elian witness what so concerned them. Bael pulled enormous amounts of adani. That was neither news nor mystery. Only from up high and from a distance could Elian see how it pulled massive amounts of adani through channels never meant to carry so much, breaking them as it rushed toward Bael. The dragon's attention dropped deep into the land and forced Elian to pay attention to the connection between Bael and the Great Heart, a thread of adani thicker than any rope.

What Bael pulled from the Great Heart was only a small fraction of what the Great Heart possessed, but it was pulled from the world and forced into the void, which did not return it. A small amount, simply gone, meant nothing.

But as the dragon returned his attention to the sky and then returned Elian's sight to his eyes, Elian understood. This was only one small battle, with more expected. Bael was just one warrior, but Samora, if she returned, would be another, and Bael hoped Elian would be a third. Each by themselves meaningless in relation to the Great Heart, but even an enormous bucket of water could be emptied one ladle at a time.

Elian looked around the circle, and then his eyes settled on the elder woman. "Can it be replaced?"

"In time, provided the hearts are properly cultivated, probably. There is much we don't know, and the situation is not without hope. Samora has brought more adani to the land than we ever imagined possible, but it pales in comparison to what this war promises to cost us. It may be that if too much adani is used, the only future for our planet is one of a slow decay."

"As if our victory against the Debru had never happened," Elian mused. The thought cut deep, that even after all they'd endured and fought for, it might still amount to nothing. "What wisdom would you offer? You've shared with me your worry, but we must still fight the emissaries. Without the transformations, what hope do we have?"

"That is the very reason this council was convened. Unfortunately, no answer has been forthcoming. We risk doom by fighting, but our end is certain if we allow the emissaries their desires. For now, we can think of no better option than to fight, but we believed it necessary you understand the risks that you run."

Elian bowed deeply once again to the elders. "I will bring this information to Bael, and if an answer is found, I will pass word along through one of the dragons helping us."

The elders bowed as one, which stirred the adani in Elian's spirit. He didn't want to let them down, not after they put their trust in him. He left the gathering on the back of the same dragon he'd flown in, his spirit heavier than before.

17

Elyn's foot slid as she dislodged a piece of loose stone. It only slipped a little, but she cursed at her treacherous footing. The slight decline had become steep enough she had to plant each foot carefully or risk a tumble. Her eyes roved around the gaping wound, but the dark stone and soil revealed little in the dusky light. The sense of Void was stronger, though, and she grew even more certain that at the very least, some remnant of her master lay below.

It wouldn't be long before she could no longer walk down the slope. The decline would become a nearly sheer cliff, and if she wanted to proceed, she'd need to climb down.

Before she reached the cliff, though, she saw signs of an old path, a thin, ragged trail that wound through the shattered stone toward the hole. Stones had fallen across the trail in some places, but it had to lead somewhere, and so Elyn followed it. She picked her way along the trail, curiosity overwhelming any exhaustion she might have felt upon her return. Her stomach rumbled, but the nearness of her master gave her strength.

Twice she feared she'd lost the path to rockslides, but each time she found it again. She didn't allow herself to question her actions, but kept walking, placing one foot in front of the other, until she looked up and realized she was about to drop into the hole itself. Darkness made estimating the diameter of the hole difficult, but it was enormous. A dragon could have flown inside and circled comfortably. She battled a wave of vertigo as she tried to find the bottom, but it was swallowed by darkness.

Elyn returned her focus to her feet. Placement had been important before, but as she neared the cliff's edge, it became a matter of life and death. Thankfully the path here was easier to follow. Any rock that had fallen this far had continued into the hole. She walked slowly, keeping one hand against the cliff face as the path carved a thin ledge into the stone. As she descended, her eyes adjusted to the lack of light and she saw a hole in the cliff face, which was almost certainly this path's destination. Her spirit quivered when she looked into that darkness, as though it quailed before a dragon, mouth open and eager to devour her whole.

She looked down into the hole once again and imagined how easy it would be to simply tip over and fall. For a long, glorious moment she would be free of all her worries and all her doubts. Then a quick, painless end, and an eternal rest. Would her adani find its way back home, or would it be trapped on this world forever? The question kept her pressed to the side of the stone, and once the desire passed, she stepped forward carefully once again.

With her gaze on her feet, the sudden widening of the path and the arrival at the cave's mouth caught her by surprise. She looked up and peered into the gloom. Her sight didn't travel far, but far enough to be certain there was nothing natural about the cave. Its floor was flat and slanted downward and the stone of the walls was smooth, as though shaped by master masons.

Elyn walked in, and as she did, she found she could see a few paces deeper than she had before. She stepped deeper into the cave and once again could see a few paces farther. The pattern repeated until she looked back and realized her sight only carried as far behind her as it did before her. The light from the opening had vanished completely, encasing her in this bubble of shadow and gloom.

She continued to follow the path, and though the way seemed barely lit, there was always just enough light to continue. She didn't allow herself to ask why, but kept marching forward. Void grew stronger yet, so strong now she sensed its presence without any effort on her own. The path descended and twisted but the smooth floor allowed her to walk quickly. Answers waited at the end of the trail, and she wondered what shape they would take.

The monotony of the tunnel and the overwhelming sense of Void dulled her senses, and she walked directly into the web of void strung across the tunnel. It was a subtle weaving, but strong despite its lack of substance. It wrapped around her the way a spider web did when she brushed her hand through it, but it sank into her skin and straight to her core. Void wrapped itself tight around the adani in her core and she grunted in pain, but the weaving was curious about the void she possessed.

It reached out to explore the void, the tips of its gossamer threads playing across the gift granted to Elyn by her master. After a brief examination, the slight weight of the weaving fell from her spirit.

She resolved to be more careful as she traveled deeper. The weaving had felt like a trap, searching for any light in the darkness to destroy. It hadn't known what to make of her, half void and half light, but had decided to let her pass. She might not be so fortunate if she walked into another.

Once she was well and past the weaving her vision expanded so she could take in the entirety of her surroundings with a glance. The smooth tunnel ended in an enormous room, which she would have called a cavern except there was nothing natural about it. Square stone pillars, each side twice as wide as she was broad, connected floor to distant ceiling. The edges of each pillar were sharp, as though the masons had put down their tools and declared the job well done just a day or two ago.

The scale of the vaulted ceiling made her weak in the knees. Thanks to Aunt Samora, humanity had recovered many of the lost secrets of their ancestors, and buildings two, three, and even four stories were now common in the cities. When she'd been younger, she'd stood in awe of the buildings that rose as high as trees, but this, this was so far beyond what she'd guessed was possible. She was underground, beneath a weight of stone she couldn't begin to calculate. How did one even begin to build such an edifice?

Stranger yet was her ability to see any of the room. Light from the surface was a distant memory, and these walls were untouched by the soot of flame, yet she could see every line and decoration carved into the stone pillars as though she stood under the light of a blazing sun. A shiver ran down her spine. This was not a space designed for one like her. She was too small, too weak, and too fragile to belong here.

A sphere of void floated above a stone pedestal at the other end of the room, pulling at Elyn's spirit with a gentle yet demanding persistence. She brushed the tips of her fingers against the stone as she walked toward the sphere. The pillars were warm to her touch. Closer now, she saw the sphere slowly spun, imperfections in the void visible to whatever senses she used to see in this place.

Elyn stopped before the sphere and looked behind her. Such a hall should have been used for feasting and celebration, as hundreds could have fit with ease. It never had, though. She was as certain of that as she was certain the heart of the void lay somewhere beneath her. The void would never tolerate so much life, and though the thought wasn't new to her, in this place, it chilled her to the bone.

She didn't dare put names to her feelings, didn't use reason to attack her doubts. She reached out to the sphere and put her hand upon it. Nothing happened until she connected with the void in her core, when she dropped into memories that weren't her own.

It was, in many ways, much as when she'd experienced dragon memories as a child. She found herself in another time and another place, her spirit housed in a different body she had no control over.

The only difference was that she didn't belong here. She knew as soon as she entered the memory. The sphere had been a monument, a physical reminder of memories long past. Not something mortals were meant to explore.

Unfamiliar smells made her want to vomit, and she strode across a battlefield filled with more bodies than all the cities of her home world added together. The ground she found between the fallen bodies squished beneath her toes, blood turning the once rich farmland into mud that swallowed her foot up to her ankles. She used the butt of a spear to steady her shaky legs as she picked her way back toward the line of the battle.

Elyn's host's thoughts were empty. A mind can only experience so much before it surrenders any attempt to understand, and that line had been crossed before the sun had reached the midpoint of this bloody day. Now only a quarter of the day remained, but the horror raged on.

Some voices asked for help. Others cried until their chests stilled and their tears dried on their cheeks. Many cursed, but she ignored them all. When bodies moved beneath her and tried to stop her, she slammed the butt of her spear against the offending arm. If they still resisted, the sharp end convinced them to release her.

Elyn didn't sense the void, but the emptiness of her host's mind was familiar, though Elyn couldn't say why.

Her host crested a small rise and took stock of the battle, fought with a force similar to adani. Golden spears fell like rain as lightning erupted from a cloudless sky to fell the warriors below.

The powers at play were near the limits of Elyn's comprehension, the equivalent of hundreds of ascended adanists fighting at once, with a handful being at least as strong as Bael had become. The ground trembled beneath her feet as clouds of dust rose in the distance.

Her fist clenched and Elyn's focus was dragged into the body of her host, which reminded her uncomfortably of the way Father's adani channels had expanded over the years. Her host wasn't what Bael had become. Clear boundaries still existed around the channels, a line that separated host and light, and yet her host was still almost entirely channels of light. Channels that had no doubt been formed over a lifetime of training, but were now empty.

She couldn't grasp the light. Her constant companion over all the days of her life, only it abandoned her now, on the day she needed it most.

She continued forward, her steps growing stronger as a trickle of light returned to her body. A tentative seeking, using the barest sliver of light, confirmed her worst fears, the reason this war had started in the first place. The light was leaving their world.

They'd first noticed it years ago, as arable farmland turned to dust and sun-scorched brush. Their best minds had searched for the cause and found it easily enough. The light was fading. Test after test confirmed it.

Her host's mind wanted to jump from memory to memory, but the thoughts were banished quickly. The years of argument that devolved into a civil war no longer mattered. Only now remained, and the opportunity to save their world was growing shorter by the moment.

She couldn't bring herself to care. There had been so much fighting and so much suffering. Even if some sliver of the light survived, all that it would mean was a longer period of suffering for those who lived to see the next sunrise. The light would never return to the way it had before. Too much had already been lost. Still, she walked toward the battle, for what else was there to do? Better to die among both friends and enemies than linger until the end.

She felt—something—growing within her, an all-consuming emptiness where a massive amount of light had once been. She explored it with another gentle seeking, risking yet another sliver of her light to discover the truth of it. Upon contact, the emptiness swallowed the light whole, and her body warmed as though she was standing naked under a bright sun. It grew stronger within her, and she fed it another slice of light, which it devoured as hungrily as the first. Once again, the warmth spread through her, more comforting than any memory of better days.

On a whim, she fed it everything, every scrap of light that remained within her body. It was pitifully little compared to what she had once possessed, but it was everything. Such a gift, on any other day, would have killed her.

She swore her heart stopped, and for a moment she possessed peace, a true and perfect contentment.

Which vanished a moment after, replaced by the same emptiness that had been stalking her thoughts since before this battle began. Now, though, the emptiness had form, and she could command it. A sphere formed at her fingertips, and when she threw it at a wounded soldier begging for mercy, it drilled a hole through his chest, swallowing up all the light he possessed. A shudder ran through her body as the void devoured the light of another, a pleasure deeper than any she'd felt before.

She created sphere after sphere as she ran toward the battlefield, dancing among the bodies the way she'd once danced through the fields as a child. She was a child, in some sense, reborn through a power she didn't fully understand. Death followed in her footsteps, and by the time she reached the line of the battle, she had become an unstoppable force. The emptiness within her knew no limits to its hunger, and it devoured what little of the light remained in the world.

When it was over, her world was quiet, and there was no more suffering, as there was nothing left alive to suffer.

The memories skipped forward in time, pulling Elyn with them. They were all variations on a theme, though. Her hunger was all-consuming, and it wasn't content with just one world. It found a way to seek out other life and to travel from one place to another. It devoured as it traveled. In time, the host's physical form deteriorated, or perhaps it was more accurate to say that it was no longer needed. Like a Vada, or an emissary, or whatever it was Bael had become, it became nothing more than spirit and force. It had birthed the emissaries and spread itself across the worlds, always consuming more.

There was more. So much more. Eras of life, followed by a sudden opposition. It wasn't light alone that opposed void, but the memories came to a sudden end, and she was left with the sense that the end had been caused by something else, something the sphere couldn't show her.

Elyn wasn't sure if she pulled her hand away from the sphere or if she was ejected from the memories, but she'd seen enough, and she found herself once again in the empty hall, her hand floating just above the surface of the sphere. She jerked her hand away as though she'd held it too close to a fire.

She couldn't rid herself of the memories. They were a part of her now, as though she'd lived them herself. She wished they weren't.

"You were like us once," she whispered.

She shook her head. She'd been here too long if she was starting to talk to herself.

Still, the revelation unsettled her. She'd always thought of Void as a force, equal and opposite of adani. But it wasn't.

Elyn asked her question of Void, but its attention was no

longer on her. It—no, she—spoke with the emissaries, attention focused on a distant, rebellious world.

There was another tunnel that traveled yet deeper under the surface, closer to where her master protected herself. If she wanted answers, they were there. Even as she studied the tunnel, she sensed another emissary being pulled into a conference with their master, no more than a few miles away.

She shook her head. She'd seen enough, and she needed time.

Elyn turned from the hall and began the long journey back to the dim light of the surface.

❧ 18 ❧

Bael wished he'd accepted Shayna's offer to join him, but when he considered the matter again, he supposed he was glad that he hadn't. Whatever happened, it was better that he learn himself, first, then share the news with her. He could sense her from across the camp, waiting in their tent for him to return.

Not for the first time, he thought that she deserved better than what he could offer her. She'd never wanted a normal life, even by the wildly different standards of a wandering clan, but that didn't mean she wanted the constant chaos and fear he worried would define most of his life.

He hadn't announced his arrival, but Grandmother apparently had endured enough of him pacing outside her tent, because she emerged with a questioning look on her face. "Did you want something?"

Bael forced himself to stop pacing. "I was hoping you and I could speak."

"Of course. You know you're welcome at any time." She stood there, waiting.

"Somewhere privately, perhaps?"

A quizzical look flickered over her face, but she nodded. "Did you have someplace in mind?"

"Maybe the training grounds Elian had been using while he was here?"

His great-uncle still hadn't returned, and when Bael had gone searching for him with adani the day before, he'd found Elian among the dragons. They'd gathered, which was unusual, but Bael believed he would have been invited if his presence was desired, and so he waited eagerly for Elian's return to learn what the meeting was about.

Grandmother nodded again and vanished, her movement between places as fast as thought. Bael paused a moment to admire her quick learning. Granted, she'd learned many of her techniques from him, but she'd picked them up faster than he expected. Some elders lost their adaptability with age, but Grandmother hadn't suffered from that particular curse. Now that she had joined Bael, he expected she would keep learning until the end of time.

He let his body dissolve and reform in the training ground.

"Is something wrong?" Grandmother asked.

Bael squirmed under her questioning gaze, though she'd asked nothing untoward. Some matters simply weren't easy to discuss. He looked straight at the ground and thought of Shayna, which gave him the courage he needed. "Maybe. I would like it if you would check my health, please."

Though he couldn't see her, Bael could hear the frown in her voice. "What is there to even check? Your body isn't a body anymore, at least, not the way we understand it."

"I know, I know. It's only—please?"

"I can try. Give me a moment."

Bael expected the feel of her hand on his shoulder or his forehead, the same way she had when he was a child and he'd taken ill. He'd always welcomed her gentle but firm touch, because it had meant that she was near and that he wouldn't be sick for much longer. Legends swarmed around Grandmother the way flies swarmed around dung, and it was sometimes hard to know what was true and what wasn't, but Bael had always known one fact for sure: Grandmother could heal anything that could be healed. She didn't need to be in contact with him anymore, though, and he found he missed the reassurance of her hand on his shoulder. All he felt was her adani run through him, as quick and light as a rabbit on the run. The search only took a few moments.

"I don't sense anything you wouldn't expect," Grandmother said.

Bael pressed his lips together so he wouldn't sigh. He'd hoped she'd find something and start the discussion, but she left him with little choice. His cheeks flushed and he pointed. "Could you check here, please?"

He was glad he wasn't looking at her, though he imagined her face without problem. She'd have one eyebrow arched in disbelief, and she'd be shaking her head.

"Why?"

The question was asked with such tenderness, Bael looked up. All he saw on Grandmother's face was genuine concern and a worry that she'd already guessed the reason. Knowing she felt the same gave him the courage to answer. "Shayna and I have been trying to start a family."

There wasn't anything more than needed to be said.

"When did you start?"

"Essentially right after I returned. Our efforts have been ... consistent."

The corner of Grandmother's lips turned up in a smile, but there was a sadness within she couldn't hide. She made no effort to check him again. "Sometimes these things just take time," she said, and Bael wasn't sure who she was trying to convince.

"I'm aware, but—" Bael couldn't bring himself to say it. He struggled to find the language to describe the sensation, but something had changed upon his return. The end of his and Shayna's lovemaking remained pleasurable, but yet somehow … less.

Grandmother nodded. "I'll check."

He felt the light touch of her adani once again, this time more focused. The pressure increased as her focus sharpened, although not enough to become painful. Eventually Bael sensed her adani retreat. She didn't speak, but Bael couldn't bring himself to look at her.

"I cannot be sure, but—I'm sorry, I don't think you can," she said. He didn't have to look to know that she was crying.

A knot tightened in his chest, and he blinked away the tears that threatened to form in the corner of his eyes. He'd worried, of course, and then became increasingly certain, but part of him had refused to believe. As Grandmother had said, sometimes these things just took time.

He'd always wanted children, and a lot of them. Enough to someday form the roots of an entirely new clan, if they so chose. Shayna, too, had been eager, and after his death and return, they'd wasted no time, for they were suddenly aware of how little time was guaranteed to them.

"How sure are you?" he asked.

"Mostly, but not completely." Grandmother sniffed, then gathered herself. "It's not something one would notice unless they were looking. Adani flows through the area like it should, and is little different than any of the others I've ever checked. But at a closer look? There's something missing. An essence, perhaps, though that doesn't describe it well. In most men, the adani gathered there has a feeling of potential, of energy untapped. Yours does not. It's just adani, with nothing else."

"Is it something I can fix?"

The rustle of fabrics told Bael that Grandmother had shrugged. "I wish I could tell you. My instinct is to say that you can't, but I don't know what the limits of your ability are. My instinct, though, is that the answer is no. I'm sorry."

Bael shook his head. "It's not your fault. Thanks for checking, though. I appreciate it."

He didn't move. "How am I going to tell Shayna? She's been worried she's the problem, and I'm glad that I can tell her she isn't, but what does it mean for us? Should we even be bonded if I can't father a family for her?"

Grandmother moved and put her hand on his shoulder and his thoughts calmed. "I don't know, but I'm also not the person you should be asking. I believe in both of you, and you'll figure it out together."

Bael forced out a crooked grin, though it was nothing but a lie. "I hope you're right."

They bowed to one another and Grandmother vanished, reappearing a moment later outside her tent. Bael gathered his thoughts and his courage and followed her into the camp, where the love of his life waited for his devastating news.

BAEL FOUND Elian and Capricia sitting alone around a fire that night, deep in conversation. They'd arrived earlier that evening, but Bael had been with Shayna and that had consumed all his attention. The sight of the two huddled close, as they often were, lifted Bael's spirits, although they were so low it wouldn't take much.

Elian looked up, saw him, and raised a hand in greeting. He didn't smile, though, as he usually did when he saw his nephew. Bael raised his own hand and Elian gestured for Bael to join them next to the fire. He gladly did so, grateful for the warmth of the flames. It wasn't cold outside, but he felt frozen inside.

"How was your trip?" Bael asked, trying desperately to summon a bit of enthusiasm.

"It was good to see everyone one last time," Elian said.

Bael stared into the flames. "I'm not so sure that transformation is a wise choice, anymore."

Elian didn't seem as surprised by the admission as Bael thought he should be. Instead, he looked as though he'd just found a clue to a riddle that had been bothering him. Bael knew Grandmother hadn't yet spoken to Elian, for he hadn't sensed them anywhere close to one another, so Bael surmised Elian's meeting with the dragons was to blame. Elian, though, kept things close, not revealing anything about what he'd learned. "Why do you say that?"

"I've learned more about the transformation since you left."

"Such as?"

Bael couldn't keep the bitterness from his voice. "Such as the fact that once one transforms, one can no longer father children. I assume, likewise, that Grandmother can no longer bear children, either."

There'd been a hint of amusement playing at the corners of Elian's lips, but that fell at Bael's words. "I'm sorry to hear that. Very sorry."

Capricia echoed the sentiment, and Bael was grateful they didn't push for more information.

Elian said, "I can't imagine what you're going through, but if there's anything you need, all you have to do is ask."

Bael bowed in gratitude. "I appreciate it. Shayna and I have had some difficult conversations, and there are more to come, but that isn't why I'm visiting."

"That's good, because if you're hoping to convince me not to transform, telling me I can't have children anymore isn't your best strategy. Those days are long behind me."

Bael shook his head. "It's not about that, either. Talking to Grandmother today sent me down a trail of thoughts I hadn't considered." He looked down at his hands. "This transformation is powerful, and until a few eighthdays ago, I would have told you

that there were no costs to it. That we needed as many transformed as possible. Now I'm not so sure."

"You're growing wiser than you look," Elian said.

"Why?"

"I've found that in life there is almost always a cost to every
gain. If you can't see it, it might just mean that you haven't been
looking hard enough. I'm glad you're learning the lesson earlier
than I did."

"Not early enough."

"Try not to think about what can't be changed. It'll do you no
good. There's something else you need to know. I spoke with the
dragons yesterday."

"I sensed you with them. A large gathering."

Elian poked at the fire with a stick, rearranging the logs so
they would burn more evenly. "They have concerns about the
transformation as well."

"What kinds of concerns?"

Elian told Bael of the dragons' worries about adani, how they
feared Bael's direct connection to the Great Heart might, in time,
pull more adani from the Great Heart than could be replaced by
the natural cycles of life. Bael hung on every word, Elian's report
only deepening and solidifying the doubts that had been slowly
gaining form in his thoughts. When Elian finished, Bael asked,
"Knowing all this, what do you think?"

Elian stirred at the fire again as he thought. Enough time
passed that Bael began to worry that Elian had forgotten the
question completely. He was about to remind Elian when the
older adanist said, "I don't know enough to make any claims with
certainty, but I am still sure enough that I need to follow your
transformation."

"Even after everything we've learned in the past few days?"

"Even then."

"Why?" A few days ago, Bael had been fighting Elian to accept what he considered an inevitable transformation, but now their roles were reversed, and he wasn't sure how he felt about it.

"Some of the reasons are the ones we've already spoken of. We don't have enough strength to overcome the emissaries, and as I am, I'm of limited use to the clan."

Elian stopped, but Bael felt as though he'd only been given half the story. "And?"

"You'll think me a fool."

"I find that hard to believe."

"I have come to believe that this transformation is what I'm meant to do."

His confusion must have been apparent, because Elian gave him a broken grin. "Told you."

"I don't think you're a fool. I just don't understand what you mean."

"You've heard Samora talk about how when she was younger, she believed that adani guided her, right?"

Of course he had. "A belief that the dragons share."

"And one that's growing on me, too. I don't feel any tug of adani, like my sister did, but I do feel a certain—inevitability, perhaps—to everything. This body is broken beyond any healing, I'm incapable of protecting those I love, and our greatest threat is at our very doorstep. All this, right when there's an opportunity to transform and address all these problems at once? It doesn't feel like coincidence to me, if there even is such a thing."

"But what about the dragons' warning?"

"I take it seriously, but even the dragons acknowledge the fact we need your strength now. I don't think I have to avoid transformation, I just have to think about how I can be a good steward of adani. We all do."

"I'm surprised. Between my doubts and those of the dragons, I thought you'd balk at proceeding."

Elian shook his head. "No. I had a wonderful chance to visit with my family. I saw the other wandering clans, larger than they've been since any time I've been alive. We flew near the cities, too, and although they've been wounded, there's a strength there, too, that I don't fully understand. They'll grow and heal in time, if we can give them that time. This land is teeming with adani. I've fought for a long time, and I can honestly say I've left the world a better place than I found it. The work isn't over, especially now, but I'm starting to understand it will never be over. I'll still fight, as long as I can, because that's what I do, but I think I can let go, at least a little."

"So you're going to do it, then? When?"

Elian glanced at Capricia and gave her a smile that was warmly returned. She dipped her head down slightly, then raised it. He turned back to Bael. "Now."

Before Bael could object, Elian embraced adani, filling his body beyond what Bael had thought was possible for a mere ascended. His uncle made no effort to control the adani, but let it flow freely wherever it wanted. The boundaries between Elian and adani vanished.

Elian looked at them both and smiled wide, and it looked like the first smile that hadn't hurt since Elyn had nearly killed him. "I love you both," he said.

And then he was gone, pulled into the Great Heart of adani.

19

Elyn sought relief in the martial forms she'd been taught as a child. If she'd been of a mind to reflect on the decision, she might have found it odd, but she needed to move, needed to not think, for thinking only led in circles that spiraled quickly into doubt and then despair.

She couldn't put her finger on what, exactly, bothered her so much about the knowledge she had gained in the hall. Nothing about the distant past changed any of what mattered now. Void wasn't the force she thought it was, but it was still a force of unbelievable power. Knowing its origin did nothing to change what it was capable of or what its goals were.

She punched at her imagined opponent, then spun on the ball of her left foot and lashed out with her right. She imagined fighting Father, but the thought brought her no joy. When she replaced Father with Bael, she was reminded of the last time they'd fought and his undeserved mercy.

She swore and kicked at the ghost of him, but even in her imagination he wouldn't fight back. She punched at him anyway, but none of her attacks brought her closer to a decision.

Elyn swore again. What decision? She'd lost the right to

choose her future when she'd pledged her loyalty to Void. When she'd killed adanists for Void. All that was left was obedience, the peace that came from surrendering to a higher power.

Except it wasn't a higher power, at least, not as she'd once thought of it. It was a woman from a tortured world who'd given birth to the ultimate destructive force, and Elyn had no desire to obey someone who'd once been a mere mortal.

Small stones crunched behind her, and Elyn twirled around to find Void's head emissary standing there, face severe. "You've been given the greatest gift in all the worlds, and you kick and punch like a mere child?"

Elyn would have thrown a punch at the emissary if she wasn't convinced the woman hoped for just such an outcome. She didn't bother bowing, heedless of the risks she ran. "What do you want?"

The emissary scowled and Elyn prepared for a beating, but it never came.

"You entered the halls of our master without permission. Servants have been killed for less."

The threat on her life lacked any punch. "Then why am I still alive?"

"Because our master needs you. I am here to address your behavior and your doubts."

The emissary sounded as though she'd rather be sticking needles into her arm.

Freed from the fear for her own life, Elyn spoke without worry for the first time since her emissary had died. "Why do you hate me?"

"Because you're weak. You've been given the gift of void, a gift you're proficient with. You could easily rise to the rank of emissary, but you barely qualify as a servant. Your will is pathetic."

"It was strong enough to destroy my own father."

The emissary waved her hand dismissively. "And that, right there, is the source of your weakness. I don't entirely blame you.

Your emissary should have recruited and trained you differently. Void doesn't care about your petty revenge. It doesn't admire your conflicted feelings about your parents."

The emissary continued, "You latched onto our master as a way to realize your revenge, and your emissary did nothing to deter you. Encouraged you, even, because he saw it as the path to buying your loyalty. A short-term gain for a long-term loss. You don't truly understand our master."

"I've seen our master's past with my own senses."

"Seen, but not understood. Void doesn't seek revenge. It doesn't judge. It brings peace. A permanent, final peace. *That is all.* Even now, as we speak, I can sense that a part of you desires this peace. It's why your heart beats the same even when I threaten you with death. We bring that gift, the very one a part of you seeks, to wherever life can be found."

The emissary's claims stabbed like tiny daggers under Elyn's skin. When she had no immediate reply, the emissary said, "You doubt because you've had your revenge, and that revenge hasn't been returned with the hate you need to justify further revenge. You have one foot in the void and one foot in the light, and you lack the will to take a final step in either direction."

Elyn couldn't deny the truth of the claim, so she didn't bother. Her friends and family would call Void evil, but at the least, it was brutally honest. She'd always respected that about her.

"What of it?" Elyn asked.

"Watch your tongue. Our master may see a use for you, but I do not, and it needs me more than it needs you."

Elyn noted that the emissary used "it" instead of "she." Was it possible the emissary, so close to Void, didn't understand its origin? It didn't seem wise to press the matter, but Elyn held the possibility close. Another question demanded a more immediate answer. "You speak of need and of use, but what makes me so special?"

The emissary squeezed the bridge of her nose with thumb and

forefinger, as though Elyn's question had created an unbearable headache. "You're not *special*, but you could become very useful to our master. It needs a servant with an impressive sensitivity to adani. You were the first candidate the emissaries found."

"Why would our master need a servant with adani?"

The emissary released a long-suffering sigh. "You're supposed to be clever. Can't you figure it out on your own?"

Elyn's thoughts already raced that direction. Void needed adani for a reason, and her emissary, the man who had recruited her, had often spoke of her becoming the ruler of her world. She'd thought, at the time, it had been an appeal to a desire for power she didn't possess, but perhaps there'd been more to what he said than she'd thought. Perhaps he'd been serious. He'd known her too well to think she wanted to rule.

She wasn't fast enough for the head emissary. "When your emissary attempted to harvest the red hearts, he used almost every servant under his command to control your people. He embedded them in cities, villages, and near the wandering clans. Combined, they were enough to keep track of your movements and activities, at least until your warriors learned to mask their adani."

Elyn finished the thought. "But with a truly skilled and sensitive servant, you wouldn't need so many servants. One would be enough to keep an eye on everything."

The emissary's nod was the same as an instructor would give to a slow student who had finally mastered a basic concept. "The emissary that recruited you had many more servants than most. He was gifted at recruiting from across the worlds. Great as our master's strength is, our physical numbers are small. Even your smaller wandering clans outnumber the total number of emissaries."

"But it hasn't mattered in the past," Elyn realized out loud, "because of Void's purpose. This is the first time it has tried to control instead of simply destroy."

"Precisely. You see, now, why healing you and leading you to accept our master was so important to us. You are sensitive to adani and could fulfill the role with ease."

Which brought them back to the crux of the matter.

"Except I'm not convinced our master is worthy of my obedience."

"It isn't a matter of obedience. Our master has no use for it."

"But—"

"None at all. Our master doesn't seek obedience, but belief. Another lesson you need to understand. We don't care if you follow some set of arbitrary rules. We only care if you believe, because if you believe, your actions will be correct. My predecessor convinced you that your father and the wandering clans deserved the gift of the void, but your belief extended no further. That's where we begin today."

There was no point in lying, not with the void within her core, and so she said, "What of those that don't deserve to die?"

The emissary blurred forward and put the tip of her finger on Elyn's forehead. "Let's dispel your illusions, shall we?"

ANOTHER MEMORY, lived as though it was her own. She walked the streets of a city grander than any she'd ever known. Buildings rose to heights trees didn't dare dream of, and the sky was filled with what looked like boats that hung from enormous, elongated constructions of fabric and rope. Everyone walking the streets around her appeared to be of roughly the same age, but a memory that wasn't hers told her the others were all much, much older. She wore clothes not too dissimilar from those she was used to, a tunic and pants belted loosely around her hips. The cloth was finer than what she knew, but they allowed her to move easily. The others wore a dizzying variety of styles, their clothing layered, colorful, and decadent. Elyn lacked the vocabulary to describe what she witnessed, but she instinctively understood this society had grown far beyond anything her world had achieved. Even her distant ancestors, who'd known more about the world than the wandering clans did, didn't compare.

Elyn's host's feet carried her to a house larger than some of the villages close to her farm. The stern-faced men at the gates allowed her in without so much as a greeting, and once she was within the house she went to a small closet and pulled out a bucket and a mop. She filled the bucket with water from a pipe, and Elyn stared at the flowing water, amazed it could be summoned so easily. Everything from the perfectly smooth floor to the lush, thick fabric of the curtains revealed the wealth and level of craftsmanship of this world, but Elyn's host moved through the rooms without a hint of wonder.

In one room a woman lay sprawled upon a couch, her eyes glazed. If not for the gentle rise and fall of her chest, Elyn would have feared she was dead. A tray with a gray-green powder lay on the side-table, and Elyn's host cleaned under it and replaced it as though it were a valuable family heirloom.

In another room a man ate at a table alone, the food before him enough to feed an entire wandering clan on the move. The only sound in the room was that of his teeth slowly working their way through the succulent meat. When he was done, he left more of it untouched than eaten.

It wasn't adani that ran through this world, but a close cousin, and Elyn sensed its overwhelming presence everywhere. Had Samora been here, she would have been ecstatic. This kind of energy was what she'd dreamed of when she'd first started planting the hearts around the land. If her home was left alone, in many generations, it, too, might have as much adani.

Everyone she passed drank freely from the deep well of strength, except for Elyn's host, who had access to less than even a child of the cities on Elyn's world. That, then, was why everyone looked so young. They were, at minimum, the equivalent of an ascended among the wandering clans.

It wasn't until much later, after she'd cleaned many rooms, that she came across another young man, who was actually a young man, dressed in clothes no finer than her own. A belt of unfamiliar tools hung from his wide belt, and he was covered in so much dirt and grime he might as well have come from wrestling a pig. He gave Elyn a cursory nod, but nothing else as he shouldered his way past her, trailing dirty footprints across the floor she'd just cleaned.

Not long after, when she was still cleaning the footprints from the hall, a woman accosted her. What looked like hearts were in her hand, but they were not hearts, for Elyn didn't sense any adani from them. "You stole one!" she shouted as she backhanded Elyn across the face.

The force of the blow caught Elyn by surprise. It nearly lifted her body off the floor as she spun around and collapsed. Elyn knew, as her host had known in the memory, that she was innocent, but the accusation wasn't met with anger. Inside her host was only that same sense of emptiness Void so loved to inhabit.

"Where is it?" The question was accompanied by a kick that sent her skidding back across the hall, and her host's dark thought was that now at least she was still cleaning the floor.

There was no point in denying it, but what else could she do? "I didn't take anything," she said.

The beating that followed was administered by one who understood their own strength. She'd have bruises and cracked ribs, but nothing serious enough to seek help for. She was ejected from the house after the beating was over, without so much as the pay she'd earned over the past several days.

There was no point in complaining. No point in anything, really. Why even survive, if this was all she had to look forward to?

ELYN GASPED as her consciousness was returned to her. In between breaths she looked at the emissary and saw a hint of emotion, long buried, in the depths of her gaze. "That was you?"

The emissary nodded once. "You speak of those who don't deserve to die, and I'd challenge you to name one person who is truly innocent. We are born as vicious creatures, only satisfied when our own selfish needs are met. Even children do nothing but take from their parents until they're old enough to take from others. The world I came from had everything. More than enough for everyone. And yet, well, you saw well enough for yourself. The very essence of life is suffering."

Elyn trembled, not from fear, but from the scars the memory had seared across her spirit. She was no stranger to hopelessness, but to see such abundance coupled with such cruelty, that she wasn't prepared for.

The emissary placed her finger on Elyn's forehead once again, and Elyn shook her head. "Not again, please."

"Until you believe," the emissary said.

Elyn lost count of the number of worlds they visited. One was torn about by war as another cousin of adani was consumed by the world's adanists. Yet another sank into starvation. Another was like the emissary's world, rich beyond measure, but full of sloth. In every memory, a world ripped apart by the force of light.

Just like her own family had been torn apart by adani. Like how her father, a good man according to most, had hurt her so terribly.

In vision after vision, she began to see. Began to understand. Yes, there may be small moments of joy and peace, but they were the exception and not the rule. Her own life and her own suffering, in comparison to all she witnessed, seemed like nothing at all.

Was Void right?

She'd never believed. Not truly. Now, though, she began to wonder. What was the point of life, if all it meant was more suffering?

Maybe Void's solution was terrible, but perhaps it was the most merciful. It was the only way of ending the suffering. The only way.

When the emissary finally lifted her finger, Elyn collapsed to her knees.

"Do you see?"

Elyn nodded, and she did. Maybe not with the belief that the head emissary would have wished, but something close, a cousin, perhaps. The emissary nodded. "Good. Then come with me. There is work to be done, and quickly."

20

Nothing felt right to Samora. In most regards, her body felt like her own, except for the incredible amounts of adani she could funnel through it. Funny, that once she'd thought a single small heart was more than her body could take. One life spanning three full generations, and she'd seen firsthand how much could change in so little time.

Younger Samora had loved the world. Full of mysteries to uncover and questions to answer, she'd been eager to bend it to her will. And she had. The hearts, the gathering grounds, even the cities had their roots in decisions she'd made and actions she'd taken.

She still loved the world, but the quality of that love had changed. She didn't hold on to it as tightly as she once had. The world belonged to the young, and she only lingered to ensure it would be theirs to live in.

Aldrick's absence was a constant ache that didn't fade with time. She'd known she relied on him, but hadn't realized how much until he was gone. She missed him when she sat around the campfire at night, and she missed him when she was training her new abilities with Bael. Her body no longer required sleep, for which she was grateful, because the idea of spending a night alone in their tent gave her the chills.

Bael wouldn't join her overnight, as his presence was needed at Shayna's side. Samora had taken to letting her body dissolve and allowing the web of adani to pull her spirit into its warm embrace. The longer she spent, pushed and pulled along the currents of adani, the more convinced she became that if she wished, it would be a simple matter to let her spirit dissolve back into the world. Will alone kept her spirit intact, and that will had been battered by recent events. Aldrick waited on the other side of a single, simple action.

Samora couldn't allow herself to stay too long, for if she did, she was certain that she wouldn't return. Better to visit nightly and return before the breaking of the dawn. Bael, of course, sensed her departures, but said nothing of them. He knew her heart well enough to know the struggle she faced.

Sometimes, when she found herself skirting close to the Great Heart at the world's core, she tried searching for any trace of Elian, but there was none to be found. She would have worried more except for Bael reminding her it had been no different when she had disappeared into the Great Heart. Just because they couldn't sense him didn't mean he wasn't there.

She rose to the surface before dawn broke over the clan's camp and joined the other men and women who started the campfires to prepare the clan's breakfast. She didn't take part in the conversations she once had. Better to keep a bit of separation so it was easier to leave again.

Before they had finished preparing breakfast, the emissaries arrived. Samora felt them like rodents crawling across her skin, dark voids that forced adani around them. So many. They'd speculated, endlessly, on how many emissaries Void possessed, and though their arrival wasn't an answer, it certainly made a statement. Samora couldn't count them all at once, but there were nearly fifty.

The number didn't matter, though. Not really. At their best, Samora figured she and Bael could fight maybe half a dozen emissaries. Had Elian returned in time, she might bump the number up to ten, but even that was a generous estimate. Any more than ten was simply rubbing salt in the wound. They could no more fight than they could stop a summer storm from rolling over the camp.

It wasn't just emissaries, though. The lone aura of an adanist had returned, appearing right outside their camp.

Samora's throat tightened. Elian should be here to speak with his daughter, but of course he wasn't. It was just another bitter twist of fate he'd have to endure.

She summoned adani from the Great Heart and prepared to fight, but the emissaries made no move to destroy the camp. They could have with little more than a thought. Instead, one of the emissaries separated from the others. Elyn's adani joined it and they walked slowly toward the camp.

Bael appeared beside Samora. His eyes darted around the camp as though he was searching it for answers, but he showed no other outward signs of panic. Adani stormed within him, though, raising the hairs on the back of her arms. "Any ideas?" he asked.

The emissary and Elyn stopped not quite halfway between the other emissaries and the camp. They formed no spheres of void, nor threw up any shields. Samora didn't doubt they were ready to respond in a moment to any aggression, but they were still, otherwise. "It seems they came to talk."

"Do you trust them?"

Samora chuckled bitterly as her adani swept over the emissaries. "I don't think it really matters, do you?"

Bael looked to the horizon and some of the tension dropped from his posture. Samora grunted to herself. All those emissaries, and his first thought had still been to fight, to find a way to win. He reminded her so much of Elian when they'd been younger, simply oblivious to the odds of failure. Hopefully, he'd still have the chance to lead the clans onward as Elian once had.

"I suppose not," he muttered, as though he still didn't quite believe it.

"Come, let's see what they have to say."

She offered her hand, but he did not take it. He stood by her side, nodded, and they walked together.

Strange that they should walk, she thought, as they made their way through camp. Faster means were available, but the choice to walk felt the right one. It gave the other adanists courage to see their leaders walking steadily, and it gave them all time to deal with their fears in whatever ways they knew best.

They still reached the emissary and Elyn too soon. The emissary's loose black robes flapped quietly in the breeze, but the hood was pulled down to reveal the face of a young woman. A stern woman, with a mouth that looked like it had forgotten how to smile. Their irises were black, which was disconcerting if stared at for too long.

Elyn looked well, though, and Samora thought Elian, wherever he was, would be glad to hear it. As much as Samora hated to admit it, the healing the emissaries had performed on Elyn had given her back her life. Samora had been able to do little to help her, but Elyn now looked stronger and healthier than she had since that terrible day she'd tried to ascend.

Elyn's eyes weren't black, though she wore the loose black robes of the emissaries. She wasn't an emissary yet, even though she stood beside them. Her gaze traveled between Samora and Bael, then over to the camp, as though she expected another visitor. Samora could guess well enough, but Elyn would have to ask before they spoke of it.

"Where's my father? I don't sense him anywhere," she said, in a tone that made it sound as though she expected a trap.

The whole truth was too long and revealed too much to the emissaries, so Samora settled on what she considered a partial truth. At the very least, she hoped it was only a partial truth. "He's dead."

The words seeped into Elyn slowly, like water trickling through layers of soil and stone before reaching a cave. She blinked once, then twice, as though Samora had spoken in a language she didn't understand. Her face paled, then, and her composure faltered for a moment. Only for a moment, though, before a glance from her companion was enough for the mask to fall across her face again. She tried to put some steel in her response, but it sounded like a very brittle steel to Samora's ears. "Very well, then. You two will be sufficient. We've come to deliver the terms of a new agreement."

"Have you, now?" Samora challenged.

The emissary now spoke, the sound of its voice cold and harsh, like wind blowing over ragged ice. "Watch your tongue when you speak to a servant. Our patience with your world and your petty rebellion has come to an end. Your only options are obedience or destruction, so I would advise you to choose your words with care."

Samora bit back the retort before it left her lips. She had half a mind to threaten the emissary with a painful death, but her threats, at the moment, were empty. Something in Elyn's expression convinced her that this emissary spoke true, and that a wrong word, now, might be the end of the world. She clenched her jaw.

A thought crossed her mind, dark but amusing. Elian would be furious with her if he returned only to find humanity destroyed because she couldn't control her temper. She was supposed to be the calm one. The out-of-place thought broke the fury that built in her and gave her the strength to reply calmly. "Fine. What new agreement?"

Elyn answered, which Samora hadn't expected. She was clearly subservient to the emissary, and the emissary had no issues speaking with them, so why did they bring Elyn at all? The emissaries weren't fools, so they wouldn't believe that by simply having Elyn repeating their demands, they would find more compliance among the wandering clans. Samora kept the question in mind as she listened.

"From this day forward, this world belongs to our master. The only reason it isn't destroyed is because of the red hearts that can be harvested. The growing and harvesting of the red hearts is to resume immediately. At first, the harvest will be supervised by the emissaries, but once obedience has been firmly established, the duty will be handed off to servants," Elyn recited the words as though she'd practiced them several times before arriving.

"What does that actually mean for us?" Bael asked.

"For now, nothing more than it meant under the previous emissary. The wandering clans are free to wander and live their lives as best they see fit, so long as they do nothing that interferes with the harvesting of the hearts. At this time, the same rules are in place as they were before. No further adanists may ascend, and no ascended adanist will be allowed to seek the transformation you two have experienced. Short of that, you may do as you please." Elyn glanced at the emissary for confirmation, and apparently the lack of response was affirmation enough.

"May wandering clans enter the cities?" Samora asked.

"You may do whatever you wish. We no longer attempt to hide our purpose. The ban on entering cities, if I recall, came from the cities themselves and not the emissaries. That is a discussion to have with them, not me."

"But you'd allow us to enter one of the dead zones the previous emissary created?" Samora wasn't sure why she pushed the issue, as there was no reason she could conceive of for visiting the sites. Only she wanted to know just how free this cage of theirs was going to be.

Elyn began to sound as though she only had one answer. "Again, you may do whatever you wish, so long as you do nothing that interferes with the harvesting of the hearts. That judgment will be made by either an emissary or a servant, and the punishment will be immediate."

"Punishment?" Bael asked.

"You've figured out already that adanists are important to the creation of the red hearts. Any adanist who attempts to attack an emissary or a servant, or otherwise interfere with our efforts on this world will be executed without question. But there will be another punishment as well. For every adanist involved in any effort to interfere with the harvest, a hundred citizens, chosen randomly, will die. For every emissary or servant who dies on this planet, for any cause, a thousand citizens, also chosen randomly, will die."

They were the first words that it looked difficult for Elyn to say, but if there was any hesitation on her niece's part, the words were backed up by the unyielding expression of the emissary standing next to her. Samora felt some of the blood drain from her face. "For any cause?"

The corner of the emissary's face almost showed something that could have been a hint of a smile, but it was Elyn who answered. "Yes. If you wish to protect those who live here, they'd be served best if you helped to protect the emissaries and their servants."

It was a monstrous agreement, of course, and though Samora hadn't expected anything different, hearing the words, especially from her niece, cut her to the bone. And the only other option was destruction. For a brief moment, Samora even considered whether that might be for the best. It didn't matter if the method was the red hearts or the void, this world was as good as dead. Why prolong the suffering?

She dismissed the thought almost as soon as it crossed her mind. The point was always the same. To find a way. To survive. Difficult as life was, it was worth living. If nothing else, agreeing gave them time. Maybe Elian, when he returned, would have some plan, some bold idea only he could come up with.

Samora didn't believe he would, but better to hold onto the hope.

She'd been so distracted by her own thoughts she didn't notice Bael until his anger exploded. "You can't do this! This is our world!"

"It *was* your world," Elyn said, "but not anymore."

"We'll kill every single one of you! We don't want your cursed agreements, and—"

"If you don't silence yourself, we'll finish this the way we always should have," the emissary said, and the ice in its voice was enough to freeze even Bael's anger. It helped that every emissary behind it summoned an enormous sphere of void.

Samora wondered if swallowing his anger and pride was the hardest feat Bael had ever accomplished. A year ago, even, she didn't think he would have been capable of it, but the emissary's arrival had forced him to grow, to become the leader she'd always suspected he was capable of becoming. He clenched his fists but dipped his head, and she was glad she didn't have to force him.

She didn't make him say the words out loud, though. That would have been cruel. "We'll agree to your terms. What would you have of us?"

"For now, spread the word to the other wandering clans. Only if they hear of your submission firsthand will they bow their own heads," Elyn said.

Samora wasn't so sure of that. Those who hadn't joined Bael before had all bowed their heads plenty quickly under the last emissary, though now they'd had a taste of victory, so it might be different. She nodded. "And Bael's clan?"

Elyn glanced to the emissary, who shrugged the question off as though it was of no importance. Bael's fists clenched so hard Samora swore she heard the bones cracking. He'd formed the clan specifically to fight the emissaries. To be dismissed so easily was an insult he wouldn't bear lightly.

Elyn turned back to Samora. "Again, you may do as you please. Live out the rest of your lives in peace."

The emissary and the emissary's servant shared another look and Samora sensed something unspoken running underneath their gazes. The emissary gave Elyn one quick nod, then vanished into mist.

Samora's adani twisted as Bael's temper broke free of its restraint. But the agreement had already been struck, and Elyn was as good as untouchable. Not that knowing that would quell Bael's anger. Samora turned to him before he could lash out. "Do you think it's wise for you to be here?" she asked.

She put enough command in her voice that it broke Bael's rapidly narrowing focus on his cousin. He gritted his teeth and shuddered, but the adani within him calmed a little. "Probably not," he answered.

"Take some time. Walk it off. Punch a tree. When you're calm, you can start informing the other clans. They'll need to hear it from you."

Bael took one deep breath, let it out, then nodded and vanished.

Samora wasn't sure her own control would last long near Elyn, but for her brother's sake, she would try.

"Thank you," Elyn said, "if something had happened, she would have destroyed the world. It's what she wants."

It was probably more than Elyn meant to reveal, but Samora kept her face blank, as though she hadn't just learned something that might become important.

"Is it what you want?" Samora asked.

"No—I would never ..." Elyn stopped and took a deep breath. "I'm not sure. There are times I think it might be for the best, and others when there's nothing I want less."

"And yet you stand by the emissary and deliver their words as though they were your own."

"You wouldn't understand."

"You haven't tried to explain."

Elyn held out a hand. "I didn't come to argue, and I don't mean to stay."

"Why are you here?" Samora interrupted.

"Excuse me?"

Samora's eyes narrowed. The emissaries did nothing without cause, and knew Elyn could be tracked. Why would they risk her?

The answer came in a flash of insight. "You're the one who will track us using adani, aren't you?"

The look on Elyn's face was answer enough. She snarled. "My purpose here is my own concern."

"It won't take long for the others to figure it out, and once they do, you'll be in danger."

"I'm protected by the agreement."

"And you think that will stop everyone who thinks you deserve death?"

Elyn shook her head and took a step back, as though she could distance herself from the truth. "Is what you said about my father true?"

"Of course."

"Was it—because of what I did?"

Samora crossed her arms. "He was perfectly healthy before you crippled him and left holes in his body with void."

Her answer was cruel, but in this case, Elyn deserved it.

"Did he suffer?"

"Every day. Everything from chewing his food to moving from tent to tent felt like being stabbed with spears. He could never get comfortable, never feel a moment without pain. Death, when it came, was probably a mercy."

Samora wished she could read the expressions that passed across Elyn's face as she spoke, but they were too subtle and too quick for her. It could have been satisfaction or sorrow, or something in between. Maybe all of the above. She was starting to believe that not even Elyn knew how she should feel. Her niece was well and truly lost.

Despite her anger, seeing that confusion instilled some small measure of sympathy in her. She let her arms drop to her side.

"He would have welcomed you back with open arms, even after, you know. You're only alive because he begged Bael to spare you, time and time again."

Elyn suffered the verbal abuse silently, and Samora thought she might leave, but she stayed and said, "I can't leave."

"Why not?"

"It's a part of me now, the same way that adani is. I don't know if she's right, but I'm not sure that she's wrong."

"About what?"

"That life is suffering, and that the only cure, the only thing that can end suffering, is to end life."

Samora scoffed. "Are you serious?"

A glance was enough to tell her that Elyn was.

"Elyn, life *is* suffering. Of course it is. But that doesn't mean it lacks value. At times, it's suffering that teaches us how valuable life is."

Her niece shook her head slowly. "There was a time I might have believed you, but that time is past. I've been shown too much across too many worlds. When there's so much pain, I start to think it's better to simply end it all."

Before Samora could argue, Elyn formed one of the dark portals and stepped through, vanishing to another part of the world. Samora didn't bother tracking her.

Elyn was better than this, a kind soul at heart, twisted by ideas and influences that poisoned her spirit. Samora feared the poison had worked its way too deep, though, and that there would be no chance of saving her.

❧ 21 ❧

T he laughter that greeted Bael's announcement didn't contain so much as a sliver of mirth. If captured into a drink and brewed, it would have been more bitter than a sour beer, and more cynical than an elder who hadn't done a chore for themselves in years. Coming from one person, it would have been hard enough to bear, but the laughter spread among the small assembly the same way the darkness of the emissaries spread across the land, and it was almost more than he could take.

"You're the pup that risked all our lives in your foolish attempt to kill the first emissary, all because you were so desperate to prove you were just as much a warrior as Elian was. And now you return, tail between your legs, and tell us we need to accept the terms of the surrender you negotiated? Ha! And they say fate doesn't have a sense of humor."

The speaker was a small man with a lean, sinewy frame. The chair he sat on had been made for a much larger man, but his presence made up for his lack of size. He wore a coat of hides and furs even though Bael suspected it had been several eighthdays since he'd been out hunting in the mountains.

Erhart was the leader of the Scorpions and had been for nearly a decade, and he was one of the first Bael had chosen to visit with news of the emissaries. The two of them were aware of each other, but Erhart was from Bael's father's generation, and they'd had little cause to meet before now. Killan and Elian both had all the respect in the world for him, but Bael couldn't see why.

"Elian fought by my side," Bael reminded Erhart.

"That he did, that he did. Which was why I didn't raise a stink when you came and persuaded so many of my best to leave at your side. I didn't agree with you then, but Elian always had a gift for making the impossible happen."

Bael summoned adani from the Great Heart, filling the room with the strength at his command. "And you think I don't?"

If Erhart had any fear of Bael, it didn't show on his face or in his adani. It flowed as smoothly as a summer stream, unperturbed by the massive amount of power Bael flooded the room with.

Bael let the power go. He was still angry from his surrender, and Erhart's words only hurt because they struck so close to his spirit. Every word the Scorpion leader said was true, even if he said them from the safety of his fortress on the eastern edge of their lands. Nothing that had happened here meant he needed to act like such a fool.

He forced himself to offer a small bow of apology. Erhart had gathered all the elders of his clan, as well as some of the more accomplished warriors who hadn't yet become elders. What was decided in this room was as good as done throughout the eastern mountains, but he'd lose what little respect remained for him if he didn't set things right.

"Apologies, sir. The surrender is a bitter medicine to have to swallow."

"A medicine you wouldn't have had to take if you'd listened to sensible advice earlier. Surrender was always going to be the end of this. How could you not see it? Even when the weakness with the servants was discovered, you had to know you were starting a fight you couldn't hope to win."

Was that true? Bael wasn't so sure. He had believed, perhaps foolishly, that they could win. How could he have led his friends into battle otherwise? Then he was no longer a leader, but a murderer.

Regardless, Erhart would only take such a confession as a sign Bael was an even bigger fool than he thought. Instead, he said, "You may be right, but that didn't mean the fight wasn't worth having. I refused to lay down and let our world, our people, and our hearts be taken without a fight. It would have ended with death, anyway."

He sensed some signs of agreement among the assembled warriors, but Erhart answered before his elders could be swayed. "I'm sure you believed that, but what evidence would you give? Think of the dragons. There was a time when they would have sacrificed everything to protect the hearts they had gathered over the ages, and surrendering them to your grandmother must have felt like surrendering everything that mattered. And yet here they are today, three generations later, as strong and as numerous as ever. We cannot predict the future, no matter how much we may believe otherwise."

Bael didn't have a good answer. He still believed he had been right, even if Erhart's wisdom argued otherwise. Perhaps it was as simple as knowing that sometimes the right path wasn't always the wise path. He held back the grin that threatened to bloom on his face. Erhart wouldn't be enamored of that answer, either. They might not see eye to eye, but he didn't believe Erhart had anything but the best interests of his clan in his spirit.

"Perhaps you are right," Bael acknowledged, "although I'm not convinced. Regardless, Grandmother and I both agree that surrender is now certainly in our best interest."

Erhart scoffed and shook his head. "Of course it is. Does that mean you'll be returning those warriors of ours idealistic enough to follow you?"

"They'll be free, as they always have been, to do as they wish," Bael said.

Erhart's eyes narrowed, and he waved his hand. "Fine. Tell them they're missed, and we'd like to have them back."

Bael bowed and left, vanishing back into the web of adani in an instant, a not-so-subtle reminder of what mysteries he'd uncovered.

That had gone every bit as poorly as he'd expected.

And he still had several more to go.

THE SUMMONS CAME ALMOST a week after he'd finished speaking to the last of the clans. More than one clan leader had been as rude as Erhart, but Bael figured he deserved nothing less. Grandmother hadn't meant to shame him when she'd sent him from clan to clan, but that had been the result. A few of the clans had accepted his news about the surrender without much comment, but he felt the weight of their judgment on him regardless.

He hadn't found much peace within his camp, either. The other clans had argued that he should have surrendered to the first emissary, while those who had risked everything to follow him argued he should keep fighting even now. They were the ones most angry with him, and no small number, when they'd learned he was surrendering like everyone else, had left his clan. They'd once been over a hundred strong, but between the battles that had taken so many lives and now this, his clan barely deserved the name. He'd gone out with hunting parties that were larger.

Even his own tent was a source of strife. He didn't doubt Shayna's love and support, not even now, but having a family had always been important to her. How many times had they spoken about kids? Until he'd died, it had been a contest to decide who wanted more. Now it didn't matter how many they wanted, the number they would have was zero.

She loved him, of that he was sure. She would support him, always. But she hadn't decided whether or not she was going to stay with him, and Bael didn't pressure her either way. He could claim he was the same man he'd been before from sunrise to sundown, but there was no denying he was different. Shayna would grow old and die, and though that process might last generations thanks to her ascension, it wouldn't last forever.

If she wanted the chance for a different life, Bael didn't think he had the right to say otherwise, but it meant the comfort he'd normally find in her arms was gone, too.

So when the summons came, there was really no doubt about what he was going to do. It arrived via the dragons, who maintained the ability to speak to one another over vast distances, and the dragon passed it on to the rider in Bael's camp, who passed it on to him one night after most everyone else had gone to bed.

The purpose of the meeting wasn't stated. Only that it was important, that it would be held on the night of the full moon, and that it would be attended by warriors whose names Bael recognized. From the list of names, he could discern the purpose of the meeting without being told. They were planning a resistance. Many were the names of the warriors who had left his camp when he'd announced he planned on surrendering.

The thought of telling them to give it up never crossed his mind. Instead, he wondered what they had found and how they planned on resisting this impossible occupation. He told no one of his plans. Elyn, without doubt, would sense him as soon as he moved, but she hadn't been concerned when he'd gone from place to place in the past. Whatever standard the emissaries were using to judge "interference," it didn't preclude Bael from meeting with whoever he cared to.

On the night of the meeting, he simply walked out of the camp until he was out of view, then vanished from sight. He could sense the adani of those who'd summoned him and appeared a few paces away from where they had gathered. There were other warriors there who had not been named in the summons, but Bael recognized many of them as well. Fighters all, from oldest to youngest.

They greeted him warmly, and after a few more warriors arrived, they began. The council, if it deserved the name, was started by a man who stood a head taller than Bael named Coll. He'd known Coll for years now, and the fact that he was the one who fashioned himself as the leader of this meeting didn't bode well. Coll was an ascended warrior of no small skill, and if they were in a fight, there were few warriors Bael would rather have protecting his back.

But Coll was no leader. The only part of him stronger than his arm was his temper, which flared to life under the smallest of provocations. Bael didn't think Coll had ever stopped twice to think about anything, because he wasn't sure Coll had ever thought once about anything. The man was all spirit and instinct, traits that served him well in battle but not in life.

"Friends, thank you for gathering here. It's time for us to strike back at the emissaries who seek to control us," Coll said.

They were gathered around a small fire in a forest clearing. Less than a dozen, all told, and yet Coll spoke as though they had gathered to take on a mighty quest. The others all nodded with such solemnity Bael almost laughed out loud. What did they think they were going to do?

Coll continued. "We know the emissaries can't sense adani as well as a trained adanist can, and so we're reasonably certain the reason they're using Elyn is because she'll be able to sense us. Thus, any attempt to fight against the emissaries must begin with her removal."

At this, Coll stared hard at Bael, as though expecting him to speak up in defense of his cousin. He'd get no argument from Bael, though. Cousin or not, and Elian's mercy or not, Elyn had sided decisively with the enemy. If their strategy focused on killing Elyn first, Bael wouldn't argue. He still wrestled with his decision not to kill her back when he'd had an easier opportunity. Bael nodded.

If anything, he was impressed others had figured it out so quickly. He and Samora had decided as much a few days ago, when they'd been asking themselves why Elyn had been given such an important role in the emissaries' plans. They hadn't been sure until they'd sensed Elyn stretching out her adani across the continent, though. That had been evidence enough. She was their first line of defense, but Bael hadn't said anything to others. He didn't want a rebellion, so there was little point in informing others of the emissaries' weaknesses.

Coll continued by saying, "Fortunately, Elyn isn't all that strong. She was only able to destroy Elian because she was working with others, and because she was his daughter. She does possess void, but we know how to overcome that. Once we kill her, my plan is to move on to the emissaries. We'll have to work together, but with Bael and Samora helping us, we should be able to take them one at a time."

Bael blinked, but the others around the circle were nodding.

"That's your plan? Attack them one at a time? What happens when they start traveling in pairs, or in even larger groups?" Bael asked.

"We'll adjust, but if we strike hard and fast, we should be able to kill at least a few before they wise up to our strategy."

Bael shook his head. "They're connected to one another, like the dragons are. They'll know as soon as the first one is killed."

Coll waved the concern away. "They can't congregate too much, not if they want to keep control of their red heart harvest."

"What of their threat to kill civilians for every action we take against them? Do you have a plan to protect innocents from the consequences of our actions?"

Coll looked at Bael as though Bael was ruining a celebration. "I believe they're bluffing. They need us."

"They need adanists, but civilians are nearly worthless. There's nothing stopping them from attacking the cities, or wiping out a village. It wouldn't bother them a bit."

Coll's expression hardened. "Then that's a risk we'll need to assume. This is a war, and though we might not like it, sometimes the innocent get hurt."

No one objected to Coll's brutal philosophy, and when Bael looked from face to face, he realized he was alone.

That didn't make him wrong.

He turned to face Coll. "That's not good enough for me. When we became adanists we promised to protect those who couldn't fight for themselves. That has always been the promise of the wandering clans."

"Protecting as many as possible sometimes means sacrificing others. They'll all die if we do nothing, right?"

"I won't be the reason hundreds, if not thousands, of civilians die."

"You won't be. They'll die because the emissaries killed them."

Once again, no one came to his aid.

Coll's demeanor softened. "It sounds cold, and it is, but we're running out of choices, Bael. The longer they have a foothold upon this world, the harder it's going to be for us to get rid of them. Their arrival spells the end of the world, one way or the other. By fighting back, at least it's on our terms. You were the one who taught us that."

He had, hadn't he? He heard the echoes of his old arguments, thrust back at him. But then he imagined the devastation a single sphere of void could unleash upon a village and his resolution was strengthened. "I still believe we can find a better way."

"If so, what is it?" Coll asked. "Tell me, and I'll follow you without a question. But from where I stand, we either fight and accept the terrible consequences, or we don't and accept a slow decline until the end of our civilization. We die as slaves to a void that will use our strength and our blood to destroy other worlds. I don't want that burden on my spirit, either."

"I don't know, not now. But I promise you all that I'll find a way or die trying."

"I'm sorry, but that's not good enough. It's not that I don't believe in you. What you've accomplished is incredible. But we're against an enemy that needs to be fought now. We need your help. You're the only one that's killed an emissary so far. Will you join us? If Elian was here, you know he would."

Bael wasn't so sure that was true, but his spirit wavered all the same. The warriors here were his friends, and he was proud to call them such. But he hadn't given up hope for something better, and he couldn't follow them down this path, not yet.

He shook his head slowly. If he didn't join them, then they'd have no chance. He wouldn't convince them with words, but he could leave them with no other options. "I'm sorry, friends, but I can't join you. Not like this."

Without another word, he vanished back into the web of adani, and hoped it was enough.

22

E lyn didn't trust peace. She wanted to, but the wandering clans were bred to fight. Samora had worked hard to convince them to use adani for purposes beyond mere destruction, and they liked to style themselves protectors, but when all was said and done, they were raised to fight. It was in their blood and in their bones. Take away their swords and they'd attack you with daggers. Take their daggers and they'd strike with shovels.

She didn't like the peace any more than they did. It gave her time to think, and thinking led her to places she didn't want to go.

Father was dead.

The thought snuck up on her, like the adanists wished they could, and struck at random moments. She would be bathing in a tub of warm water only to think of the baths he'd forced her to take when she was barely old enough to talk. She couldn't remember them herself, but the stories had been legendary among her family. Or she'd be training, which never failed to bring up memories of them together.

She told herself she didn't miss him. That he'd gotten what he deserved. If she said it often enough, she could almost believe it.

So she didn't think. She trained and traveled, never spending too much time in one place before shifting to another. The void allowed her to make and use as many portals as she wished, and she never spent more than a day or two in any place before moving on. It wouldn't do anything to stop Bael or Samora if they decided she needed to die, but it would prevent any other adanist from targeting her. The emissaries agreed. If the clans were to strike, they'd strike at her first.

She sometimes visited villages. Other times she camped in the wild. She surrendered the robe the emissary had given her, opting instead for thick traveling clothes that allowed her to blend in. She didn't enter any villages where she might be known, and when she visited the cities, there were plenty of people to use as cover.

When she wasn't training, she used adani to keep track of the wandering clans. The emissaries' arrival had thrown the clans into confusion for a bit. Bael had lost a fair number of his followers, and Elyn paid them particular attention as she watched for trouble. Most seemed to have rejoined their original clans, although a handful had kept themselves apart. They were the ones Elyn suspected would attempt an attack. Bael had met with them one night, but they'd had no contact since.

Bael and Samora were the true threats, and Elyn grew to despise them. Like the emissaries, they could appear out of nowhere, without more than a moment of warning. She knew she would sense them if they appeared, but she couldn't help but snap her head around at the crack of a twig or the rustle of a dry leaf in the wind. It was never one of her family, but she feared that one day she wouldn't look around and they'd be there, a bound dagger of adani in hand. They'd be foolish enough to try it, given their stubbornness.

She walked into a small village, a pack on her back, looking for all the world like another traveler. The mountains that belonged to the Scorpions rose in the east, a stunning backdrop the villagers accepted as a matter of course. This was one of the villages that produced the metals the growing cities demanded, and the sound of hammers striking steel was loud in the air.

The first women she crossed greeted her warmly, and she asked them if there was a place where she might have a bite to eat and bathe. They suggested two places and offered directions, and Elyn thanked them. A handful of children kicked a leather ball around the street, nearly catching her in the back of the head as she passed.

Fortunately, she avoided the ball. The emissaries had their eyes on her. They probably wouldn't demand consequences for an honest accident, but she couldn't be sure. No small number of emissaries were waiting for an excuse to slam their heels down on the necks of the population.

This village was closer to the wandering clans than she usually came, but there was a hot spring that was a day's hike up in the mountains she had always wanted to visit.

An empty pursuit, perhaps, but what else did she have to do? Her duty was to watch, and adani allowed her to watch from anywhere. The emissaries remained firmly in control, and they never consulted her, except to ask if she'd sensed any danger, and so there were no decisions to make. The weight of her world rested on her shoulders, but there was nothing for her to do.

She took refuge in the first inn the women had recommended, soaking in a bath long enough that the water was cold by the time she stepped out. She informed the innkeepers she was famished and ate enough to feed a family, though it did nothing to satisfy the gnawing void within. With so much food in her stomach, she decided to take a walk as the sun fell behind the mountain peaks. The streets were more crowded than she expected, but if the demand from the cities continued, more people would come to the village for the work and the coin. It would be its own city before long.

The thought of the village turning into a city was on her mind and she wasn't paying attention to her surroundings.

A young girl, barely older than Elyn had been when she'd attempted to ascend, was about to pass her, but instead drew a long dagger from some hidden pocket and stabbed at Elyn.

The girl had some training, but not enough. Elyn caught the sudden movement and shifted her weight, instinct taking over. The girl stabbed out, but she wasn't quite tall enough to aim directly for Elyn's heart. She aimed instead just below Elyn's ribs, and as Elyn shifted away, the dagger cut deep and nicked the bottom rib. Elyn gasped and shuddered as steel pierced flesh, a sharp, burning sensation that spread from the wound outward.

The girl pulled the blade out and blood spilled from Elyn. She brought her arm back to stab again, but Elyn's hand snaked out and clasped her by the throat. The girl's eyes widened as her lungs failed to pull in fresh air, and Elyn pulled the girl's face close to her own. "You better run," she said.

The girl, thankfully, obeyed. She dropped the dagger and fled, even as the commotion drew the attention of others. A kindly-looking older man hurried over, but Elyn backed away.

She couldn't be here.

Already she could feel the void reverberating. Eager. This was the moment the head emissary had been waiting for.

She called for a portal, and it opened before her. She stepped through and into the first place she had thought of, the farm she'd called her own. The front door was only a few paces away, every bit the same as she remembered leaving it. She stumbled forward and threw open the door. No one was inside. Not that she expected anyone, but this would be among the first places they set a trap for her.

Her vision quivered and her legs almost gave out. She clutched to the side of the door and kept herself upright, but barely. What had that cursed girl cut?

And for that matter, where were the cursed emissaries? The

void still reverberated, echoes of an argument she couldn't guess at, but if she was so precious to them, why were they letting her bleed out in her own home?

She needed to clean the wound, but water was out back, in the stream that ran behind the house, and she had no fire. She swore as tears gathered in the corners of her eyes, blurring her vision. What she'd give for a friendly adanist.

Another wave of nausea almost brought her to her knees. She needed to sit, but her bed called to her. Maybe if she laid down she could focus her adani and heal herself. Decades ago, she'd been able to do so. She only needed to remember how. She only needed to focus.

Her thoughts wandered, and she thought she saw Mother standing beside her, but she reached out with her arm and found nothing but air. She squinted and was alone.

Elyn fell on her bed and stared up at the ceiling. How had they found her? She must have been recognized, but to send a child after her?

It was monstrous.

And now the village was at risk. The fools.

Her stomach clenched tight and she groaned. Focus. She needed to gather her adani and repair the wound.

Except her vision darkened around the edges and she couldn't hold onto her thoughts, slippery like fish squirming out of her grip. The void reverberated, but it didn't answer her calls. She wasn't abandoned, but put aside, as other discussions were apparently more important.

She blinked and when she opened her eyes it seemed darker outside. The burning in her stomach had spread.

She started to close her eyes again, but there was a light, and then a smile, and a deep voice that should have been dead.

She knew she was safe, even as the darkness took her.

WHEN SHE WOKE it was daytime outside, the sun streaming through open windows. For a long moment, it was as though she'd jumped into her past and it was one of the normal days she'd lived when she was on the farm. She raised her arms and stretched, only then realizing that she should have been hurt. She'd never woken up in this bed without some form of pain.

The past came rushing in. The child and the dagger, and no one to help. Then a dream. It had to be a dream.

"Morning," Father said.

He was on a chair she'd built herself, a sturdy but boxy build that was barely more comfortable than sitting on the floor. He was leaned back against a wall so only the back two legs of the chair were touching.

It was Father, but a younger version, one that should have only existed in her memories.

She still felt as though she was in a dream, not entirely convinced this was real. "You're not supposed to be here."

Maybe she was dead, and this was whatever came after.

He smiled, but it was the sort of smile one might offer when they were trying to hide a great sorrow from the world. "Believe it or not, I think you're right. But you were in pain. I'd been having trouble finding my way back, but I felt your spirit calling out."

"You came for me?"

"Of course."

It was too much. Too much weight, dropped on her all at once. She curled into a ball and her body shook. She wouldn't cry. Couldn't cry, but it was the only way to expel everything she couldn't contain.

Father didn't speak, didn't even move, as near as Elyn could tell. He just sat and waited. Patient now, because he had all the time in the world. She reached out and brushed against his adani, and there was no doubt it was him.

In time, her body stopped shaking and a calm fell over her like a blanket. She gathered herself and sat up. Her fingers traveled to where the girl had stabbed her, but there wasn't so much as a scar. "You don't know how to heal this well."

"You're right. Samora came and did the healing, then left."

"She did? Even after the last time we met?"

Father gently pushed off the wall so the chair rested on four legs again. "Why do you always think that love is conditional?"

Any other day, that question would have sparked a fire in her she wouldn't have known how to extinguish. Today it barely caused the embers to spark. She was tired of being angry. "You're the one that taught me that."

Father went unnaturally silent, and it was only then she realized that he wasn't breathing. Her heart pounded for a moment before she realized he was like Bael and Samora now. He didn't need to breathe. After a time, his chest started to rise and fall again, a comforting illusion. "Please forgive me, but how did I teach you that?"

The flames in her chest stirred, but the hurt on his face doused them quickly.

"When I was little, you were only proud of me when I exceeded expectations, when I worked harder than anyone else. You told me, never out loud, but in a hundred silent ways, that you loved me most when I did what no other child could do. Then once I failed, I saw that you would never love me the same way again."

She expected him to argue, to tell her she was wrong and that he'd always loved her the same. The fire in her chest was burning now, waiting to ignite into a vast wildfire when he denied it yet again.

"I never meant to make you feel that way. It's true that I was most proud of you when you learned faster and performed better than anyone had before. And yes, I was hurt when your ascension failed. I was angry, and felt guilty, and for all my strength, I didn't know how to fix it. It's no excuse, and I like to think I tried my best, but every parent has moments we fail. I'm sorry, though."

He stood.

"You're going?"

He gave her a knowing look. "You don't want me to stay. And I know that no matter what I say, you aren't ready to accept my apology. Your adani is flowing smoothly again and you seem healthy, so I'll take my leave."

"You always leave."

Dying, it seemed, had made Father more patient than he had been before. He answered softly, "It's because every time I've visited, you've made it clear, in hundreds of unspoken ways, that you don't want me here. It hurts, but I've always tried to respect your wishes. Do you want me to stay? Because if you do, I'd be happy to."

She wanted him to stay, but he couldn't. That little girl had started something. She could once again feel the void within reverberating, quieter than before, but still clear. Father shouldn't be here. It could harm both of them. His honesty deserved hers. "I do want you to stay, but I don't think you should. I don't think the emissaries have decided to move yet, but they're thinking about it. I can feel the rumblings of their power in movement, as though they're gathering in anticipation. It's too dangerous for you to be here."

His lips turned up, as though she'd told a joke, and he stepped toward the door.

When his hand was on the door she asked, "Why don't you just kill me?"

"You're my daughter and I love you. I could never, not even if it costs me the world."

"You're a fool."

He grinned at that, and it was like he was a young man again, someone she'd never actually met. "I've heard that before. If you ever need anything, just let me know. I'll keep you as safe as I can, though I expect things will get tough, soon."

He opened the door, but before he could step out, she called after him. "Wait. You said, when I woke up, that you didn't think you belonged. What did you mean by that?"

He looked at her for a moment, then shook his head. "I can't tell you now. But if you ever come to me, I'll let you know."

With that he was gone and Elyn was alone, and that was about all she was certain of anymore. She sat down on her bed and stared out the window, expecting to see Father fly away, but there was no need for that anymore. He took a few steps, turned back to her and waved, then vanished.

23

Elian traveled through the web of adani at the speed of thought, Capricia's distinctive aura his guide. She was away from the camp, most likely hunting, her timing fortuitous. He wasn't yet ready to reveal his presence to what remained of Bael's clan. Bael knew he'd returned, his senses attuned to the slightest fluctuation of adani across the land, but Bael had also known at whose home he'd appeared and let him remain there undisturbed. They would have time enough to speak, soon.

Now that Elyn was safe, Elian returned to his wife. He burned a massive amount of adani as he approached so that she wouldn't startle at his arrival. He appeared beside her a moment later, willing adani to form a physical body. It was simpler than he'd expected it to be. His spirit remembered his form, and when he was embodied, it was as a younger man, long before Elyn had crippled him.

Capricia turned at his arrival. The first strands of gray were beginning to creep into her hair, and though she had many years of life ahead of her thanks to her ascension, those hairs served as a reminder that even her span of years was numbered. She smiled when she saw him, and it was more beautiful than any sunset or mountain peak. "You made it back," she said.

He stepped toward her, and they embraced tightly, like they had when he was younger and had returned from fighting one of the lingering Debru. "It's good to see you," he said.

They stepped apart and she looked him up and down. "It even feels like you."

Elian let her gaze linger for a moment, then said, "Did Samora tell you about Elyn?"

Capricia shook her head, and so Elian shared what he knew and what he'd done. He ended by saying, "She's fine for now, and I still hold out hope for her. She's not so far gone."

"I hope you're right, and thank you, for taking care of her."

"Of course. You and she and all the rest are what matters to me most, now. If I can ensure that you are all safe, I'll consider my life a success."

Capricia didn't miss his implication. "You sound like someone who doesn't think they're going to be around for much longer."

Elian looked down at his hand. "I can't say for sure, but since I've been back, something feels wrong. Not in a corrupted-by-shadow way, but even though this looks like my body, it's not. When I was broken from my wounds, it was still my body."

"Does Samora or Bael feel the same?"

"I'm not sure. I doubt Bael does. Samora might, though we haven't spoken of it, yet."

"But you're certain?"

Elian nodded slowly. "I am. The feeling may fade with time, but right now, I'm not so sure."

Capricia stepped close. "Well, I, for one, am still glad that you've returned. You came back looking a few decades younger, too."

Elian grinned. "It's what felt natural."

He held her close again, treasuring the feel of her skin against his own. Whether or not he belonged here, he had missed her. In time, though, she was the one who broke away first.

"What will you do next?" she asked.

Elian's grin grew wider, and he felt like a much younger man, more like he had back when he had been fighting the Debru. "I'm going to speak to Bael. We need to think about how we're going to get the emissaries to leave this world once and for all, and I've got some ideas."

Capricia returned the grin. "If that smile of yours is anything to go by, it's the sort of idea that will drive Samora mad, isn't it?"

Elian kissed her. "You know me too well, my love. Shall I tell you?"

Capricia shook her head. "If you don't, then I won't have to lie when Samora wonders if I knew. Go on, now. See what you can do."

He kissed her again. "I think I will."

Before she let him go, she said, "If nothing else, it's good to see you like this."

He stopped, curious. "Like how?"

"Like I remember you best. A challenge in front of you and the belief that no matter what happens, you'll find a way. You were always at your best in times like these."

Elian grinned and offered a quick bow with a flourish. "And you, my love, are at your best at all times."

Capricia stopped just short of rolling her eyes. "You better get going before I force you to go."

Elian laughed. "As much as I'd like to see that, I hear and obey. I'll be back soon, though. It's good to see you again."

"And you, too. Now, go!"

Elian had always believed the way of wisdom could be found in listening to one's wife, and he did so now, vanishing with another bow.

H e a p p e a r e d b e s i d e B a e l, who was helping Shayna butcher a deer for the camp. Despite the nearly endless amount of adani at his disposal, he used a steel knife, forged in the fires of the Scorpions' mountains. His blade worked the hide off the muscle and bone in smooth, practiced cuts, while Shayna pulled out the entrails and began to sort them.

His arrival attracted little attention beyond the couple's. The camp was busy with the tasks of daily survival. "May I join you?" Elian asked.

"Only if you don't mind helping," Bael said.

Shayna's eyebrows rose at that, but she said nothing. Elian had always known the pair to be close and affectionate, but there was a distance between them that hadn't been bridged yet. Elian simply nodded, formed a sharp knife of adani, and went to work on stripping the hide from the other side of the animal.

"Welcome back," Bael said.

"Thanks. I assume you've been keeping track of me?"

Bael nodded.

"I'd like to visit the emissaries. Care to join me?"

Bael's knife stopped for the first time since Elian had appeared. "Why?"

"Well, I figured I could use the company, and I wouldn't mind having your sharp eyes by my side. I miss things in my old age."

Bael scoffed. "I meant, why are you visiting the emissaries?"

"We need a better way to fight them. The best way to get started is to go visit them."

"They'll kill us."

Elian shrugged. "They might try, but they wouldn't succeed. I don't think we'll have to worry, though. So long as we don't pose a threat, I think they'll leave us be."

Bael's expression made it clear what he thought of that idea, but Shayna was grinning. "I think it's a great idea," she said.

Bael almost jumped. "You do?"

"Sure. You haven't learned anything watching them from a

distance, so it makes sense that getting close might work. And besides, you weren't made for sitting around. Better to stir things up and see what happens."

"You say that now, but you might be singing a different song when you find out what we stirred up."

Shayna's grin didn't diminish. "Unlikely. You should join him. I can finish up here."

Bael was about to ask if she was sure, but a look from her silenced the question before it could leave his lips. He nodded, cleaned off his blade, then sheathed it and put it down. "Very well. You have one in mind?" he asked Elian.

"Their leader."

Bael laughed out loud. Then he nodded. "You really are something else. Fine. Let's go stir up the hornet's nest and try not to get stung."

Bael vanished into the web of adani, and after bowing to Shayna, Elian followed him. It was easy to track his nephew's spirit, a burning ball of adani that put even a dragon's deep reserves to shame. They appeared a moment later in a forest clearing. Elian sensed the emissary less than a mile away, but here they were alone.

"Probably best not to get too close right away. It'll be better if it senses us coming."

Elian agreed with the logic. He didn't want it to appear like he was launching an ambush. He found a thin trail of worn dirt that ran through the woods, a game trail used by animals traversing this area. It ran in the direction they wanted to go, and so he took it, Bael following behind him.

"How are things with you and Shayna?" Elian asked.

"Getting better, I think, but slowly. The issue of children is still a difficult one, but I think she'd rather stay by my side and not have a family than start a family with someone else."

"A hard decision."

Bael nodded. "And one I'm worried about. It's her decision to make, of course, but I fear that one day in the future she'll wake up and realize she was mistaken and that all she really wanted was a family, and that she'll regret choosing me today."

"I hope you two find your way through. You two are good together."

"Thanks. Did you and Capricia ever have arguments?"

Elian laughed at the thought he and Capricia might not have had arguments. "Not often about anything that really mattered, but there were a few."

"Any advice?"

Elian shook his head. "I'm not the one to turn to for such questions. Capricia could answer better. All I would say is this: after everything that's happened in my life, it's the relationships that have come to mean the world to me. Family and friends. I think that so long as you treat your relationship with Shayna as something that really matters to you, you'll find a way. It's when people start thinking too much of themselves, or when they take their relationships for granted, that they get in trouble."

"Thinking of Elyn?"

"I am. I don't think I deserve all the blame she lays on me, but I can't help but think that if I had done better, if I'd just found a way to give her something more, none of this would have happened."

The game trail they were on intersected with a human path that Elian took. It led through the tall oaks until a small house came into view. Its construction was crude but sturdy, with enormous logs cut to form the walls. Smoke rose from the chimney, and Elian and Bael both stared for a moment, as their sense of the emissary told them it was within and alone.

The emissary emerged before they could approach closer. It glanced at Bael but focused most of its attention on Elian. "We believed you were dead, and before that, crippled."

Elian stepped forward and gave a friendly bow of his head. "Just for a bit. Had to walk it off. It's a pleasure to meet you."

The emissary looked between the two. "Give me one good reason why I shouldn't kill you where you stand."

Elian rose and kept a smile on his face. "I'm not sure you can, for one, but according to your own rules, we're allowed to live in peace so long as we aren't interfering with the harvest of the red hearts, and so long as we don't harm either an emissary or a servant. I believe we're well within the bounds of our rights to visit."

The emissary looked as though it couldn't believe the words it was hearing. "Why are you here?"

"I wanted to talk." Elian spoke as though he was visiting a long-lost friend.

"No amount of talking will stop what needs to happen," the emissary said.

"I'm not here to convince you of anything. I want to know what happens when you disagree with another emissary. Do you fight each other? Do you kill one another?"

The emissary's placid mask dropped. It shifted and stood right in front of Elian, but he sensed the movement. Its spirit was void, and even though it could move its body and place it somewhere else, that movement could be tracked. If he'd been so inclined, he could have had a spear of adani ready for it. The emissary relied too much on its threat and its belief it understood him.

Unfortunately, it wasn't wrong about him. Elian wouldn't strike it without significant provocation, which it was trying to goad him toward. It loomed over him.

"Why should I tell you anything?"

Elian shrugged. "You don't have to, if you don't want. I'm simply curious, is all."

The emissary seemed to realize how close it was and shifted back to where it had first greeted them. "Leave, now."

Bael looked inclined to agree, but Elian said, "No. I'd like to stay."

The emissary's stare might have killed a lesser adanist, but

Elian refused to be intimidated. "You will leave, or I will kill you and say that you attacked me."

That would have to be enough, then. Bael had one hand on Elian's wrist, but he needn't have worried. Elian bowed again, then vanished into the web of adani.

His nephew followed him, and as soon as they reappeared somewhere far from any of the emissaries, in an open plain, confronted him. "What were you thinking? You could have gotten us all killed."

Elian barely heard. His thoughts were on the encounter. "Did you notice it?"

Bael had been about to continue his tirade, but Elian's question unbalanced him. "Notice what?"

"How it reacted when I asked if they fought among themselves."

"I noticed. I thought it was going to attack and we were going to have a full-fledged war on our hands. Have you ever seen an emissary act like that?"

Elian shook his head. "It's not that we've had that many experiences with the emissaries, but the first one always seemed cold and impersonal. It was something more for this one, and my questions really got under its skin."

"Maybe it was mad you were prying. Maybe it's not used to be questioned."

"That might be some of it, but there has to be something more. We get the most upset when questions or insults get too close to the truth."

Bael looked as though he didn't follow, so Elian explained. "If I was to call you a slug, that wouldn't bother you very much, because you know it's not true, right?"

Bael nodded.

"But if I said that you're a hotheaded fool who's not fit to lead the clans, you'd have a much different reaction, true?"

His nephew's stony expression answered for Elian. "You're

upset because when I call you hotheaded, you know that's close to the truth. It's something you've worried about yourself. I'd guess it's the same for the emissary. I poked at something close to a truth it worries about. So what truth?"

Bael took the lesson to heart. "You think there might be a way to defeat the emissaries, if we keep prodding?"

Elian grinned. "I'm not sure how much prodding they'll let us do before they make some sort of new rule enforced by the threat of violence, but yes, I think we can get them to reveal their weakness if we push hard enough. Even today, the emissary didn't attack, though I certainly antagonized it. We need to better understand how they think and how they'll react. It's the first problem I had to solve when we fought against the Debru, too. It's hard to defeat an enemy you don't understand."

Bael was giving Elian a look he couldn't quite decipher. "What?"

"This is what you were like, back when you were fighting the Debru, wasn't it?"

Elian hadn't considered it in that way before, but he supposed it was. "Fighting an impossibly difficult enemy seems to bring it out, I guess."

"I'm honored to witness it myself. Scarier, though, than just hearing you and Grandmother talking about those days."

Elian rested his hand on Bael's shoulder. "If we win, then someday you'll be the old man sitting around the fire, regaling the youth with stories of the past."

Bael winced, and Elian regretted the words, but he couldn't take them back.

All any of them could do was poke their way forward in the dark, hoping they didn't lead humanity to its end.

24

E lyn knew she should have left, kept moving, never allowed herself to stay in one place for too long. She'd given up her life with the wandering clans but still she was forced to wander, like it was a disease that had settled in her bones. She was tired of running, tired of feeling like her thoughts were running circles around her. Staying home was a mistake, but she couldn't bring herself to care.

After the world of the void and sleeping wherever her body ended up at night, the simple comfort of her worn bed tempted her more than adani ever had. Her bowls, spoons, and chairs had been shaped by her own hands, as familiar to her as the fields beyond the front door.

Funny, that for so long she'd felt like this home was a cage, its walls closing in and squeezing the breath from her lungs. Now she welcomed the small space, hesitant even to step outside and face the expanse of fields she'd once called her own.

Elyn decided she wouldn't think. She wouldn't give her mind one idle moment in which to swirl around the events of the past months. She puttered around the house, sweeping away all the spiders and cobwebs that had made their homes in dark corners.

An old rag, dipped in a bucket of water she'd pulled from the stream running full behind the house, caught the dust that had gathered in her absence. She washed the sheets until her hands burned from the cold, then hung them out to dry on a line she tied between two tree branches. Every action served as a shield, protecting her mind from intrusive thoughts that threatened to spear her spirit.

She used the last bit of daylight to chop the wood to heat her home overnight. Adani would have made the task a simple one, and taken her no more than the length of a thought, but she chose her familiar axe, the handle worn to nearly a shine from years of use. She carried the wood back to the house and left it to dry, then used up some of her seasoned wood to light a fire, using a shred of adani for the first time that day. The kindling caught quickly and before long she sat in front of the blazing fire.

She'd always loved to stare at flames. It danced and twisted as the wood turned to ash. Not destruction, exactly, but transformation. The fire kept her thoughts at bay until her eyelids drooped, and she summoned just enough strength to put on two more logs before she rolled into her bed and fell instantly asleep.

She woke in a house being warmed by the first rays of the sun, and she didn't dare move, for as soon as she threw the covers aside, there would be no more hiding. A wiser woman might have extended her adani to see what schemes, if any, the adanists considered launching, but Elyn couldn't bring herself to care, even with her greater strength. She elected instead to pull the covers higher over her head, and it wasn't long before she was once again asleep.

When she woke again, the sun poured in through the open windows and the breeze brushed the curtains against her face. She yawned, stretched, and rose from the bed. It had been a long time since she'd slept so well, and she felt even better. She stepped outside and let the sun warm her face. It was a cloudless sky, which meant that she could see for miles.

Which meant, in turn, that she could see the flight of dragons approaching in the distance. Three of them, so she was probably looking at twelve guests or fewer. There was no good reason for three dragons to be heading her way, which left only poor decisions. The head emissary had expected the adanists would eventually make a try on her life, but she'd hoped they wouldn't be so foolish.

A growl rose from the back of her throat. They were mad, thinking that attacking her would solve their problems. It would serve them right if she remained and forced them to deal with the consequences of their actions.

She didn't want their deaths on her hands, though. She couldn't say for sure where her loyalties lay anymore, but nothing good would come of a fight. Void answered her call and a doorway appeared, not more than a few steps away. The sight of her home, freshly cleaned, made her hesitate, though, and nearly cost her everything.

A giant golden ball of adani, the type of weaving preferred by most dragons, struck her home from behind, from the direction of the stream. Instinct took over and she threw up a shield of void, which saved her life. The adani smashed into the house before releasing its tremendous pent-up energy. The wooden frame, which Elyn had painstakingly built by hand, which had survived brutal winters and scorching summers without complaint, cracked and broke like dry twigs beneath her heel. Debris and adani struck her shield, which absorbed it all like a starving child inhaling a feast. What wasn't devoured by the void flew past her, violently plowing unwanted furrows in the field and burning the weed-filled crops.

She stared at the place where her home had been, now only a smoking ruin. Nothing recognizable remained, her years of toil wiped from the land with less effort than she'd taken in sweeping her floors the day before. Her gaze rose to the lone dragon and rider approaching from the opposite direction, then dropped to the house. She looked to the portal, still open and waiting to take her away.

Elyn closed the portal carefully, as though she was folding up clean laundry to store it. A sphere of void no bigger than her hand danced above her right palm, and she thrust it at the dragon with all the speed she could summon. It sped through the sky fast enough she could barely track it. The void cut through the dragon's scales and feasted upon its deep well of adani.

Her sphere didn't kill the dragon instantly, but the void disrupted its ability to fly, and it folded its wings and plummeted. Elyn watched as dragon and rider hit hard on the other side of the stream. After the dust settled, it was clear that neither would rise to bother her again.

She turned to address the rest of the flight of dragons approaching her field, but before she could send any spheres in their direction, someone was standing beside her. Instinct took over and she twisted, releasing a handful of spheres even as she sought to dodge any adani that might be pointed at her. The unexpected guest vanished, and Elyn caught a glimpse of Bael's dark hair. He appeared again on her other side, and this time she had the presence of mind to hold her attack.

She saw that he was looking at the wreckage of her house, and at the dragon and rider, both bodies lying at odd angles. He opened his mouth to speak, but the bright golden glow of adani from the sky prevented any discussion. Elyn threw up a wall of void wide enough to protect them both and the adani uselessly expended itself against the shield.

"They attacked you?" Bael asked.

She nodded.

"You should leave. I'll speak to them."

"They destroyed my home."

"And that will only be the beginning of the destruction if we aren't careful," Bael said.

A third voice joined them, colder than a frozen lake on a blustery winter day. "A noble sentiment, but too late. The agreement has already been broken."

They both turned to see the head emissary standing behind them. She threw a handful of spheres in the direction of the dragons, who weaved through the sky to avoid them. While the dragons were otherwise occupied, she turned to Bael. "I've been looking forward to ending you."

Bael embraced adani, so much that Elyn had to take a step back or risk being burned. "I'd like to see you try."

Other emissaries appeared behind Bael, misting into existence from wherever they'd been before. Three, then half a dozen more. Then more than Elyn had ever seen in one place. The void within her core vibrated, not with any message, but with the sheer amount of power granted to the emissaries. They'd been preparing for this.

Bael shifted, but a dozen emissaries shifted, too, each moving as fast as thought. Elyn lost the ability to track the fight only a moment after it started, but her field was the first friendly casualty. Adani burst upon it as Bael tried to kill emissaries with waves of golden light, but they weren't so easily dismissed. Void swallowed entire chunks of her field at a time as emissaries aimed for killing blows and missed.

The dragons above moved much slower, but the void that had embraced her after the destruction of her house had crumbled. She formed a sphere and launched it, but her spirit wasn't in it, and the attack was easily avoided.

At least one emissary hadn't forgotten about the dragons, though, and a sphere of void bigger than her house struck one dragon behind its hind legs. A chunk of tail fell to the surface as the dragon roared in pain. It flapped its wings like a baby bird trying to fly for the first time, but it couldn't keep to the air. The adanists riding upon its back leaped off at the last moment, but they jumped onto a battlefield far beyond their skill.

Two more bright lights appeared, not far from Elyn, and she

turned to see both Samora and Father, standing side by side. Father glanced at her once, and then they joined the battle.

Elyn wasn't sure what hurt worse, that they would ignore her presence as inconsequential, or that they were right to do so. It was no better than being a child again, unable to partake in the adult activities.

As the ground rumbled beneath her feet, though, she wondered if this wasn't a war she was better off having no part in. She was no more equipped to fight these battles than the adanists now trying to flee from the spheres of void that rose into the sky after their dragons.

More shadows appeared, emissaries appearing to lend their aid in what was quickly becoming the battle that would decide the fate of their world. It had happened so quickly. She'd only been awake for a while when the first blast of adani had destroyed her house, and only a few moments more for every major power on this world to show up at her doorstep. Both sides sought a decisive advantage, but the battle would never end in the adanists' favor.

She couldn't track the battle, but the sheer number of emissaries guaranteed that Bael and the rest of her family would soon be overwhelmed. It was their own fault for getting involved in a fight that didn't have anything to do with them. Even more shadows appeared, but by now the two surviving dragons had turned around and were fleeing from the destruction with all the speed their wings could create.

Something blurred in front of her, and there was an explosion as an adani spear struck no more than ten paces in front of her. She closed her eyes and turned her head away as rich soil pelted her in the chest and cheek.

As quickly as it had begun, it ended. Elyn couldn't see her family's departure, but she could sense as their adani vanished back into the web. They'd done enough to save the adanists from the deaths they deserved, but were wise enough to realize they had no chance of winning this fight. Elyn wasn't even sure they'd killed a single emissary, for she hadn't felt the void reverberate with the loss. They'd tried, but had proved insufficient for the task.

She was glad they had escaped, and she was pondering that when the head emissary appeared before her. The emissary had a deep cut along her cheek which healed as Elyn watched. Elyn had expected anger, but instead, she saw only pleasure on her master's face. She smiled, and it was every bit as terrifying as seeing a dragon open its jaws and prepare to bite down on her head.

"The time has come. It's time to show these adanists what it means to serve Void."

✦ 25 ✦

Bael wished that all his problems in life could be solved by simply using more adani. He could always pull from the Great Heart, and his problems would simply vanish, swept away like dust before a broom. A younger Bael had been guilty of thinking as much. How many times had he pushed himself beyond his limit, thinking that if he could just become a little bit stronger, all his problems would be solved? More times than he could count, that much was sure.

No amount of adani would solve the puzzle in front of him today, though. News of the failed attack on Elyn's home had spread through the clans like wildfire. Given the amount of adani he, Elian, and Samora had used in their fight against the emissaries, it would be a surprise there was an adanist on the continent who *didn't* know a fight had happened. They'd sent inquiries to Bael's clan and he'd responded with the full story.

Clan elders and leaders had fallen upon his little camp like locusts. He hosted them as well as he was able, but his clan was more a memory than a reality, and he didn't have food or drink to welcome them with.

Not that they noticed. They came prepared to fight, not to eat, and there wasn't enough liquor in the world to stop this fight from happening. They sharpened their words and formed alliances with dizzying speed, and before Bael had finished greeting the last arrival, they'd gathered around a small campfire, seated, because they expected to be here a while.

"They need to be caught and punished. It's the only hope we have of avoiding the emissaries' wrath," one young man argued. Bael didn't even know who he was. A Hawk, but Bael didn't recognize him.

"It doesn't matter what we do to them. The emissaries will do what they want, regardless. We should be thinking about how we can save as many as we can," said Amelyn, an elder from the Scorpions.

The arguments came fast and heavy, and Bael made no effort to intervene. He was furious Coll had launched an attack that seemed so clearly doomed to failure, and in such a clumsy manner. It was nothing more than Coll would have come up with, though. His solution to every problem was to hit it as hard as he could.

But Coll had paid the price. He'd been the rider attempting to sneak up from the back side of the house, the unfortunate rider struck down by what Bael assumed was a void from Elyn, launched in response to her home being destroyed.

There was plenty of blame to go around, though. He'd known they were planning something and hadn't tried to stop them. Elyn should have kept on the move if she hadn't wanted to risk unnecessary lives. And Coll should have been smart enough to know when he was stirring up trouble he couldn't contain.

None of it mattered, though. He could throw blame around all day and hit plenty of worthy targets, but it did nothing to change what had already happened. All that mattered now was finding the way forward, and he didn't know that, either. He didn't know the emissaries well enough to know how they'd react. The three transformed adanists hadn't even killed a single emissary, and

Elyn was unharmed, so if they chose, they didn't need to respond.

Bael's hope in that future was slim.

It grew even slimmer when the head emissary appeared in the middle of the circle, silencing the argument with little more than a glance. Most of the elders shifted and fell backward in surprise. Bael grasped adani and held it close, but didn't lash out. It looked ready to vanish with a thought, but it made no move to strike the elders down.

If it had wanted to land a devastating blow to the wandering clans, there would be no better opportunity. One sphere of void, dropped here, would leave each of the wandering clans leaderless.

It was certain chaos, but Bael didn't think that was what the emissary wanted. It wanted order and a docile group of adanists. Killing them here worked against its goals.

His guess was confirmed when the emissary said, "You have broken your agreement, and as such, will suffer the consequences explained to you when we arrived. Every adanist who survived the attack must be turned over to us within one of your eighth-days. We counted ten who were involved, and per our agreement, we will kill one thousand civilians, a hundred for each adanist who thought they could stand against us."

Shouts rose from the circle, as did an angry wave of adani. Bael held his close to his chest, afraid that if he extended it at all he wouldn't be able to resist striking the emissary. It wanted him to; of that he was certain. A handful of elders had spears in their hands, but none were so bold as to throw. They cast glances at Bael instead. Only now did he become important to them.

Bael stood and took a step toward the emissary, which had the effect of silencing the pointless shouting. Older warriors spread their feet as they prepared for battle.

"You should leave," Bael said.

"But what if I want to stay?" the emissary asked, delighting in turning the tables on its antagonists.

"You'll find no welcome here."

"It didn't stop you and Elian from disturbing my peace."

Bael took another step forward, partly to show he had no fear of the emissary, but partly because his proximity to the emissary would hopefully keep anyone's temper from boiling over. They stood within two paces of one another, close enough that either could possibly kill the other with a single move. It appeared calm, but something in its eyes told Bael it was as ready to kill or flee as he was.

"Why do you want us dead? Your master wants our hearts."

"Which is a mistake. Your world should be destroyed, no different than any other. Give me an excuse, and I'd be happy to end it all for you."

Bael asked, "And if we don't deliver the adanists?"

"Then your innocent will suffer the consequences. Your cities are filled with sacrifices yet to be made."

Amelyn interjected. "You will have your adanists. You have the word of the Scorpions."

The emissary turned to the elder, as did several of the other leaders, their mouths hanging slightly open at the betrayal. Amelyn didn't flinch from their stares. "It's not even a question worthy of debate. If we don't, more innocents will suffer. All of you took the same oath I did, to protect those who can't fight for themselves. This is what that means. Coll and the others lost their right to live when they betrayed the agreement their leaders made and launched that foolhardy ambush."

It was the reasonable choice. The choice that left them with the most options and the most time, so why did he hate it so much?

The emissary, probably realizing it wouldn't inspire an attack today, nodded briskly. "Very well."

"Will you still execute a thousand civilians?" Amelyn asked.

"Of course. Those were the terms of the agreement. One thousand, but no more. You have our word on that."

"Where and when?" the Scorpion leader asked.

"Best we don't say, but within the next few days. An opportunity to inspire you to turn over the traitors who attacked us."

The emissary started to mist away, but before it left, it looked squarely at Bael. "And just so you all know, there were only seven surviving adanists who fled on the dragons. The other three who fought against us and survived were Bael, Elian, and Samora."

It vanished, but Bael swore he heard it laugh as it disappeared. The silence it left behind was deafening, its parting blow devastating.

All eyes turned to him, and it was Amelyn who led the questioning. "Will you abide by the decision of this council, no matter which way it falls?"

"You know that by having the three of us surrender, you give up whatever small hope we still possess."

"We are all aware, but the question still remains. Will you abide by the decision of this council?"

His chest felt as though someone was piling boulders on top of it. He no longer needed air, but he still felt as though he was choking. "We were trying to save the fools," he said.

Amelyn looked like she was about to ask the question again, but Bael held up a hand to stop her. Would he allow himself to end, even if he was convinced it was wrong? The part of him raised on stories of noble sacrifice wanted to say yes, that if it was what the clan desired, he would obey.

He couldn't convince himself. Surrender was a failure.

"Honestly, I do not know. I will have to think on it."

Amelyn accepted the answer as good enough. "Perhaps it would be best if you left us to debate on our own. We know well your spirit, and we know what the emissary is truly asking of us. Is there anything more you would have us know?"

Bael searched his thoughts, but there wasn't. He didn't always agree with the clan elders, but he trusted them to make a decision they truly thought was best. He shook his head, bowed to the circle, then took his leave.

SHAYNA WAITED for him inside their tent. He reported all that had happened, and she listened until he finished without interruption.

"Are you leaning one way or the other?" she asked.

He would have hedged with anyone else, but Shayna deserved the full truth from him. "I don't think I'd obey if they ordered me to surrender, but that might change. I suppose it depends quite a bit on what Elian and Samora decide, too. No point sacrificing myself if they won't."

"But if they decide to, you might?"

"It would certainly make it more likely."

He closed his eyes, surrounded by the familiar odors of the tent. Since returning, he'd come to appreciate the details of his life that he hadn't before. Smells and textures were things he'd barely thought of before, but now they reminded him that he was alive, and for all the warmth and peace of adani, it lacked the vibrance and variety of daily life. He didn't want to leave.

Shayna said nothing, but from the way she shifted frequently, Bael guessed there was something else on her mind. He considered prodding her but elected instead to wait her out. She would speak when she was ready.

It didn't take long. She cleared her throat, then said, "There's something I've been thinking about, but it's a big question, and now probably isn't the time."

Bael opened his eyes and rolled onto his side so he could face her. Shayna would hold onto him as he dove a dragon between two cliffs without fear, but whatever was on her mind made her nervous. She looked like she wanted to be pacing their small tent instead of laying beside him.

"What is it?" he asked.

"Did you know that Coll had a child?"

He hadn't had even the slightest inkling. The idea of Coll being bonded had never crossed his mind. "Really?"

Shayna nodded. "He was bonded with another adanist from their clan about three years ago. Their child, a little girl, is just shy of turning two."

Bael's thoughts were yanked back to the memories of the battle around Elyn's house, and to the dragon and its rider that Elyn had killed. "Then Coll was even more of a fool than I thought, if he was willing to risk leaving his wife without a husband and his daughter without a father. Especially for so little chance of gain."

His wife's face fell. "It's a more tragic story than that. His wife died in childbirth, so the women in the clan have been nursing her and helping Coll raise her. Now that Coll's dead and his name is disgraced, they're not sure what they want to do with the child."

Bael raised himself up so he was propped on one elbow. "What are you thinking?" he asked, even though he was certain he already knew the answer.

"That we should raise her as our own. If her clan doesn't want to raise her, we should do it. Not only will it bring some new life to our tent, but it will give her a chance she wouldn't get otherwise."

Bael didn't need to sense her adani to know Shayna's feelings. She tried to keep her voice even, as though they were discussing what they might eat for the next few nights, but she more excited by the prospect than he'd seen her in some time.

It would solve several problems at once, but that was no way to think of bringing a new child into their family. Could they offer the love and support the little girl would need? Would it be best for Coll's daughter?

A glance at Shayna made him think that the answer was yes.

Clans usually cared for orphans as well as they could, and from what Bael understood, it was far better to be a clan orphan than to be without parents in most cities. Clans rose and fell together, whereas people in cities tended to think more of themselves and their immediate relations.

Shayna, though, had love to give, and Bael knew well how much she wanted a child. They'd argued the topic often enough since finding out he'd never be able to have children, so there was little to discuss. Only one question mattered.

"How sure of you are this? How sure are you that what you're offering is best, not just for us, but for Coll's girl?"

She answered without hesitation. "Perfectly sure."

Warmth spread through his chest, a welcome reprieve after bearing the burdens the clan elders and the emissary had piled on his ribs. They were going to have a family, despite the fact they wouldn't share blood with their child. He didn't mind. He was going to love that child as though it were his own. Maybe he couldn't have followed Coll on his doomed mission, but he could offer his old comrade this, at least.

"Then I suppose I have even more reason to stay, don't I?" Bael asked.

Shayna broke out in a wide smile that stretched nearly from ear to ear, and she wrapped him up in an enthusiastic embrace.

They lay together for a while after that, talking about the details and making the necessary plans. Bael quickly realized that Shayna had been thinking about this for a while. He didn't know how long ago she'd learned of Coll's orphan, but the idea of bringing a child into their family clearly wasn't a new one. He rode the wave of her enthusiasm, and for one precious afternoon, there was hope in the world.

A messenger came for him just before nightfall, and he followed the messenger back to the central fire. The elders were still gathered there, and they looked exhausted, as though they'd survived some battle for the ages instead of a dispute between leaders.

Amelyn seemed to have taken the role of leader, and she spoke first. Bael appreciated that she didn't mince her words. She was a strong elder and a tribute to the clans.

She said, "Bael, as a council we've decided that you, Samora, and Elian, should turn yourselves over to the emissaries for execution one eighthday from now. We're sorry, but we believe it's for the best."

❧ 26 ❧

Elyn didn't know the head emissary well, but she'd never once seen the emissary truly pleased, and so when she appeared within the forest clearing that served as Elyn's temporary home smiling, Elyn wondered what had happened.

The emissary didn't keep her in suspense long. "Our judgment has been delivered to the clans, and they didn't even put up a fight."

"You wanted them to fight?"

The emissary waved away the question. "Yes, but this is a win either way. If they fight back, they die and we can put this world behind us, but if they surrender, which they will, we earn the power to finally strike a fatal blow against the light. They hold onto their promise to protect those weaker than them as if losing nobly makes them somehow victorious. Our master chose our strategy well."

"What was the judgment?"

"No more than what we had originally promised. Ten adanists were involved in the attack against you, and our agreement was a hundred civilians for each adanist involved."

"A thousand people …" Elyn murmured. The number didn't seem real, though she knew plenty of towns that held so many.

"And the adanists must turn themselves in for execution, including Bael, Samora, and Elian."

Elyn couldn't hide her surprise. "They didn't attack me."

"No, but they attacked the emissaries who arrived to defend you. They're lucky they were too weak to kill any of us, for their punishment would be ten times worse."

"Will they do it?" Elyn asked.

The emissary shrugged. "It doesn't matter. If they do, it's the end of this world's resistance. If they don't, we'll have all the justification we need to hit the clans again and again. They'll bend the knee, one way or the other."

Elyn bowed, mostly to hide the emotions she couldn't keep from her face, but also to buy herself a moment to collect her thoughts. "Congratulations, master."

"Thank you. There is one other piece of news that will be important to you, though."

Elyn's stomach knotted up as she rose. "Yes, master?"

"My fellow emissaries are already preparing the town that will be destroyed. We chose the Scorpion village in which you were ambushed the first time. As we speak, they are ensuring that exactly one thousand people will be there."

Elyn's blood ran cold. She knew she was among destroyers, and a part of her wanted to be numbered among them, but she had been promised destruction without malice. They brought peace. Perhaps, if she stepped far, far away from what was transpiring, she could see how their actions would eventually bring that end, not just to this world but across all the stars, but from where she stood, it looked an awful lot like murder.

It was the smile on the emissary's face that bothered her most. She wasn't performing a brutal but necessary duty. She *liked* this.

Elyn was trapped, though, her decision made what felt like a lifetime ago. Obedience was all that remained. "How may I help, master?"

The emissary's grin grew wider. "For now, you must keep yourself safe. But I will summon you soon, and you shall be the one to destroy the village."

Elyn blanched as she understood the head emissary better. Void sought to destroy light and life, to end the suffering of all, but that destruction was carried out without malice.

The head emissary, in contrast, served Void to bask in the power denied to her during her mortal span of years. She delighted in forcing others to endure the suffering she'd lived in for so long, in making them feel powerless against her. She cloaked her intent in the language of their shared master, but the motives behind her actions shared little with those of Void.

"Me?" Elyn asked.

"You are not the first servant who has experienced doubts. Our mission is a difficult one, and not for the faint of heart. But you have had more time than most to give yourself fully to our master. The time to commit completely is now. Either destroy the village when we command you to, or your service to our master comes to an early end."

ELYN HAD NEVER KNOWN that three days could pass so quickly. She hadn't been able to sleep and spent most of her nights wandering the woods, wishing the majestic silence of the trees had some answers for her. Food no longer agreed with her stomach, and whenever she attempted to eat anything more filling than a handful of berries, she found herself bent over, hands on knees, heaving the food up.

Worst of all, the fact that loomed above all others was that she didn't know how long she had. Her adani couldn't tell her exactly how many people were in the Scorpion village, and it seemed the emissaries had stopped moving people in and out the day before. The moment of her summoning couldn't be long now, but there was no word from the head emissary.

She'd even thought of running to her family, but she didn't think there would be any help from that quarter. She'd chosen her lonely path. Now she had to walk it.

The head emissary arrived in the late morning of the third day, and Elyn was no closer to a final decision than she had been the moment she learned of her duty.

"It's time," the emissary said, and Elyn bowed.

The emissary summoned a portal for her, and Elyn stepped through, blinking as she stepped from the shade of the trees to the bright light of a clear sky. The sun burned overhead as though it was trying to do its part to push back the darkness. Mountain peaks glistened with small packets of snow that had clung to the stone even as the late summer sun melted it away. The Scorpion village spread out before her, the outermost homes no more than a few hundred paces from where she stood.

It was close enough to hear the cries for help.

The emissaries had encircled the town, and as Elyn arrived, she saw one young man sprint from the shadow of a house and run toward the foothills. He'd barely made it twenty steps before an emissary shifted in front of him and drove the air from his lungs with a single, devastating punch. The young men fell, and the emissary picked him up by his belt and dragged him back to the town, throwing him into the alley he'd emerged from before shifting away again.

A handful of bound adani spears rose from a distant rooftop, aimed for one of the emissaries to Elyn's left. The emissary formed a wall of void that devoured the adani, but made no other effort to retaliate.

"Do they know that it's now?" Elyn asked.

Her question was answered by the townspeople themselves, who launched a coordinated attack of adani upon her location.

Like all other adani spears, the attack was as good as useless. Judging from the spears' strength, none of the adanists trapped within the village were ascended.

The head emissary confirmed her guess. "We let them know that if they had any final actions to take care of, now would be the time."

Elyn studied the emissary, now convinced her earlier realization was correct. Two possibilities existed. Either she offered the townspeople a small mercy, or the news had been a final form of torture she could inflict. Elyn was sure now that the answer was the latter.

The emissary gestured toward the town. "Whenever you're ready."

"That's it?"

The emissary nodded. "That's it."

Elyn wasn't sure she could summon enough void to destroy the town in one attack, and was about to say something, but she realized it wouldn't matter to the emissary. One attack or a dozen, so long as the people within were dead at the end, her master wouldn't care. She'd probably prefer a dozen attacks to draw out the terror.

Elyn formed a sphere of void. Not because she wanted to, but because what choice did she have?

It was Father's voice, from a memory long forgotten, that she thought of them.

There's always a choice.

She let the sphere of void unravel. "What if I refuse?"

The emissary looked as though she'd been expecting the question, and she probably had. Elyn's spirit was too well known to the void. There was no hiding from it anymore. The corner of her mouth turned up in a malicious smile. "If you refuse, you can join the rest of the citizens in that town. We'll choose one person randomly and allow them to flee, so that the count remains exactly one thousand. No one will be able to say that we didn't keep our word."

Elyn looked to the town. Kill a thousand or save one, at the cost of her own life. If Father had been in her place, faced with the same decision, it would have been made faster than she could snap her fingers. He hadn't been able to protect her, but he would have sacrificed his life for a stranger in this town without thinking twice about it.

Hadn't she once wished for death, an easy end to all her suffering? Why not now, when the action was certain to save a life, at least for a time?

She didn't want to die.

She couldn't say, exactly, when her attitude had changed, but the emissary had revealed the truth Elyn hadn't been able to admit to herself. Did she want to live badly enough she was willing to kill a thousand people for the right? She was disappointed to find the answer was not an immediate no. A void of sphere almost formed above her palm before she realized what she did.

The emissary's grin never faltered. She liked watching Elyn squirm, had been hoping for a test just like this, a moment that proved she wasn't worthy of following their master.

The appearance of a second emissary, who took the shape of a young man, interrupted Elyn's ordeal. "The three of them have arrived, just as you predicted," he said.

The head emissary's eyes lit up. "Where?"

"They're hiding in the hills above the town. A rise with a clear vantage point."

"Any other signs of an attack?"

"No. For the moment, they're just watching."

The head emissary considered for a moment. "Call the second wave of reinforcements. If they think they can interfere, it's best if they understand how much of a battle they have on their grubby little hands."

The emissary bowed and vanished into mist, and Elyn sensed

the void reverberate with a message. Two more emissaries appeared, one on each side of the head emissary, surrounding her like living shields. More mist formed into emissaries around the town. Not all who served the void were upon this world, but many of them were.

The head emissary turned her attention back to Elyn. "It seems your family has arrived to observe your decision. What will it be? Will you serve our master and bring a lasting peace to this world, or will you throw your life away for some stranger in a town that tried to murder you the last time you visited?"

Put that way, it seemed like no choice at all, but Elyn couldn't choose. She didn't want to take either path, but she didn't have the strength to forge a separate one. Surrounded by so many emissaries, they could make her do whatever they wished.

She wished she wasn't alone. Her family had come, not to observe her, but to do what they could to protect the town. It would only bring more suffering to the world and the wandering clans, but they would fight. She was certain of that. It was in their blood.

It was in her blood, too, though she didn't like thinking of what they had in common.

She formed a void and considered it. Cold and empty, it would destroy anything it touched. The villagers' deaths, when they came, would be quick and almost painless. They were all going to die soon anyway, she could at least make it merciful. She raised her hand and pointed at the village, took a deep breath.

All she had to do was let go. There were few things in the world easier than that.

Except she couldn't, and she would be cursed if she allowed her life to be traded so cheaply. Her family was here, and they gave her strength.

She turned toward the head emissary, released the sphere of void at her, then formed and released another as a new war erupted around her.

❧ 27 ❧

Elian, Bael, and Samora had spoken after the council of elders had delivered their judgment to Bael and decided their best course of action, and the only one they saw that made any sense, was to watch and wait. They'd been given an eighthday reprieve, and they planned to use every moment of it.

It hadn't taken them long to discover the emissaries' target. To their sense of adani, it felt as though spirits were being pressed together into a ball, like a child packing a snowball tight in the winter months. The Scorpion town was too small for a thousand people, and there was no other reason for the sudden influx. An assault and a rescue were considered, but the emissaries were no fools, and there were always enough around to prevent any surprises. When the emissaries summoned Elyn, they knew the time had come.

Knowing what was about to happen and being able to do anything about it were two different problems, though. Elian stood out in the open, staring down at the village below, his mind racing. He'd never visited, and it was smaller than he'd expected, their streets currently filled with uninvited guests banned from leaving. Given the size of the deadlands in the middle of the cities out west, Elian was confident that any emissary could destroy the village without problem. One blast, and it would all be over.

Except the emissaries seemed content to draw the process out. They knew Elian and the others were present. Not long after they'd arrived, another wave of emissaries had appeared to ring the village, prematurely killing any plans Elian might have had.

There were too many emissaries, and it was too difficult to defend the village. All an emissary needed was one spare moment and it would be done. Nothing the three of them could do would stop that.

He tried not to focus on Elyn, for she only served to distract him from the larger problem at hand. He still held out hope that someday she would choose a different path, but today, the lives in the village mattered more.

Bael elbowed him in the side. "Do you see what's happening with Elyn?"

Elian shook his head. "I'm still trying to figure out how we might save the villagers."

"Well, it might be worth a look."

Elian allowed himself a moment of distraction, then swore to himself. Elyn stood with the head emissary and two others, a sphere of void floating above her palm. It was pointed straight at the village.

"They're going to make her do it."

Any chance of bringing his daughter back and making her a part of the clan again would die if she did. Her crimes already spoke volumes against her, but he wasn't sure even he would find forgiveness in his spirit for her if she was the one who destroyed the village. No doubt, the emissary at her side knew as much, too.

Elian stared, waiting for the slightest twitch of a finger, the slightest relaxation of the tension running through her body. He convinced himself that she couldn't. Not his daughter, who he'd raised to protect those who lacked the adani she'd been gifted with. She might be misled by lies and make mistakes, but surely she'd never do anything so terrible as this.

His faith was rewarded a moment later, when she turned her attack on the three emissaries standing together and released it. As near as Elian could tell, she took aim at the head emissary, but the two standing guard were too quick. Dangerous as she might be to the unsuspecting, she wasn't even an ascended adanist, and the emissaries had to be prepared for her to turn.

They weren't fools.

Her sphere of void struck one of the emissaries square in the chest, and the darkness that was the emissary faded against Elian's senses. It hadn't shifted or fled.

It had died.

Void, it seemed, destroyed *everything* it touched, including itself.

The reaction against Elyn's betrayal was immediate. The second emissary guard had a sphere of its own raised against his daughter, and in the blink of an eye, Elian sped through the web of adani and appeared before the emissary. Fast as the emissary was, it had become too fixated on Elyn, and Elian's arrival wasn't expected. He didn't bother with a bound sword, for this physical form had become his weapon. He stabbed out with his hand, sensing the core of darkness that resided near the emissary's navel. Adani bit into the protective layer of void, the negative reflection of the adani that formed Elian's own physical form.

As always, void pulled adani from him, like an oversized mosquito drinking a bucket of blood, but he was connected to the Great Heart, and the void shattered against his immense reserves. He grasped the emissary's core in his hand and squeezed. The core cracked, then transformed to something like sand that slipped between his fingers. The emissary and its attack vanished before it could hurt Elyn.

He searched for the head emissary, but it had disappeared in the moment he needed to kill its guard.

Did they run or fight? What surprise they had was lost and they were sorely outnumbered.

"Can you form a portal and escape?" he asked.

She shook her head. "The doorways are controlled by Void, and I don't think she's going to want to help me escape her vengeance."

Then it all came down to Elyn, as so much did. "We fight, then."

Bael and Samora appeared beside Elian.

"Plan?" Samora asked.

"She can't run, so we fight."

Samora could have argued. Would have been wise to do so. They were too valuable to risk, even for family. Losing here doomed everyone. Samora only nodded.

Elian addressed Elyn. "Use the void against them."

She nodded, but then their brief reprieve came to an end. The sphere appeared in the very center of the Scorpion village, and Elian only noticed the growing darkness after it was too late to resist. He'd expected the emissaries to attack him directly, and it never crossed his mind that they would have other plans.

Because he would never think the way they did.

The sphere expanded from the center of the village, swallowing flesh, forged steel, stone, and light with equal ease. Screams echoed down the narrow streets and burst into the open space beyond, but sound moved so much faster than feet, and the sphere grew fast enough to overtake even the quickest messenger.

Not that it mattered. There were no open streets to sprint down, and the mass of humanity crushed itself even as the sphere overtook it.

The sphere devoured the screams of the innocent, and the nature of its force was such that neither wood nor stone cracked as it vanished into the expanding maw of darkness. The destruction was silent, and when the last home was consumed, the sphere simply vanished, leaving the head emissary at its center. A new deadland had been created, the death substantial enough more red hearts could be harvested.

Elian could only hear the quiet, the loudest sound the wind that rushed to fill the new emptiness. Life was noise, from the soft footsteps of a mother slipping away from a sleeping baby to the clang of steel on steel as smiths forged the steel civilization needed. He wanted no part of the peace the emissaries brought.

He had no memory of forming the spear that he found in his hand, but he hurled it with all his might, even as he knew it was useless. Defiance, though, needed to be shouted, and best to make his point with something sharp.

The head emissary absorbed the spear with a wall of void, then shifted until it was behind a line of other emissaries. Not one, then to lead its warriors from the front.

His anger spent, Elian took a breath and thought. He, Bael, and Samora could leave if they wanted, make their escape and live to fight another day. Elyn could not, but he wouldn't leave her behind. He didn't see how they won, though.

Bael vanished and reappeared among the emissaries, a golden blade of adani flashing as he cut at them. They shifted around him like a cloud of insects, and though he was faster than any single emissary, they were all too willing to retreat and protect one another, limiting him to shallow cuts that did no real damage. Samora threw darts of adani, but her hope of catching the emissaries by surprise was in vain.

Bael vanished again and Elian blinked, only belatedly realizing he couldn't follow his nephew's movements. The emissaries couldn't either, and Elian felt two of them die before they organized themselves, casting shields around one another while others dropped spheres of void from above.

He began to fear that Bael wouldn't be able to escape for much longer, but then Elyn threw several spheres of void into the crowd gathering around her cousin.

That caught their attention. Some emissaries shifted away while others lashed out with a return volley of spheres. Elian and Samora's layered shields kept them safe, but not for long.

It was a better fight than Elian thought they'd put up, but its conclusion seemed inevitable. No matter Bael's strength, the emissaries were too numerous.

When Bael vanished again, it was to break away from the fighting and join the rest of his family. He had a smile on his face, and Elian wondered how much he'd been like that when he'd been younger. Those days seemed a long time ago, now. Bael threw up a shield to help with the next wave of void spheres. Each sphere cracked and destroyed a shield, but between the three of them, they were able to put up enough shields to absorb each of the attacks.

The head emissary threw up a hand, and the gesture was mirrored by nearly thirty others. Countless spheres of void appeared in the air above them, and there was nothing Elian or his family could do to stop them. If only there was some way to get Elyn away from here.

Elyn stepped forward. "Thank you, but it's best you go now."

She looked back at Elian. "I'm sorry."

Even as she spoke, dozens of void spheres formed around her, more than Elian had seen around any emissary. They were small, and put him in mind of one of Samora's earliest techniques, one he was certain Samora had taught Elyn as a child. Samora had used adani, but his daughter had found a new medium, and it was one that served her well.

He wished there was an artist nearby, someone who could capture what he saw in that moment and preserve it after his memory had faded. His daughter stood tall, not proud, exactly, but accepting, as though she'd finally found some sliver of the peace she'd been seeking for so long. She was surrounded by the power of their enemy, but she had turned it to her own purposes.

His heart pounded heavy in his chest, filled with a warmth

that had nothing to do with adani. She'd not become the woman he'd dreamed of her someday becoming, but that didn't mean he would leave her to die.

Elyn threw her spheres first, the entire process from their birth to their delivery taking no more than a beat or two of his proud heart. The emissaries were caught flat-footed as they prepared their own attack, and the spheres above them vanished as they rushed to throw up shields.

A handful raised defenses in time, but more were struck, Elyn's tiny spheres punching through limbs and torsos with impunity. Elian hadn't believed a single attack could do so much damage against the emissaries. Samora followed Elyn's devastation with one of her own, hundreds of small weavings of adani that descended upon the emissaries like a soft but deadly golden snow. The ground rumbled as her attack landed and the darkness receded against the onslaught of light.

Elyn didn't relent, nor did she wait for the smoke or debris from Samora's attack to clear. She formed another volley of small voids and threw it forward. She advanced with Bael, Elian, and Samora at her side. Together they dropped a mountain's worth of devastation upon the emissaries.

Elyn stopped after they'd advanced another ten paces, then held up her hand to stop the others. The last of the explosions faded, though the cloud of dust had risen to block out most of the sun.

Elian cast out his senses and noticed what Elyn already had. The emissaries were gone, but the way Elyn held herself made him think they weren't dead.

His daughter closed her eyes, then shook her head. "They're up to something."

"We need to find a way to get her out of here," Elian said.

Elyn shook her head again. "There's no hiding for me. I'm connected to the void, so no matter where I go, they'll find me.

It's better that you should go. There's no point in throwing away your lives."

"We drove them off this time. We can do so again."

Elyn's disagreement was written on every line of her face. "You can't feel what I feel. Whatever they're planning is big. They're bringing everybody they have on this world, and they know I'll be fighting against them, so they'll be prepared."

"It doesn't matter if we overwhelm them."

"We can't overwhelm this, Father."

"I'm not leaving you behind."

"Why not? I left you once."

"That doesn't mean I need to return the favor."

Elyn clearly wanted to argue the point, but knew her father well enough not to bother. Once his mind was made up, there was no changing it. She turned her attention to Bael and Samora. "You two, at least, should leave. I know there's no convincing him."

"Leave? I'm just starting to enjoy myself," Bael said.

Bael wasn't his grandson, and Elian wished he was. He'd be as proud of the young man as he was of Elyn.

"A whole family of fools," Elyn said, but there was no condemnation in the comment. Then she tensed. "They're coming."

The emissaries arrived all at once. In one blink of an eye the adanists were alone, the next they stood halfway encircled by emissaries. Their enemies gave no thought to defense, and their assault began the moment they were solid enough to summon the void.

Elian threw up hasty shields, barely strong enough to absorb the blow of a single sphere. He pulled adani from the Great Heart with abandon, his will and spirit a channel and nothing more. Samora and Bael cast shields faster than him, still more used to the external manipulation of adani than he'd ever be.

Elyn formed another volley of spheres and threw them in the

air, needing to avoid the chaotic swirl of void and adani battling between the two forces. Her attack was too slow, though, and the emissaries only shifted enough to protect their cores.

An emissary's sphere snuck through Elian's defenses and punched him through the shoulder. He gritted his teeth against the pain and the sudden loss of adani, but in a moment his shoulder was repaired, and he continued their desperate defense. Samora and Bael also took hits, and without a word they each stepped back, forming a wall of transformed adani between Elyn and the emissaries. Their bodies healed quickly, but each hit took them out for a precious moment, allowing the emissaries to advance.

The battle seemed to slow. Elian didn't feel any of the desperation he'd felt when facing the Vada. Maybe it was because he'd believed he had a chance against the Vada and all he had here was the cold certainty they would eventually fall. Maybe it was just because the fight wasn't in him the way it had been when he was younger. There'd been so much more he'd wanted, back then. Now, so long as Elyn survived the day, he'd be content.

He watched Elyn throw up another two dozen spheres and slam them down, but the pressure against their defenses barely lessened. More spheres snuck through their defenses before they could rebuild their shields, and they were forced to take another step back. Bael took one sphere to the side of the head, shearing off his left ear completely, but he just ground his teeth together and redoubled his efforts.

Adani pulled at Elian's thoughts, an offer he hadn't dared consider, with a cost he hadn't been willing to pay before.

About time it spoke to him the way it used to speak to Samora. He accepted without hesitation.

"You need to leave!" He shouted to Samora.

She glanced at him and shook her head, too busy forming shields to respond.

"SAMORA!"

He'd never shouted at his sister, but it caught her attention, and she wasted a precious moment looking at him. They no longer shared the connection they had when they were mortals, but they'd still known each other from their earliest days. They didn't need it. She couldn't know exactly what he meant to do, but she didn't have to. She nodded. "Just tell me when."

His chest swelled, and he nodded. "I'll always love you."

"You, too."

He stopped forming shields and stepped behind Samora, placing himself just ahead of Elyn. "Whatever happens, stay right behind me."

She also knew him well enough not to argue, so she nodded.

Elian thrust his adani deep into the world, opening up a new, wider channel with the Great Heart. Adani built beneath him and he tapped Samora's shoulder. She didn't look back, just dropped her shields and somehow pulled Bael down into the web of adani and away.

The adani from below raced toward him just as the emissaries' spheres did, the final result too close to predict. He couldn't spare a thought for shields, and could only offer his body to protect Elyn. Spheres struck, and fought against the flood of adani pushing through every muscle in his body. They dug deeper, even as he shaped the adani. One cracked his core, but it no longer mattered. This had only ever been going to end in one way.

He sensed *himself* weakening, the spirit that was Elian, but there was enough of him left for what was needed. He released the adani, straight from the Great Heart. Beams of golden light burst from his core, bending like snakes even as they stretched toward the horizon. They destroyed everything they touched. Stone exploded upon contact, and the beams swallowed up the spheres aimed at him without slowing.

The emissaries' attack faltered and stopped as the beams whipped and snapped toward them. Walls of void rose between

Elian and the emissaries, but they weren't strong enough. An emissary's void could only absorb so much adani. Enough adani to give life to a village, yes, but Elian pulled so much more. Enough to shape a mountain range. Enough to bring life to a desert and guide that life to civilization.

The emissaries couldn't stand before it. Those that tried had their cores destroyed, and after the first dozen fell, the head emissary, standing near the rear, must have realized it couldn't win. Not against the raw power of the Great Heart unleashed upon them.

It ran, and took all the emissaries with it, and Elian's last act of will, the one he worried he wouldn't have enough strength to complete, was to cut himself off from the Great Heart. He collapsed to his knees, and when he blinked, he was in Elyn's arms.

Which was backwards. He was the one who was supposed to care for her. To protect her, and to carry her when she stumbled.

Wasn't right that she should be holding him up.

He reached up and wiped a tear from her cheek.

And then he was gone.

28

Elyn was empty. Not in the way she was when she embraced void. That was a cold despair that wanted to expand, to spread itself like a disease in her field. This was an emptiness that threatened to collapse upon itself. It wanted to be filled, to be made whole again, but a part of her she hadn't even known existed had been ripped out. She tried to fill the emptiness with tears, but like a cup with a hole in the bottom, it didn't matter how many she poured in, it wanted more.

The emissaries were gone. Not for long, but Father's last attack had revealed an ability they weren't prepared for. They'd lost more warriors in moments than they'd lost since Void had begun her long war against the light. Void was rightfully furious, the fragment of her within Elyn's core vibrating like a string pulled tight and plucked.

Void would order the world destroyed. Elian had forced their enemies into a corner. Samora and Bael were also transformed, so were also likely to possess the same ability, now that it had been seen once. The emissaries would never be strong enough to control the world.

The thoughts were no more substantial than echoes, though,

for all that mattered to her was the space where Father had been in her arms. She sensed, in intimate detail, how the fragments of his spirit had returned to the world, and knew that though he had transformed once, he was never coming back.

A shadow passed overhead, and she looked up to see a dragon swirling in the air above. It came down to land, and Samora appeared beside Elyn. Her eyes were rimmed with red. She sniffed and wiped her nose, but she held herself tall, unwilling to bend even under this last burden. "I've come to take you home."

"Where is that, now?" Her family was divided between different wandering clans, and the place she had called her home for decades was gone.

"With your mother. She's asking for you. The rest of the family is gathering, too. Bael is summoning them to his camp."

Elyn shook her head as she stood. She wanted nothing more than to run to Mother, but she couldn't. "There's not enough time. Father bought us a reprieve, but it won't be long. Once Void decides how we're to be destroyed, that will be all for this world."

"That's their plan?"

"I can't say for sure, but it has to be. We only lived because Void thought she could use the red hearts to strengthen her warriors."

"She?"

"Void used to be a person."

Samora grunted, which was less of a reaction than Elyn had expected. "I think it's worth you visiting Capricia, right now. The dragon will have you there in little time. Bael and I are there planning how to defend the world."

"You can't. There's no way to be everywhere at once. The emissaries don't need to fight you."

"Maybe we can discuss this on the dragon?"

Elyn supposed she might as well. She couldn't think of any better plans, at least. She climbed on and Samora sat behind her.

"You don't think there's any way of fighting the emissaries?" Samora asked as they took to the sky.

Elyn thought for a moment, then said, "No. I assume you and Bael could do what Father did?"

Samora nodded. "Though I don't know that I would. The entire world is groaning from that attack. He used up many generations worth of adani in the blink of an eye."

"Regardless, we're limited by the fact we can only use that attack twice more, and Void knows it. If I were in her place, I would attack the world directly, ignoring you and Bael."

"We can stop the emissaries wherever they appear."

"There's only two of you. Void only needs three emissaries to be in more places than you can be at once. You two might hold the world for a moment, but no more."

"Do you have any suggestions, then?"

"If I could get to Void, where she lives, then maybe I could kill her." The thought had been building for a while, and had only been confirmed by the emissaries' reaction to her attacks. Void destroyed anything she touched, including other void. No wonder Void demanded such strict belief from her adherents.

"She can be killed?"

"She was a person once. Void has a core, and it's on the world where I was healed and trained as a servant. But we have no way to get there. Void will never let me through with a portal, not now that she knows I've betrayed her."

Samora thought this over for a moment. "I can get you there. Or, better yet, I can teach you a weave to get there yourself. Now that I'm thinking about it, actually, it might be the only way."

"What?" How could Samora, of all people, get her to another world?

Samora nodded. "Back when I was studying the history of the Debru, I learned that they originally came from this world. Do you remember that?"

Elyn was offended Samora thought she might have forgotten.

"Of course. They learned the weave to create portals, too. It's how they traveled to other worlds and became corrupted by shadow."

"And our ancestors taught those weaves to the dragons, who have taught it to me. I can make the weave, but without a destination, it's always been pointless, and I've never wanted to engage in the search for other worlds like our ancestors did. But I can teach it to you, which will help you get there and back."

Elyn's heart raced. Were they seriously considering this? It had been nothing but a foolish idea back when she'd been sure there was no way of traversing the worlds on her own. Samora spoke as though the decision was as good as made, but Elyn wasn't even an ascended adanist. She couldn't possibly lead a strike against their greatest enemy.

The dragon landed at Bael's camp before she could sort out the answers for herself. Samora dropped off the dragon with her, and together they made their way toward the tent Father and Mother had shared. Elyn didn't recognize it. When she'd left, they'd had a bigger tent, suitable for their larger family. They'd traded it for something smaller sometime after the last of their children had left, but Elyn hadn't been to visit them since she left as a young woman. All their meetings since had been when her parents had come to her.

With the benefit of hindsight, she felt a fool, but there was nothing for it now.

If she could lift the threat that hung over their heads, she could return with her head held high. For now, though, she froze outside the tent, certain she didn't belong there. Samora nudged her forward, but Elyn couldn't move. She couldn't face Mother, not after, well, *everything*.

Mother didn't make her enter. She came out of the tent, tears running freely down her cheeks, and she wrapped Elyn in an embrace so tight Elyn couldn't breathe. Mother whispered hoarsely in her ear. "He loved you so, so much."

Elyn's legs threatened to buckle, but Mother's strength kept her upright. "I know, Mother—I know."

It seemed impossible, but Mother held her even tighter then, and Elyn worried she'd never breathe again. Then Mother broke off the embrace. She took a step back, then dug in her pocket. She pulled something small out and held out her fist to her daughter.

Elyn couldn't accept whatever it was. She dropped to her knees and pressed her forehead to the ground. "I'm sorry."

It wasn't enough. It wasn't nearly enough, but it was, at least, a start. She'd work for her forgiveness for the rest of her life, but depending on what happened next, that might not be very long.

Mother kneeled beside her, then guided her back to her feet. She held out her hand again, closed tightly around something. "Elian lost this when he transformed, but when he returned, he gave it to me. He told me that when you came home, I was supposed to give it to you."

How could Father have known she was going to return? Had he somehow seen the future, or was his faith in his daughter so strong?

Elyn didn't deserve whatever Mother wanted to give her, but if this had been Father's wish, who was she to argue? She held out her hand and Mother dropped a small gem into her palm. It was surprisingly small and light for someone whose legend was so large. "It was his heart. The one he ascended with against the Vada."

Elyn wrapped her fingers tight around the stone and pressed her fist to her chest. She didn't try to stop the tears that burst from her, and she welcomed Mother's strong arms around her again. Without them, she might have collapsed and never moved, even as the world ended around her. She buried her head in Mother's shoulder and wept.

She was sitting alone, just outside the camp, when Bael appeared beside her. He gave her a moment of silence, then said, "I'm sorry we don't have longer to mourn, but Grandmother said you had an idea for attacking Void."

Elyn wiped the tears from her eyes. "Now we know that Void destroys everything she touches, including herself. If I can get close to her core, all I need to do is strike her with one fragment of her own power and she should die. If we're very lucky, it will kill all the emissaries as well. They're part of her."

"You make it sound simple."

"It is simple, but it won't be easy. She can summon emissaries to her, so as soon as we appear, we'll have to fight through an impossible number."

"It's that or nothing, though, isn't it?"

Elyn nodded. "I think so."

Bael brushed off his pants as he stood. "So, when do you want to leave?"

She looked up. She'd intended to ask Samora, as she had less holding her to this world than Bael did. Bael seemed to see into her thoughts. "I believe this is why we were granted this power. This is the reason. If we don't come back, then so be it. As long as we can protect those we leave behind, I'll be satisfied."

She bowed her head to him. "Thank you."

He waved away her gratitude and nodded at her hand. He could sense the heart's adani. "Elian's?"

She nodded once.

"Are you going to ascend with it?"

She needed a full moment for her mind to understand what he'd asked, but once she understood, she was on her feet. "I can't ascend!"

Bael wasn't flustered. "Can't you?"

The simple question silenced her before she could unleash a tirade upon him. The thought of ascending had never crossed her mind, not even with a heart in her hand. She'd learned her lesson well enough the first time. Why should it be any different now?

She stared down at the small heart, so clear she could see through it without a problem. Maybe it would be different because she was different, shaped by decades of experience she hadn't had before. Her mind and body weren't the same. Her eyes snapped up and locked on Bael. "Do you know something?"

"Nothing for sure. It … feels right, and I'm coming to learn to trust that feeling more than I have in the past. Besides, if we're going to visit the very root of Void, it would be helpful if you were ascended."

"It'll do nothing to my abilities with the void."

"Maybe not, but you'll be faster and stronger, so you'll be easier for me to protect."

Elyn bit her lower lip, then shook her head. "There's another reason I can't ascend. The void only found root in me because of that emptiness that adanists use to host the heart. If I ascend, I might lose my ability with void, which we need."

Bael shrugged. "Have you tried?"

"How?"

"Connect with that heart and draw enough adani to open that space again. Prepare to ascend. See how the void within you reacts."

She was a fool for not having thought of that first. There was no need to jump into the stream to see how deep it was. She could wade slowly in.

"Will you stay with me?" she asked.

"I will, but let me get Grandmother first. She's more sensitive to the flow of adani, and would be the first to catch if anything goes wrong."

Bael vanished, then reappeared a few moments later with Samora. Her aunt approached and brought her hand up. "May I?"

Elyn nodded, and Samora rested her hand on Elyn's shoulder. Samora closed her eyes. "Whenever you're ready."

Elyn looked down again at the stone. She felt as though she was running downhill toward an edge of the cliff and there was no way to stop. This was all too fast. Just this morning she'd been in the service of the emissaries, preparing to destroy a town on their behalf. But there wasn't time to think.

Her own heart pounded in her chest, beating like a war drum. The last time she'd tried this it had destroyed her life. Thankfully, she didn't have the time to think, to worry about what might happen. She only had to keep running downhill.

Elyn connected with the heart, and her body filled with adani. She breathed in deep, formed a spear, then a dart, then a sword, adani eagerly bending itself to her will, as though it had only been waiting for her to return. She bound the small spheres of light that Samora had once taught her, testing the limits of her ability. As a child, she'd bound over thirty, but today she held more than fifty and could have done even more. The lights hung over their heads, warming the air and making her feel as though she was under a clear night sky in the middle of the day.

Void had given her strength, had given her the ability to affect the world once again, but it hadn't made her feel alive. Not the way adani did. She gently unwound the spheres of adani, letting their strength return to the world. She held out her other hand and bound a small sphere of flame, remembering that day, so long ago, when she'd wished she could have summoned the flame to kill her diseased plants.

She let the flame vanish and looked at Samora. "There's really no need for the void, is there?"

Samora, her eyes still closed, her senses focused on the smallest changes in the flow of adani within Elyn's body, frowned. "What do you mean?"

"Life and death are already inextricably linked. One doesn't exist without the other. Adani has always been telling me, but I haven't been listening. With it, we can create and we can destroy. Void is simply an evil we don't need."

"The world doesn't, but I fear that you might," Samora said.

"What?"

"Do you sense what's happening within you?"

Elyn hadn't. The return of adani and her ability to manipulate it had captured all her attention. She sent her awareness inward. Adani flowed smoothly through her body, the lasting gift of the emissary. No matter what the emissary's purpose might have been, she would always thank him for the healing. She sensed the two surprises at the same time.

The more obvious of the two was void, cold and angry as adani surrounded it, but still a part of her core. Separate, and not equal, but present. Curious, she summoned a sphere of void, which appeared above her palm on command. Then she bound a sphere of adani in the other hand. Light and dark hovered before her, each seeming like they belonged. She grunted, satisfied. If nothing else, it meant her plan had some slim chance of working. She could manipulate adani and void at the same time.

The less obvious truth, hiding in the smallest of spaces between the void and swirling adani, was the same emptiness she'd sought so desperately when she was younger. The place in her spirit where a heart would fit. It remained, even though she'd welcomed void into her body.

Father's heart felt heavy in her hand, and she could imagine it sinking into her flesh, becoming a part of her. Her physical heart raced so fast she felt she might burst, and every instinct but one told her to stop, to break the connection with the heart and think this through.

Father wasn't here to push her this time. The decision would be hers to make, an adult with full knowledge of the consequences.

Or maybe Father was still here, still pushing her. Maybe that was why he'd given her the heart.

She didn't think so, though. There was no secret ambition for his daughter hidden within his final gift. Only love.

Before she could doubt herself, she accepted the heart. It felt as though it melted into her skin, part physical object and part spirit. Somewhere far away Samora shouted a warning, but Elyn's focus remained settled on the heart. Though it was nothing but adani, it was also her father, becoming a part of her after she'd refused him for so long. She would carry more than his memory, but a fragment of his strength.

The heart traveled up her arm into her chest, and she was sure her physical heart was about to beat its way out through the cage of her ribs. The stone of adani settled deeper into her core, drawn toward the emptiness like a moth toward the flame. It nestled into the space like a cat settling into a warm spot in the sun. There was a slight shift as the heart repositioned itself, and then everything went white.

❦ 29 ❦

Bael laid his cousin down gently, making sure she didn't hit her head as she fell. He looked up at Grandmother, who was shaking her head. "Is she hurt?"

"No, she'll be fine, but no thanks to herself. That was a cursed foolish thing to do."

"You weren't sure she'd ascend?" Bael could feel the power rushing through Elyn's adani channels, and there was no doubt she'd succeeded on her second attempt at ascension.

"I'm still not sure what went wrong the first time, but my biggest worry was the void within her. It's attached to her spirit like a parasite, and I feared that if she attempted to ascend, it would kill her."

Bael could sense the void still within his cousin, too. "I'm glad it didn't."

"Me, too. It will take her a bit to recover, but then I imagine she'll want to leave. It won't take me long to teach her how to weave a portal out of adani. So long as she can find the world Void is hiding on, there won't be long. You'll be going?"

"Of course. I'll take the chance to go say goodbye to Shayna."

Grandmother nodded. "I wish I could tell you there was no

need to go, but with Elian gone ..." her voice trailed off, and Bael wished he could take some of the pain from her spirit. She'd lost both her husband and her brother in short order, and that was on top of the many she'd watched die already. It didn't seem fair to have to bear so much loss.

Although, if he lived through this, such would be his fate as well, to linger on while everyone he knew and loved grew old and passed away. Unless he convinced others to transform as he had, but because of what the dragons had told them, both Samora and Elian believed it wrong.

That was a problem for another day. It assumed that he would live through today, which was far from certain. "Is there anything you need from me?" he asked.

Grandmother shook her head. "Say hi to my granddaughter, and my great-granddaughter, if she's there already."

"I will. She'd probably like to meet you someday soon."

"When this is over, I will."

"I'll hold you to that."

Bael took one last look at Elyn, somehow afraid that if he left, he'd never see her again. She'd been gone for so much of his life he barely knew her.

Grandmother seemed to have a window into his thoughts. "She'll be ready."

Bael nodded and vanished into the web of adani. Shayna's spirit called him home and he answered, rushing toward her as fast as his will could carry him. He appeared in front of their tent, just in time to see Juula try to escape. The girl had a smile on her face as she looked back, hoping that Shayna would chase after her. She didn't see Bael in front of her, but he scooped her up before she ran headlong into his legs.

Juula startled at first, but after she saw who had caught her, she laughed out loud, her joy echoing across the camp. "Bael!"

"Afternoon, little one. Are you giving Mother a hard time?"

Her mischievous grin was answer enough. A moment later

Shayna emerged. There were dark bags under her eyes, and she wasn't moving quite as quickly as Bael was used to. Her hair was a ragged mess.

She looked more beautiful than ever, the effect only heightened by the wide smile on her face. "I think she likes you."

"Most women do."

Bael sounded confident, but both he and Shayna had been pleasantly surprised by how well Juula had adapted to her new surroundings. Shayna thought it was because the girl was already used to being passed around between families, and Bael figured there was a fair bit of truth to the guess. The girl had cried most of the night last night, and Bael had stayed up with her. One advantage of his transformation was that he didn't need to sleep anymore. Shayna, though, had frequently been awoken by the commotion. In time, they hoped that Juula would sleep through the night.

Grandmother had told them both about Elyn's plan earlier, and Shayna had already made what peace she could with Bael leaving again. His journey might be taking him to a different world, but she treated it no differently than if he was going on a hunt. He couldn't imagine the cost she paid to act as though all was normal, but he was grateful. Seeing her like this, it made him think that he'd be coming back after completing one last task, no more difficult than chopping down a tree.

"You're leaving, then?"

Bael handed Juula back, and the girl frowned at being returned to Shayna's arms, her escape so easily foiled. "I am. Elyn successfully ascended with Elian's heart, and so I'm going to return, and Aunt Samora will help us with the portal."

"Are you going to say anything to the rest of the camp?"

In truth, he hadn't thought about it, and his cheeks flushed with shame. Events had been happening too quickly, and since he was the only one of the clan who could travel from place to place with a thought, he'd been forced to leave the rest of his warriors behind to get to the site of the emissaries' "justice." His friends deserved something from him, though. There was no telling if he'd return.

It was only then that he realized the camp was empty except for a few families in their tents. He frowned and extended his adani. All his warriors were to the west, mingling with the dragons who nested next to the camp. "What's happening?"

Shayna's expression of pure innocence didn't fool Bael for a moment, but he didn't press the issue. He took her and Juula in his arms, held them close, then kissed her farewell.

His heart broke as he turned away. In the past, Shayna had joined him for most of his battles, so there'd been no farewells. Leaving now, though, after seeing Juula and Shayna together, was almost more than he could bear. Only the knowledge that they needed him to leave if they were to have a chance to live kept his feet moving. He looked back frequently, and each time Shayna and Juula were there, waving as he left. Finally they were obscured by the tents, and he nearly turned around and ran back to them.

The mystery of the dragons and the warriors was almost welcome, though it didn't take him long to solve. His clan was only a fraction of what it had been, and there weren't more than a dozen warriors left, but all who remained were preparing to mount the dragons. Bael eyed them suspiciously. "Where do you think you're off to?"

Karoc, a small man who was among the fastest warriors Bael had ever known, grinned at him. "With you, of course."

"You can't be serious."

"We are, actually."

Bael had met Karoc when both of them were just children, not even close to being adanists. They'd gotten into plenty of trouble at clan gatherings, and he'd been among the first to join Bael when he called for help after the emissaries arrived. "If all goes well, I'll be fighting on another world."

Karoc gave him the same smile he would have when they were planning one of their troublemaking adventures. "And you think we'll let you have all the fun?"

"I'll be fighting emissaries."

"Sure, but my previous point still stands."

Bael stared, not sure what to say.

Karoc scratched at his beard, neatly trimmed for once, which was a change for him. "We know what we're getting into, but we also know the stakes. This was always why we followed you. I can't say I was planning on following you to another world, but we'll give everything to save the people here, just like we know you will. We may not be a match for emissaries, but we've got dragons and ascended adanists, and that's not nothing."

Bael arched an eyebrow. "The dragons are in on this, too?"

"They live here same as us. There are more coming in, too, once you tell us where to go. We figure it's all or nothing, and we're choosing all."

Bael had a hundred objections, but they were all variations of the same doubt, and Karoc had the right of it. There was no telling what little difference might be the piece that saved them from defeat. The warriors who gathered were under no illusions, and there was no misunderstanding he needed to correct. Leading warriors who were so outclassed condemned him as a commander, but the stakes were such he couldn't order them to stay. He would very likely need their help.

Bael bowed to them. "It's a pleasure to have you, then. We'll be leaving from here as soon as my cousin has prepared a portal for us."

He didn't miss the flickers of doubt that shadowed their expressions.

"I know. For what it's worth, I trust her, but we really have no choice. Her betrayal has given us the only weapon worth anything against our enemies, and she's the only one who can take us to the world."

Karoc nodded. "Doesn't mean I like it."

"I know, friend. I know. Were there another way, I'd take it, but we have no choice but to roll our dice and see which way they land."

There was a chuckle from somewhere behind Karoc. "Good thing you're lucky at dice, then."

Other warriors shared the mellow mirth, and the matter was settled as well as it was going to be.

The pride he saw on his warriors' faces, their determination, drove a stake into his chest. But this had always been the way, hadn't it? Even when he'd first recruited them, it had been for a fight that had seemed impossible.

When he returned to the camp, he found Grandmother training with Elyn. His cousin looked better than she had in years, and such was their focus that Bael had no desire to disturb them. He sat in the grass and watched.

The weaving of adani was simple enough, and Elyn had already learned that. Bael hadn't known her when she was a child, what with him not being born yet, but he remembered Grandmother talking about her, how she'd learned so quickly. How she and Elian had put such hope in her, how they'd believed that they'd raise another generation so much stronger than they were.

Ironic, then, that after leaving the clans and betraying them for the enemy, that the promise Elyn had represented might yet be fulfilled. Bael couldn't allow himself to think of Elian, for the loss was too fresh and the wound too raw, but the thought flitted across his mind, just for a moment, that if Elian could see Elyn now, he'd be proud. Silently, he promised himself that if he could, if there was any way at all, he'd bring Elyn home.

If they ever made it. The problem, as quickly became apparent watching the two women, was Elyn finding the world she'd been taken to. She could sense Void, swore she could feel the heart of it, but connecting the portal to the location proved difficult.

There was nothing Bael could do to help, so he watched and waited. He was just about ready to head back to Shayna and Juula when a bright disc of adani appeared before Elyn and she shouted.

She was grinning, and before Grandmother could stop her, she jumped through the opening in the world. She hopped back a moment later, grinning from ear to ear. Her nod was confirmation enough and Bael rose to his feet.

"Can you make it bigger?" he asked.

"Why?"

"It needs to be large enough to fit some dragons. Turns out, we're going to be bringing a bit of company with us."

"If that's the plan, then sure, I can make it bigger."

"Good. It might be best if we go meet them. Easier than getting the dragons through the tents."

They were halfway from the tents to the dragons' nest when they all looked to the south at once. It was no surprise Elyn felt the arrival, connected to the void as she was, but Bael didn't like the fact both he and Grandmother could so easily. Whoever had arrived, they'd come prepared to strike a devastating blow, the amount of void at their disposal incredible.

Elyn paled. "It's her."

"Void itself?" Grandmother asked.

"No. Void's head emissary. She brought help, too. I've never felt void being used like this, though." Elyn squinted as though focusing on something distant. "That's too much."

Her face grew even paler. "They must mean to destroy the world. There's too much void there for anything else. It would wipe out a city in a moment."

Bael turned south, preparing to dive into the web of adani and emerge to face them. Grandmother's hand on his arm stopped him.

"No. Go with Elyn. If there are that many emissaries here, it means there are less guarding Void. This is your chance."

"We can't leave when our world is under attack!"

Grandmother shook her head. "I'm not sure that it matters, does it, Elyn?"

"I could negate their void with my own. It's worth a shot." Bael silently thanked Elyn. Finally, she was making wise decisions.

"You don't see. If we all stay, they win. There have to be what, two dozen emissaries here? They know what Elyn can do, and they'll be prepared. They'll kill us one at a time, and then this war is over. We were always gambling our world. It's just a little more apparent now than it was before."

"What about you?" Bael asked.

"I'll hold them off as long as I can. Elian showed me the way." Grandmother laughed to herself, lightly and full of joy. It was out of place at a time like this, and Bael feared she'd finally cracked under a lifetime of pressure.

Elyn didn't seem concerned, though. "What's funny?"

"Oh, it's just that when I was younger, I was always furious at Elian because it seemed that no matter how strong or talented I became, he was always ahead of me. Turns out that is true even now, at the end of it all."

Bael embraced his grandmother, but only for a moment. "Keep them busy. Elyn and I will kill Void and end this nightmare."

Grandmother smiled. "I believe you will. Now hurry. There won't be much time. I am getting old, you know. Can't fight like I used to."

They exchanged quick bows, and then Grandmother vanished into adani, racing to fight the emissaries.

Bael and Elyn sprinted for the dragons and the home of Void.

30

E lyn took two deep breaths to calm her thoughts. Opening the portal to the other world, once she found it and understood how she had to sense it to connect the weaving, should have been an easy task. The first time she'd succeeded, though, had been under Samora's gentle instruction. It was a different beast, she realized, when it was her alone and the fate of the world rested on her completing the technique again.

The third try succeeded, and the portal opened wide enough to admit a flying dragon. She glanced back to see that everyone was still behind her, then stepped through. Her foot left the grasslands of her home world and fell upon the loose stone of Void's world. A moment later, Bael's footsteps followed her own. He looked up at the dim sky. "Is it always like that?"

"It is. Can you still use adani?"

"I'm here, aren't I?"

Elyn hadn't considered that, but it was true. They'd quickly debated, before they left, whether Bael would be any help on a world without adani. It seemed his connection to their world and its Great Heart remained.

Bael stared down at his hands. "I think you'll need to leave the portal open, though. If it vanishes, I'm not sure what happens to me. I need a connection to home."

Elyn shrugged. "I needed to leave it open, regardless."

"You did?"

"I knew how to find Void. I've done that before. I don't have the slightest clue how to find our home world, though."

Bael glanced back at the portal. "Might have been good to know that before I stepped through."

Bael quickly stepped back into the portal, then reappeared a moment later. "We should get out of the way."

Elyn was plenty happy to obey, and they stepped aside as adanists and then dragons came through the portal. The expressions on their faces were all reflections of Bael's, and she wondered if she'd looked the same when she first stepped foot here. Probably.

"Where to?" Bael asked.

Elyn felt Void near and pointed. The place where her portal had formed was near the edge of the depression that led underground.

"Any suggestions?" he asked.

Elyn looked over the flat, barren land and shrugged. "Kill anything that moves? The dragons can take to the air and cover our advance, but once we go underground, they won't be able to help. It's best if the adanists don't stay on the dragons. Makes them easy targets."

She thought of the doomed attack on her home and shuddered. They'd been fools to attack, but still.

The adanists spread out and the dragons took to the air. Elyn meant to take the point, but Bael insisted he should. At a gesture from him, the other adanists formed a loose circle around her. She almost objected, but she understood. It wasn't about her. They were protecting their best opportunity to destroy Void.

She wouldn't let them down. Not if she could do anything about it.

She listened to the sound of the breeze and of their boots walking across the loose stone, and she wondered how long it would be before the emissaries came to defend their master. That they hadn't already unsettled her, made her feel as though she was prey walking into a trap.

Or maybe Void was so confident in her own strength she didn't need to use emissaries to defend herself. Prideful and foolish, but maybe not wrong. She led her cousin and his warriors forward, hoping against hope they had a chance.

The arrival of the emissaries came almost as a relief. They appeared behind the advancing adanists but gained ground quickly.

The adanists were coming close to where Elyn had picked up the trail that led to Void's being, and she suggested they make a run for it. Bael took one look toward the hole and shook his head. "We won't make it in time. Even if a dragon picked us up and carried us most of the way, the emissaries would still catch us before we made the door. They can shift, but I can't. There's no web of adani here to travel along."

She cursed herself for not having thought of that herself. Bael's strength was every bit as incredible as before, but it hadn't occurred to her that some of his abilities were tied to his home world. "No choice but to fight, then?"

"So it seems."

Bael issued his orders quickly, revealing a side of himself that Elyn had never seen, the side of him confident about ordering adanists into battle. But why should she be familiar? In her memories, he was still the young boy who came to visit her on occasion with his family when they were traveling through her area. She hadn't been around to see all he would become.

The adanists formed groups that would hopefully be strong enough to fight against the emissaries' voids, and then those groups spread out so that no single attack could destroy them all. Dragons wheeled about in the air, as though they were simply waiting for the attacks to begin so that they could drop into the fight.

As the emissaries neared and began to separate, Elyn counted eight. A considerable force by any estimation—she'd been taught that whole worlds were usually subdued by a single emissary—and yet it seemed too few. Had so many been sent to their home world, or were more lying in wait somewhere else? She didn't sense any presences besides those that attacked from behind, but she didn't consider that conclusive evidence of anything.

Bael gave the signal, and the dragons led the adanists' defense. Huge spheres of adani dropped from the sky and broke upon the emissaries, but their walls of void swallowed the energies and kept them safe. Two emissaries maintained the walls while the other six began preparing spheres. Their movements were slow, as though they believed they had all the time in the world.

"How's this for distance?" Bael asked.

"Good, but a little closer would be better."

"We'll drag them a little closer, then. Good luck."

Elyn nodded, her first dozen spheres of void already prepared. She threw them ahead of the adanists, and the reasonably orderly battle devolved into chaos.

The emissaries had spent too many lifetimes reassured by the strength of their walls. Elyn's spheres struck and cracked the structures, and they broke a moment later, allowing the rain of adani from the dragons to fall freely. The quickest-thinking of the emissaries used their spheres to defend themselves, but several of the dragons' attacks sneaked through the weakened defenses to strike both land and emissary.

Blasts of adani turned the already small stone at their feet into deadly projectiles, and the emissaries found themselves in the center of a tornado of sharp pebbles. None would be strong enough to kill an emissary, although there might have been some small chance. Even so, the swirl of stones would have been painful and distracting, which was all Elyn and the others could ask for. She threw another wave of void spheres at the emissaries over the heads of the charging adanists. She advanced and threw again, saying a silent thanks to Samora for such a useful technique.

Bael and the other adanists took as much advantage of Elyn's openings as they could. Their adani, for so long ineffective against void, finally found emissary flesh, and it was every bit as devastating as it had been against the Debru two generations ago. One of Bael's spears caught an emissary in the shoulder, and the force of it was such that the entire arm separated from the body like a misbehaving child attempting to run from its parents.

What Bael's adanists lacked in precision they made up for in enthusiasm. The only fatal wound against an emissary was to pierce its core, the seat of its will and spirit, and though each of the adanists knew the fact well, making such blows were not how they'd been trained. They used bound swords to cut off heads and drove their spears into the chests of their enemies, causing damage aplenty but killing none.

Even so, there were only so many places in a body the core could hide, and the adanists learned quickly, altering their tactics. Three emissaries died in the initial confusion, and it seemed as though the reckless charge of the adanists might make short work of their powerful enemies.

The emissaries recovered quickly, though, and several started shifting away from the main site of the battle. None of the adanists, not even Bael, could match their speed, not here. One more emissary fell amidst the chaos, but three retreated to a safer distance, and one's attention fell fully upon Elyn. He shifted toward her, blinking from one place to the next as he checked for dangers. His advance was halted, just for a moment, as one of the dragons dropped a wall of adani in front of him. The emissary threw a halfhearted sphere at the dragon to chase it away.

The relief gave Elyn a moment to prepare her defenses, to

throw up a wall of void to protect her against the advance. The emissary's void cancelled hers as easily as hers did his, though, and none of the walls she formed lasted more than a moment.

Having her attention focused on her own defense spelled doom for the other adanists, though. The surviving emissaries, finally freed from the suffering of having their defenses destroyed, once again found themselves fighting a familiar battle. The collected adani of Bael's warriors and the dragons meant little against walls of void, and the void spheres that answered their attacks did damage far beyond the effort required to create them.

Elyn sensed the turn of the tide as adanists fell against the emissaries, but she couldn't spare them a thought. She exchanged spheres of void with the emissary attacking her and found herself wanting. Samora's technique allowed her to create more spheres than her enemy, but his ability to shift away from her attacks evened the battle. She gave up ground as he advanced, but it only delayed the inevitable.

A golden flash of light reminded her that she no longer fought alone. The spear caught the emissary from behind, and his focus had been such that he hadn't sensed the danger. It had missed his core as he had been shifting away from one of Elyn's spheres, but still it stumbled under the impact.

Elyn sent two spheres after the emissary, and though they missed his core, they struck true, hobbling it further. He snarled, but couldn't decide if the greater threat was before him or behind him. She didn't know either, for though she sensed Bael's adani, she couldn't see him behind the emissary.

A bright golden light caught all their attention, and the emissary threw a pair of spheres at Elyn as he turned around to face Bael, who held in his hand a sword that glowed as brightly as the sun of their home world. On this dim planet, it was the strongest light around.

Elyn of yesterday would have struggled to avoid the spheres sent after her, but her ascended body clearly saw them coming and had no problem moving out of the way. She wasn't aware of any limits to how often she could call upon the void, but there was no reason to test it unnecessarily. The spheres zipped past her, but before she could return the attack, Bael reached the emissary. The emissary fashioned one of the blades out of void to block Bael's cut, and the two bound weapons crashed into one another with a resounding shock that shook the stones loose at Elyn's feet.

Bael kept the pressure on the blade, as he was no equal in any contest of speed. The golden light grew closer and closer to the emissary, and though the emissary shouted for help, it was too late. Bael's blade, drawing strength from the Great Heart, sliced through the void and into the emissary, a clean cut through his core.

"The others!" Bael said, and Elyn didn't waste a moment. Spheres of void sped toward the three surviving emissaries, but they'd been warned by the death of their peer, and they shifted away from the adanists.

Whether by unspoken agreement or by a message passed through the void, the remaining emissaries turned their full attention to Elyn. They converged on her, pursued by adanists and dragons alike, bombarded by adani for every step they took. One woman couldn't shift between the various spears, balls of adani that fell from above, and dodge Elyn's spheres, and once the first sphere reached her, her battle was over. She stumbled and was immediately sought by half a dozen spears, one of which poked through her core and ended her unnaturally long life.

The fight remaining with the last two emissaries felt as though it lasted an eternity, and Elyn feared Samora wouldn't be able to keep the emissaries contained long enough for them to strike directly at Void. Details escaped her, the fighting around her too furious to track. Bael was everywhere at once, here holding a shield to fight off a determined sphere of void, there trying to cut an elusive emissary with his blade of light. Spears and darts of adani dropped among them, sometimes saving them from nearly certain doom. Blood splattered against the side of her face, and she realized it was Bael's as the side of his head vanished against a sphere of void that had crept through their defenses. He fell for a moment, but by then the other adanists were there. Slower than her cousin and less powerful, but every defense of the emissaries was stripped by her spheres of void.

She kept expecting the emissaries to run, to hide and recover, as was their wont whenever the situation turned against them, but they pushed instead, eyes wide as they tried to fight off the mass of adanists gathered around them. Their spheres felled adanists left and right, but never for more than a moment, for if they failed to consider their own defense, Elyn's attacks would kill them.

Bael's rise ended the emissaries' resistance. Combined with the surviving adanists, he possessed too much strength to defeat, and one after the other, the emissaries fell with a pained cry.

The air shook with the roar of the dragons' victory, but then the shattered lands fell silent save for the labored breath of the adanists. Their victory had not been without cost. Only five adanists remained in good health, and that was stretching the term to fit. All suffered from deep cuts and bruised flesh, but they stood tall. Three more were too wounded to be effective, and Bael sent them home on the back of a dragon in even worse condition. They complained, but not for long.

Bael's look hardened after they left. "We don't have much time left. Lead us on, cousin."

A wave of weariness crashed over Elyn, but she nodded and turned toward the hole. The path shouldn't be too hard to find from here. With a gesture, she led the adanists toward Void's heart.

31

Samora hadn't yet come to terms with Elian's death. There hadn't been any time, nor would there be. She knew he was dead, had felt his spirit burn away and join the incredible flow of adani he'd released as his final act. If anyone survived this day, it would be one more legend about him that would spread across the land and down through the ages. His spirit had shattered, but if he could take form one last time, she imagined he would be quietly smirking, humble around others, but secretly proud of one last great feat.

She kept expecting him to appear beside her, to shoulder the weight of the burden that remained. He hadn't been as present in her life as Aldrick, for obvious reasons, but she'd always known she could trust in him, that if she'd ever needed him, he'd be there.

She couldn't convince herself he wouldn't show again, no matter how untrue she knew it to be.

She could have used him, now. Adani had carried her to where the emissaries had gathered, high up in the mountains that she still remembered flying across for the first time, escorted by a dragon that hoped to show her some of humanity's forgotten past. The emissaries had appeared upon a plateau, and she'd appeared on a nearby peak. She made no effort to hide herself, so the emissaries knew she was near, but they paid her no mind.

And why should they? With the Great Heart at her disposal, she could be some threat to them, but not nearly so much as if she'd had Elyn by her side wielding some void to keep the battle honest.

She counted thirteen emissaries, and as she watched, twelve formed a wide circle. They stretched out their hands to one another, though they stood too far away to touch. The thirteenth, who Elyn had identified as the head of Void's emissaries, stood in the middle and waited for the others to take their place.

Samora wasn't sure what to do. Whatever they planned, it seemed in her best interests not to let it happen, but they paid her little mind for good reason. Most of her attacks would do no good here. She could use the same technique she'd learned so recently from Elian, but her spirit wouldn't survive intact any more than his had. It was a technique she could only use once, and so she needed to ensure it would work.

The emissaries didn't give her much time to consider. To her sight, the forms around the circle suddenly stiffened. They all stood taller, heads held high, reminding her of when she'd gotten after Killan to stop slouching when he'd been younger. Their arms were already extended toward one another, but now the tips of their fingers started to mist, forming thin ropes of dark clouds that wiggled like snakes as they reached for their nearest companions.

Samora didn't need to know what was happening to know she didn't like it. She bound three adani darts and threw them at the gathering, but the head emissary was prepared. A wall of void protected the emissaries and rendered Samora's attack pointless.

She didn't try again. There was no point wasting her adani against such a powerful force.

The ropes that had once been the emissaries' hands

connected, and the sudden surge of void nearly brought Samora to her knees. The force ran through the circle like a dark stream that rushed around in ever-faster loops. The torsos, legs, and heads of the emissaries so far remained unaltered, though even they started to mist as Samora watched.

She couldn't simply observe, and attacking from a distance was pointless, so she took a deep, unnecessary breath, then dove into the web of adani, intending to come up among them. She couldn't, though. Her adani, her spirit, was stopped by void. She pressed against it, tried to knife her way through, but nothing got her closer. In the end, she had no choice but to retreat, and when she reappeared at her viewpoint was rewarded with a malicious grin from the head emissary.

The emissaries were no longer whole, no longer took the form of humans. They had connected and become a ring of darkness spinning rapidly around the head emissary. Only heads remained, and Samora watched as they, too, became part of the spinning ring. She could sense their cores within, spinning as rapidly as anything else. The force of the combined void pressed against her like a physical weight, almost too much for her to bear. She wanted to lose her form, to become one with adani, but the world couldn't afford her laziness. She forced herself to stand against the force, to watch as the ring gained even more speed.

The head emissary spread its hands out wide and lifted them high. It started to rise in the air, and the ring gained a wobble. The higher the emissary rose, the greater the wobble in the dark ring became. The speed of the spin and the wobble made the ring appear wider than it was. Its power grew, too, somehow becoming more than the simple sum of all the voids put together. Soon, the wobble of the ring was such that it looked as though the head emissary was surrounded by a shadowy sphere.

Samora threw a dart at the sphere, more out of curiosity than any expectation that she would meaningfully damage the emissaries. The weaving, which once had brought a Vada to its knees, didn't even get close to the ring before losing its strength and unravelling. Whatever power she felt where she stood was nothing compared to the raw strength of the void closer to the ring.

If Elian was here, he would have known what to do. Here she stood, supposedly meaning to defend the world from attack, but she couldn't even land a blow. Only Elian's final technique remained, his last gift to humanity, but she hesitated over a seemingly meaningless question.

What if she missed?

The illusory sphere could move, and she only had one chance.

With a shout, the head emissary reduced Samora's options to one. The sphere rushed toward the surface, toward the plateau where the technique had begun.

Samora no longer feared death.

Only failure.

She summoned all the strength of the Great Heart, just as Elian had done earlier, and prepared to defend their world.

Bael had too little time for wonder, but as he stared into the hole in this world, he couldn't help himself. Whatever power had shaped this hole rivaled that of the Great Heart that sustained him, and it had been controlled with a determination that spoke of a tremendous will.

No matter how far he advanced, it always felt like there was more waiting for him around the next bend of the stream of time. Void and light had fought their war for countless generations, and he wondered at the stories that might someday be told.

Stories he would never hear if he didn't focus.

Through his connection to the Great Heart, he had some sense of what transpired on his home world, though time slipped, as though it passed differently here than back home. Regardless, Grandmother had widened her connection to the Great Heart, which meant she was preparing to unleash Elian's final technique. She wouldn't unless there was no other choice, and so they had little time in which to act.

He had hoped they would have reached Void by now, but it was no easy journey. They'd run from the battle, risking falling off the steep ledge of the trail to reach their destination sooner.

They'd just reached the door carved into the wall of the hole, and Elyn led them through without pause. She walked the darkness as though it was lit, but the adanists had no choice but to bind small lights overhead to see by.

"How much further?" he asked.

"There's a hall a little ways ahead. After that, I don't know. It's as far as I've gotten. A few miles, perhaps, total."

"We need to run faster. Grandmother is already connected to the Great Heart."

It was poorly worded, but Elyn understood well enough what he meant, and she took off down the hallway even faster than before. The other ascended adanists tapped into the hearts in their cores and followed her, outpacing any wolf. He wished he had the ability to shift ahead of them, but on this world, he was limited to a stride the ascended adanists could easily match.

Their run took them down the hallways and into a grand hall, so big their small lights couldn't reach the walls or ceilings. Bael stared as he ran, wondering what powers and what patience must have been needed to hollow out such a structure in the middle of a mountain.

He wondered, too, at the lack of resistance. Granted, the emissaries had been a fight, and a tremendous one at that, but was Void so weak it couldn't summon more servants? Or was it so strong it didn't feel the need?

He asked Elyn as they ran.

"I think she's out of emissaries. I got the sense from the one that recruited me that there were never that many, and that they were hard to create and train."

"Let's hope that's true."

At the end of the enormous hall was a pedestal and what appeared to be a sphere of void. Bael slowed, but Elyn pulled on his arm. "No time. If we survive this and it remains, we can see if it works for you, too. It's the history of Void."

It was the wrong thing to tell him to get him to move, and if the stakes were any less, he might have stopped. As it was, Elyn dragged him past the pedestal as he stared. They entered a second hallway, smaller than the first, and Elyn led the way, still not needing light.

"Stay well behind me. If there are any traps, I'll sense them well before you do."

Bael slowed slightly so that she could pull ahead.

The hallway's ceiling was almost too low for Bael to run. He bent over and ran at a slight crouch, then cursed when he noticed the walls were squeezing in around his shoulders. Elyn, being smaller, wasn't as disturbed by the lack of space, but it wouldn't be that much longer before Bael and some of his warriors would have to slow down.

They made quick time as they hurried down the tunnel. Bael let his focus wander back to the Great Heart, where Samora was fully connected to the core of the world and ready to unleash its power. His throat tightened at the thought. He'd known, when he'd left, that it was likely the last time he'd ever see his grandmother, but knowing didn't make it any easier. He felt her adani mixed in with that of the Great Heart, vast and powerful, and he was proud to have known her.

Elyn stopped suddenly, wrenching his attention from the home world to this strange one. She studied stone knobs that grew out of both walls and the ceiling, the first real break from the monotony of the hallways since they'd entered the tunnel beyond the great hall.

"It's a trap, I think," Elyn answered before Bael could ask.

"You're not sure?"

Elyn studied them a moment longer. "No, I'm sure. There are lines of void running between the protrusions, like wire. Run through them, and you'd find yourself in more pieces than when you began."

"Destroy the knobs?"

She nodded, and Bael wove three small discs of adani. He

threw them so that they sliced through the knobs right next to the wall. The pieces fell and Elyn gave a satisfied grunt. "We're clear."

They resumed their run, but now that Bael was focused more on his immediate surroundings, he felt the presence of Void nearing. The air grew darker and heavier, so thick it felt as though he was breathing in a dense fog, though his sight was clear. He trembled at the sense of it.

Great powers were no revelation to him. He'd swum in the currents of the Great Heart and fought against emissaries, but still the sheer magnitude of Void took his breath away. Any comparison seemed insufficient, and he couldn't believe that this strength had once been a person, a being not that different than him. Given enough time, might he reach a similar level?

Would he even want to?

The adanists behind him started to slow noticeably as the weight of Void burdened their steps. Even Bael felt as though he pulled an enormous cart laden with heavy stones behind him. He couldn't imagine how the others suffered. Such was their determination, though, that they didn't utter a word of complaint. Though the ground sloped downward beneath their feet, every step seemed as though they climbed a steep incline.

Elyn discovered one more trap, which was destroyed as easily as the first, and then the hallway ended in a room unlike any that Bael had ever seen. A perfect sphere had been cut into the stone, the edges so smooth Bael had no problem believing that Void had carved it in a moment, the same dark strength that had destroyed so many lives on his world. The hallway's end appeared to be halfway up the sphere's height. The stone curved away both below and above.

Elyn gasped, though at what, Bael wasn't sure. The darkness ahead swallowed the light from his bound adani. He thrust the light forward, but it didn't penetrate, and he needed a moment to understand what he saw. The strength of Void was so overwhelming here, it was all he sensed.

He didn't realize, at first, he was staring upon the face of his enemy. It was nothing like Elian's stories of facing the Vada.

Bael had lived for the retellings of those stories when he'd been younger. A bloody battlefield, filled with monsters and heroes, with Elian leading one side and the Vada the other. A day overflowing with sword and spear, claw and tooth. The sort of battle a young boy could imagine fighting in, day after day, as he learned the arts of the wandering clans. How many times had he stood toe-to-toe against the Vada in his dreams?

Instead of a vicious monster, he was confronted by a darkness without form. Inside the sphere of stone was another sphere, filled with an inky darkness that flowed like a thick liquid. The sphere was maybe the width of a hand smaller than the stone walls which contained it.

"Is that it?" Bael whispered.

Elyn nodded.

"What do we do now?"

Elyn formed a sphere of void. "We kill her."

Bael pulled adani from the Great Heart, strengthening limb and will for the fight to come. Elyn waited one moment for him, then threw her attack at Void. It struck—something, though Bael couldn't say what it was—and rippled the surface of Void, but nothing else happened. The substance, or perhaps the energy, that rippled, hadn't looked like the walls of void he'd become used to fighting.

Elyn looked as confused as he felt. She sent another sphere, and then another, and each time, the reaction was the same. The ripple of something that wasn't void, followed by silence.

Bael swore he could hear Void laughing at them, though there was nothing to hear beyond the labored breathing of the adanists behind them. "Should I try?" he asked.

Elyn nodded and stood to the side. Bael formed a dart of adani and strengthened it with more light than any ascended adanist could summon. He threw the dart, only to see the same ripple and the same lack of effect.

"Together?"

Elyn shrugged, as one who was almost certain it wouldn't work but was willing to try anyway. She dutifully formed her sphere and he his dart, and though the two struck right beside the other, there was no destruction. Bael shook his head. They hadn't come all this way to fail now, especially not against an enemy that didn't fight back. He gathered more adani, but stopped short of unleashing everything at the sphere. Was this why they'd been allowed to proceed with so little resistance?

Although, again, eight emissaries were hardly a little resistance.

Regardless, this didn't have the feel of a problem that could be solved by throwing more adani at it. Neither his attack nor Elyn's had done the least to disturb whatever protected Void.

He glanced at Elyn. "Any other ideas?"

She stared into the sphere as though the darkness within had the answers regarding its own demise, then sat down cross-legged and closed her eyes. "Give me some time and silence, please. I'll see what I can find."

"We don't have much time," Bael said.

"I am well aware. Now please, be quiet."

Bael ground his teeth together, then nodded and encouraged the other adanists to take a few steps back with him. They all took seats and relaxed as best they could in the darkness and oppression of Void's heart. Bael shook his head and ran a hand through his hair. He would give anything to fight a mere Vada right about now.

ELYN REACHED out to the void and searched for the answers she was sure were hidden nearby. Something was happening here she didn't understand. So far as she knew, void devoured all it touched, including itself. Their entire mission revolved around that belief. So what force was this that now stood against her in their final moments? What resisted void and adani both, shrugging them off as though they were mere annoyances?

She breathed in deep and cleared her mind of thoughts. *Something* stood in her way, but there had to be a way around. All she needed was to learn how Void protected herself. She extended her own sense of void, not sure what she was looking for but hoping she would recognize it when she found it.

Strange, that even though she faced Void directly, her master and enemy felt distant to her senses, as though they were separated by worlds and not just a few paces. The dissonance was unsettling, but perhaps also explained by the barrier. Void must have established it, somehow, to protect herself against an eventual traitor. How else would she feel confident inviting her emissaries to her?

The void within Elyn vibrated at that question, providing part of the answer, perhaps. It was attached to her core, perhaps even an integral part, now. Void's death might very well be a suicide on her part, but she didn't dwell long on that. She deserved no less for the wrongs she'd done her family and the clans.

She let void drift forward like tendrils of adani, brushing lightly against the surface of the barrier. She'd expected to find some subtle weaving of void beyond her ability, but what she found instead was a mixture of one of adani's many cousins and void, a weaving that compensated for the weaknesses of both to become something stronger than either.

Elyn stared at it in awe, for she discerned a pattern to the weaving, but it lay beyond her understanding. She could tell it existed, but couldn't mimic nor unravel it. She knew what the barrier was, but that did nothing to help them. Whoever had created this wasn't just powerful, they were inspired. Of all the weavings she'd learned, this was the greatest, stronger even than the incredible power of Void.

Stronger by far.

The thought brought a frown to her face, and it shifted her perspective, as though someone strong had picked her up by her ankle and dangled her upside down. What if the barrier hadn't been meant to protect Void, but to contain her? Was that what she had sensed, that sudden ending, when she'd explored Void's memories?

What if this wasn't a home, but a cage?

Her adani and void danced faster across the surface of the barrier, and the longer she remained in contact with it, the more certain she became. Void's own presence, intimidating as it was, only leaked out through the tiniest of gaps of the weaving.

That's why she relied on the emissaries to spread her influence.

The new knowledge raised new questions, as it always did. What had happened to the being that had created this cage? Why, if such a being had once made the effort to contain Void, did it now allow Void to slowly weaken the bonds of her cage?

This weaving, strong and durable as it was, couldn't last forever. Nothing lasted forever. So why wasn't the captor somewhere nearby?

She didn't know the answers, but she could safely assume no help was coming. They had only her and Bael's strength to rely on. She couldn't reinforce the weave, as it was beyond her understanding, so they were left with the same problem they'd come here with.

How did they kill Void?

BAEL ALMOST JUMPED out of his skin when Elyn spoke. "I don't think it's a protective barrier. I think it's a cage."

He didn't bother standing. "Cage or barrier, we still need to kill it. Do you know how?"

"No. It's a very fine weaving of both void and something like adani. Beyond my skill." She went on to describe what she had sensed, and Bael listened carefully, though he doubted he could add anything Elyn hadn't already thought of. Her sensitivity to adani was much finer than his own.

But as she spoke, she reminded him of something, a story he'd once heard, though he could barely remember it. He raised his hand to stop her. "You're saying that the influence of Void is leaking out through very small gaps?"

Elyn nodded. "Very, very small gaps."

"Could we fit an attack through those gaps?"

"The idea is sound, but I don't know how we would. I could weave adani small enough, but as soon as it comes in contact with any of the void, it would be swallowed. I don't know that I have that type of control with void."

Bael rubbed at his eyes. They didn't have time for this. "I don't think we have much choice."

"Even if I could, the strength of the weaving is too great. Poking a little sphere of void through is one thing, but so what?"

Bael finally remembered the story Elyn's tale reminded him of. "Maybe we don't have to overpower it. Did Grandmother ever tell you of when she had to pass the elder dragon's trials?"

"Yes."

"Remember how she had to make a tiny cut with adani, and then the weaving fell apart?"

Elyn's eyes lit up. "I do."

"Could we do something similar?"

Elyn considered for a moment, then her face fell, the momentary joy gone. "No. the strands of the weaving are too strong.

Even if I could create something so small, I don't think I'd have enough adani to cut it."

"But I do, if you can pull from me."

The air around them suddenly vibrated, stealing the breath from Bael's lungs. Elyn clutched at her head as tears streamed from her eyes. She fell to her side and whimpered.

The assault passed soon, and once Bael could move again, he crawled to where Elyn lay. "Are you hurt?"

She pushed herself, shakily, to a sitting position. "No, but I think we're on the right track. Void just summoned all the emissaries back home. I think she's scared of us."

❧ 33 ❧

The emissaries' final attack dropped like a stone toward the world Samora had always known as home. Samora rushed through the web of adani and appeared upon the plateau. Now that the emissaries were no longer standing upon it, she was able to place herself directly beneath the falling sphere. It blotted out more of the sky as it fell, and Samora stared for one moment. The strength of all thirteen emissaries linked together was incredible, and she couldn't help but think that if it had been put to a better use, what a different world it could have been.

Except the void only destroyed. It did not bring life.

She raised one hand above her head and summoned a single dart, the most focused and powerful weave she knew.

She'd imagined that at the end, fear would have gripped her heart, and she would have had to summon strength from some deep well of courage. Instead she found only a weary and resigned determination. She thought of her children and grand-children, already so capable and growing more so every day. She would miss them, but that, too, would pass. So many were waiting for her, having already rejoined adani.

Just this one last work to take care of.

Samora opened the connection she shared with the Great Heart, mimicking the technique Elian had used earlier. The glow of the dart intensified, bright enough that it cast shadows miles away, and yet Samora could stare at it without hurting her eyes. She roped the dart to a strong thread of adani, then threw it at the sphere.

The moment void met adani, a rippling wave of force blasted away from the point of impact. The wave rushed over Samora, leaving her unharmed, but when it struck the plateau beneath her feet the mountains rumbled. On a distant mountaintop a small avalanche released from the snowpack above and slid to the valley below, destroying any tree foolish enough to be standing before it.

Void devoured the adani, as hungry and desperate as ever. Samora's dart could have carved through a dragon and still had enough energy left over to flatten a town, but the void licked it up with the eagerness of a child devouring sweet berries. Still, Samora's attack slowed the descent of the sphere until it stood in place above her.

Her body, this form she had assumed, burned like it had the very first times she'd connected with the hearts. Any physical form could only take so much adani, and as she channeled the strength straight from the Great Heart, up through the soles of her feet and through her hand into the sphere above, she stepped far beyond that limit.

When Elian had released the strength against the emissaries, it had landed with devastating effect. Now, against this coordinated attack, all Samora succeeded in doing was delaying the inevitable. The sphere spun as quickly as it ever had. Even with all her strength, the combined void of the emissaries overwhelmed her.

She tried to channel even more adani, but this form was already at its limit, and the void was devouring more adani than Samora had thought was possible. She kept pulling, hating that she had to ask for so much from the Great Heart. Enormous as it was, it wasn't limitless, and she sensed it pulling back from adani channels it had long nourished to answer her call.

And such was the danger the dragons had warned about. Adani possessed something resembling a will, but it was a servant of life, and it answered Samora when she begged its assistance. It would continue to answer that call long after Samora's need had passed, or after Samora's cause was doomed. Even a well-intentioned adanist, when granted this power, could have used it to destroy life across the world.

Samora felt life diminish. Groves withered and died, not because shadow spread across the land, but because she pulled away the adani that nourished it. Fish died in ponds and beehives went quiet. Rich green grasslands browned and grew brittle in moments, as though they hadn't seen rain for years.

What choice did she have but to keep pulling, though?

She was a healer. She always had been, from the very first time she wandered away from their small village in search of the wandering clans. No weaving brought her more pride than a healing, and her life's work had been to plant hearts across the land, bringing life wherever she traveled.

One by one those hearts winked out, like stars going dark in the night sky. Death crept across the land, and what she sensed was only the beginning of what would be difficult years. Cows survived the pull of adani, but they had no grass to eat, and within weeks, entire herds would die out. Deer and other wild game would be no different, and those that relied on such game, like the wandering clans, would soon be at risk.

She didn't want to think about what the cities would look like.

There had to be a way to pull more adani quickly. At this rate, even if she held the sphere off for good, the world would still die, as would all the people upon it. But her spirit was already burning away, carried off by the tremendous flow of adani rushing through her body. She called for adani's help, tugged with all the will she could summon, but it was all for naught.

The sphere began falling again, and Samora wasn't sure it was because her own strength began to wane, or the sphere's strength had increased. She gritted her teeth and sought any edge, but all she could do, with the whole world's adani at her disposal, was slow it down. She wasn't enough.

Then Samora swore she felt the brush of a familiar hand on her shoulder. Could almost hear Elian laughing softly in her ear, telling her not to worry so much. Aldrick stood behind her, wrapping her in his strong arms, answering all her doubts with his mere presence. Harald's booming laughter called for another cup of ale, and he seemed to be enjoying her performance.

"You're too smart for your good, girl," another voice said beside her, on the opposite side of Elian.

"I'm not strong enough, Karla. I can't pull enough adani at once."

"You know why your foolish brother was always a step ahead of you?"

Samora had no answer.

"Because he believed he should be."

The voices faded, but the presences remained. Real or imagined, Samora pulled again, imagining her hand scooping out huge chunks of adani from the Great Heart. Backed by generations of friends and family, she threw it forward.

The sphere trembled as the additional adani struck it. The voices of dozens rose as one and the head emissary screamed. Samora thanked the others as her own spirit finally began to crack apart from the strain. Everything that she knew as herself, her very awareness, began to fragment.

No fear accompanied the dissolution. Every piece of her that broke apart was caught by one of the presences surrounding her, who then carried it with honor back toward the Great Heart. Father and Mother accepted the final sacrifice of their daughter, cradling the fragments of her spirit the way they'd cradled her body when she'd been a baby. Elian escorted his fragment as though he was holding her hand, pulling her forward as he always had. And of course Aldrick, standing resolutely beside her, waiting to catch the final shards of her spirit.

They gave her the strength to hold on, to channel just a little more of the Great Heart at the assembled emissaries, even as the last bits of her spirit were stripped away. She smiled. She was sure she'd held the technique much longer than Elian had.

When they met again, he'd be jealous.

The air vibrated as the emissaries' shrieks turned into moans of pleasure. The sphere spun smoothly as even more void filled the sphere, and it began to fall once again.

All Samora could do was watch. Her spirit was already breaking apart and rejoining the great web of adani, which she feared wouldn't last much longer. She held on to what she could, keeping the channel open for as long as she could, but somehow, she had failed.

Or maybe their world had failed. It simply hadn't had enough adani to stand against such a force.

Her sight flickered as her body began to dissolve, and the void fell closer to the surface, now beyond her ability to slow or stop.

❧ 34 ❧

Elyn held onto the void as gently as she would a wounded butterfly she was trying to heal. Her emissary had never trained her to handle void in such minute amounts, for there had been no need. Void destroyed. What need was there for such fine work, creating a sphere as small as the sharpened point of a needle?

If not for her years of training with adani, under the watchful and ever-demanding eye of Father, there would have been no chance of success. Fortunately, she'd been trained by adanists of legend, and though void didn't weave the same way adani did, the two forces shared enough principles that she learned the manipulation quickly.

Bael's pacing behind her didn't help, as he waited for an emissary to appear before them.

From the way the void around them trembled, he might be waiting for a bit. Void's desperate call went unanswered, and between Bael's senses and her own, they had a good idea why. Samora, aided by the Great Heart, battled toe to toe with the assembled emissaries.

By itself, the act meant little. The emissaries could have answered the call despite their struggle against Samora.

Except the head emissary, in control of the emissaries' assembled power, wouldn't hear of it. Victory wasn't enough. Destruction wasn't enough.

As Elyn had long suspected, it was something deeper and darker than mere destruction that drove her. She wanted those with power to bend beneath her might. She needed to be placed above them, and for them to know that she, who'd once been powerless, had come to take her revenge. So she refused Void's call, the two wills in contest with one another.

Elyn couldn't say how the contest would end. Any moment now, the emissaries might respond to the call and appear, and if Elyn's weaving wasn't complete by then, she'd never finish it. She shaped the sphere again, shaving off a piece of no larger than the width of a hair.

"Are you done yet?" Bael asked.

She ground her teeth together. "You'd know if I was, trust me. Now be silent so I can focus."

"Right. Sorry." He resumed his pacing, paused for a moment, then decided it was a forgivable sin and continued. Step, step, turn.

She didn't mind. His steps carried an even beat she could lose herself in, and she did. The weaving was more delicate than any she'd attempted, and mixing adani and void presented a fresh layer of problems. The two forces couldn't touch, exactly, but adani needed to follow immediately behind void, to rip open what void penetrated. With more time she and Bael might have been able to perform the technique together, but it would take dozens of practice attempts, which they didn't have. The responsibility was hers alone, powered by Bael's connection to the Great Heart.

Elyn shaved off another bit of the void, making it as small as she felt she was capable of. A weave of adani followed behind it, and both were stable, at least for the moment. A bead of sweat dripped down her forehead and she reached out to Bael. "It's time."

A tilt of his head summoned the others, who embraced as much adani as their ascended hearts would allow. Once they were in position, Bael put his hand in Elyn's. "Good luck."

"Better lucky than skilled, right?"

The corner of his mouth turned up in a grin. It had been one of Father's sayings. "I'd rather be both, honestly. Never could bring myself to tell him that, though."

Elyn nodded, and Bael channeled strength through the Great Heart and straight into her. It threatened to overwhelm her for a moment, until she stopped trying to hold it and instead settled for funneling it toward the weave she'd created earlier. The thread of adani was thinner than one of her hairs, but as it collected more adani it began to glow with the light of a late evening summer sun.

She grunted when she could take no more of Bael's strength. It was already more than she could weave on her own. It would have to be enough. She moved the point of void and the trailing adani, which continued to glow brighter as it neared the barrier.

Within the barrier, the darkness churned as though it was one of the swirling, destructive clouds that sometimes formed during intense storms on the plains. Void strained against her cage, but the legendary working held against the onslaught. Elyn positioned the point of void directly over the barrier and worked her way closely in. Soon she hovered the point in the minuscule gap between two threads. She took a deep breath and shoved it in.

Void penetrated, creating the tiniest of incisions that began to close as soon as it was opened. She followed it, though, with a powerful thread of adani, which wedged itself in the crack and held it open. Bael yelled as the weaving attempted to close on the adani and cut the thread.

"Let go!" he shouted, and after a moment of trying to figure out what he meant, Elyn dropped his hand and broke her connection to him.

He'd created another weave connecting him to her original thread, and he filled the thread with adani, holding it open with a strength that would have killed Elyn if she'd attempted to channel it. Even so, she sensed that he was losing the battle.

There were more contestants in the space, though, than just the weaving and the adanists, and Void saw the first real crack in her cage in countless generations. She wasn't about to let the opportunity slip her by. Needles of void worked their way around the thread of adani, fighting back the healing efforts of the barrier. Once she became involved, it was only a matter of time.

The barrier cracked, then broke apart with less than a whimper. One moment, it was the most impressive weaving Elyn had ever witnessed, the next it was simply gone, as though she'd imagined it during a fever dream.

Void, though, was more than eager to make her presence known. The darkness that had been contained exploded outward, devouring stone as though it were warm bread. One of Bael's adanists had taken position closer to the sphere, to protect against any emissaries that appeared before them, and he simply vanished before he even realized he was in danger.

Elyn only had time to gasp, and if not for Bael's inhuman reflexes, would have died as a result of her foolishness. Who were they, to think they could stand against a force as ancient and powerful as Void?

Bael surrounded them with adani channeled straight from the Great Heart, creating a bubble around them and protecting them from Void's fury. Powerful as he was, though, it wouldn't last. His protective sphere shrank against the onslaught of Void's power.

Elyn couldn't see beyond the sphere of golden light, but she could sense what was happening well enough. Void devoured all the stone that had formed her prison, and in just a few moments she had already reached the surface. Her hunger was so large it might as well have been infinite, for she'd eaten enough stone to create a range of mountains, and it hadn't slowed her a bit. Before long this world would be gone, and then who knew what next?

Void's advance slowed for the briefest of moments as the dragons on the surface unleashed their adani against it, but they might as well have tried to restrain one of their own with twine.

"Now!" Bael shouted.

His shout brought her back to her purpose, the reason why she was here. She turned her senses away from the rapidly expanding perimeter of destruction and to where they were. Her eyes went wide.

Bael's protection might have been shrinking, but he was also pushing against the vast forces emanating from the heart of Void, and he'd gotten them closer to the core of Void's spirit. She couldn't imagine the amount of strength it had taken, and when she glanced back at him, she saw his physical form fading as he fought them forward.

Elyn formed a sphere of void and Bael opened a tiny gap in the sphere. Spikes of void punched through the gap, and Elyn just slid to the side before one pierced her chest. She threw the sphere, and though it passed through the hole and created chaos as it pushed toward the heart, the amount of void fighting against it overwhelmed it.

With a long shout loud enough to shake leaves from healthy trees, Bael closed the gap and pushed them forward more. He didn't have much longer, and though they'd gotten close, they still hadn't reached the heart.

Tears ran down her face. "I'm sorry. I can't."

In spite of it all, Bael grinned, and she swore that some part of her mad cousin was enjoying this, a fight against the most powerful force they'd ever encountered. "Maybe try a spear? Shape the void like you would adani?"

A dangerous idea, but a good one. She'd never seen the emissaries form a spear, but she'd seen the swords many of the servants preferred and made her own.

Bael gave one last push of their sphere of adani, then opened another gap. Void spiked through, and two spikes dug deep into Bael's flesh. Elyn stood to the side of the opening and thrust the sword through. At first, it felt as though she was stabbing into the side of a mountain, but slowly, the void within her dug slowly, inexorably, toward Void's heart.

She screamed and thrust with every bit of strength she had left as the sphere of adani began to collapse around them. The tip bit into something that felt like flesh and she pushed harder. Then the blade slid in, and the last bit was as easy as cutting butter.

The darkness around them disappeared and they fell, but not so far as Elyn thought they would. Her ankle twisted as she landed, but she hardly noticed. The spherical hole in the stone they'd originally discovered was now the bottom of a vast hole that reached up to the sky, and when she looked up, she saw three dragons had survived and were overhead.

Of Void, there was no trace.

✼ 35 ✼

Samora couldn't hold adani any longer. Her spirit was too fractured and broken to exert her will, and she was beyond caring, surrounded by warmth and the peace she'd desired for so many years. The void fell, but there was nothing she could do about it anymore. She felt herself dissolving even as it came to destroy all that she held dear.

And then it was gone. One emissary remained, the one who'd been in the center, controlling the force of the others, but it hardly lasted any longer. Its body turned into a light mist that was gently blown away by a mountain breeze, and the air was clear.

Samora smiled. She had an impressive family, that she did.

She was leaving their world in good hands.

Adani welcomed her, and though they were transformed into something different than the wills and spirits that had defined them in life, she sensed all those she'd loved around her.

Aldrick, of course, but Harald and Karla, too, and so many who'd left to rejoin adani before her, paving the way for her own return.

And Elian. Incredible Elian, shining bright even in a sea of light.

And Mother. And Father, who'd been waiting so long to hold his daughter again.

She fell into them all, became a part of all, and was no more.

❧ 36 ❧

Bael almost felt human again. The strength and vitality he'd come to think of as his own had faded, partially because adani had faded and partially because he only allowed himself to sip at the well he'd once been happy to take great gulps from.

The damage done to the Great Heart in the battle had come close to destroying it for good. Too close. He felt its weakness as his own, as though he'd pushed himself too hard during training and needed a good night's rest to recover.

In the case of the Great Heart, its rest would take generations, at least, to regain even half the strength it had once had. As limited in scope as the physical battle had been, the ripples of it would echo for decades to come. Crops and smaller animals had died in uncounted masses, and even larger animals that were weak or injured had died in certain areas. He foresaw famine and conflict ahead, and there were many deaths yet to come. The small comfort of knowing that his people were no longer under the knife of extinction eased his mind some, but he still worried about the future.

Had Grandmother and Elian felt the same after they'd finished their fight with the Vada?

Grandmother had gone wandering for years after the final battle, and Bael now better understood why. When he considered the list of problems still facing him, it made him want to run away, too.

The wandering clans were more fractured than they'd been since he'd been born, largely due to his own actions. Nothing of his own, temporary clan remained. All were either dead or had moved back to their original clans. The youths that had dreamed of fighting a battle worthy of legend were now content to turn their adani to more peaceful purposes.

The cities still held to their prohibitions regarding the wandering clans, but Bael didn't expect those to last long. They would be among the worst hit in the coming years, and they'd need the wandering clans' assistance to survive.

Everything needed fixing. Cities, farmland, and relationships alike.

He turned at the sound of small, running feet. "Dad!"

Bael caught Juula in one arm, and her mere presence was enough to bring a smile to his face. Maybe not everything needed fixing. There were a few things that were perfect as they were. "How are you, little one?"

She ignored his question, too focused on completing her own mission to think of anything else. "Play? Mother says you have to."

Bael laughed, "Well, if Mother says so, then I have no choice but to obey."

He spent most of the afternoon chasing after her, finding her no matter where she hid. Her determination to best him was endless, and her small legs were oblivious to all fatigue. When she finally announced that it was time to be done, they'd wandered more than a mile away from the camp. He picked her up in his arms and carried her back. She nestled close to him and promptly fell asleep.

Shayna was smoking strips of meat when he returned, and she

smiled when she saw Juula asleep in his arms. "I see you finally tired her out."

"That was almost as exhausting as fighting an emissary. Did I have that much enthusiasm when I was young?"

"More. She's a lamb compared to what your poor mother had to put up with."

She stood up and helped part the flaps of the tent so that Bael could lay Juula down in her bed. Once she was covered and sound asleep, they left the tent together.

"So, what have you decided?" Shayna asked.

"She needs a clan. We need a clan. I think we should return and ask Father to vouch for us. He's not leader anymore, but his word still carries plenty of weight."

Shayna didn't look as convinced as Bael thought she would be. "I agree that Juula needs more than just us, but I fear returning to a clan won't be as easy as you think. Killan might welcome you back with open arms, but there will be arguments about allowing you in the council. At the very least, you'll be expected to follow all their orders."

They were good points, one and all, and true, also. He and Elyn might have stopped the emissaries from destroying the world, but he'd angered plenty of adanists on the journey. One would think saving their lives would earn him some good grace, but it didn't take long for old grudges to surface.

"That's fine. We have time, now, and even if I disagree with the councils, I can't imagine them doing something so foolish that I would have to disobey them like I have in the past couple of years."

Shayna arched her eyebrow, daring him to support that claim, but he just smiled. "At least, if they do, that's a battle we can fight when we come to it. There's no need to deny Juula a clan simply because we're worried what might be."

"Then I agree. When do you want to leave?"

"Tomorrow? I can call for a dragon and we can fly over."

Shayna shook her head. "I'd like to walk, if you don't mind."

Bael shrugged. "Fine by me. Why?"

"More time together as a family. More time for Juula to get used to us, and for us to get used to her. But also to give you the time to settle into more of a routine. We've been on the move for a long time, and it'll be good to slow down, especially as we transition to a more normal clan life."

He leaned over and kissed her. "You're a wise woman."

"Don't worry. I won't let you forget it."

WHILE JUULA WAS STILL SLEEPING and Shayna didn't need his help, he darted through the web of adani, only to rise again upon a field that had seen much better days. His arrival was greeted by the sound of a mallet pounding a wooden joint into position.

"It's looking good," he said, and he sincerely meant it. Building had never been a skill he possessed, and he still awed at the way some people could take raw materials and turn them into something useful. He supposed he did something similar with adani, but he'd never looked at his gift in that way.

Elyn stepped away from her new house and wiped the sweat from her brow. She still appeared alarmingly pale, but Bael knew better than to say anything. She'd snapped at him the last time he'd tried.

The destruction of Void had almost killed them both, and neither of them preferred to be reminded of those moments. She'd held onto consciousness after Void's death by no more than a thread, and he'd heaved her over his shoulder as one of the remaining dragons landed nearby. How he'd climbed onto a dragon with her over his shoulder still confused him, but he'd found himself hanging on for his life as the dragon had flown as quickly as it could toward the portal.

Bael had been sure that after everything, the portal would close before they passed through, and they'd be stranded on a dead world.

They'd made it through with not more than a moment to spare. As soon as she felt the sun on her face, Elyn had lost consciousness and the portal had closed, nearly chopping the tail off the last dragon to fly through. He'd pumped adani into his cousin, but even then, hadn't been sure she'd live. The void within her was gone, but her body had grown used to the parasite, and her survival had been in question for days.

He was glad to see her on her feet, though from the way she looked, perhaps it would have been wiser for her to remain at rest. She'd claimed, on his last visit, that her body was healing, but that the process was slow. It had gotten used to Void's presence within her.

"Thank you."

"I'll admit you've made much more progress than I expected. At this rate, you'll have the home done within another two eighthdays."

"Being an adanist again makes this build considerably easier than the first. I can cut down trees and shape boards in moments instead of days."

Bael looked over the house and at the fields, which also showed some evidence of repair. Her harvest would be poor to almost nonexistent this year, but that was the case everywhere. With her access to adani, she had a better chance than most. "You're really committed to this, aren't you?"

"I am. I'm not sure it will be a permanent decision, but for now, it seems the least I can do."

It seemed a waste, especially during a time when humanity would need every shred of strength it could lay its hands on. They'd already debated the points, though, and Elyn had been firm. He couldn't help but try again.

"Shayna and I have decided to return to Father and ask to be part of the clan again. I'd vouch for you, too, if you wanted to join us."

A haunted look appeared behind Elyn's gaze, and she shook her head. "I know you mean well, and I appreciate your kindness, but please don't ever make that offer again. I have no place in the wandering clans."

"You saved all of them. That counts for more than you think."

"In your eyes, maybe, but not theirs. I don't believe I deserve their forgiveness, and I've made my peace with that. More to the point, though, I don't want to wander. What little desire I had for exploration was satiated for the rest of my life on that other world. I want to put down roots somewhere."

"You could always do it in a city. They'll have a great need for adanists there, and no one would need to know who you are."

"Can you imagine me living in a city? I may not have a place in the clans, but I'm still too much a child of the clans to live there."

"But you've also tried living here before, and I don't remember you being that pleased by it."

She nodded at that. "True enough, but times change. Before … I think I was waiting for something to happen. For Father to come and beg forgiveness. I don't think I was truly living—more like I was waiting. But I'm not anymore. Now I'm here, building something. Maybe it's small and maybe it doesn't matter much in the larger plan, but it's mine. I think that's enough."

How could he argue against that? He let the argument go. "In that case, could you use a hand?"

"I'd love one."

"I can't help for long, but Juula's down for a nap right now."

He helped Elyn lift some boards into place and held them fast as she secured them. She worked quickly, and Bael soon lost himself in the work. So many of his problems, so many of every-one's problems, were going to affect them for years and would take slow years of constant effort and sacrifice to fix. Seeing

Elyn's house come together, in an afternoon, before his eyes, reassured him that larger problems could also be solved.

Just so long as they figured out how to build together. It would be a struggle, and would probably always be a struggle, but it would be worth it.

When he next glanced at the sun, he realized he should probably be off. Elyn encouraged him to stay for a moment longer. "There's something I wanted to show you."

He followed her around her house to the back, where the stream trickled quietly by on its long journey to a river and then to the sea.

Two stones had been set side by side, carved with adani in such a way that they fit together, and when they were together, made a circle. A name was on each stone.

Samora.

Elian.

Tears sprang, unbidden, to Bael's face as he nodded. "They'd approve, I think."

"Good. I was hoping you'd think so."

Bael wasn't sure how history would remember the siblings. They'd given everything to protect the world, but they'd exacted a cost it would take generations to repay. It was a steep price to pay to avoid extinction, but survival was all that mattered.

Perhaps they were right. Perhaps this power was too great for them to handle. He didn't know.

All he knew was what Grandmother and Elian had done for humanity, and for as long as he was around, he'd make sure to spread the tale.

"Thank you for showing me this," he said.

Elyn nodded, and with a deep bow to his cousin, he departed. He had one more stop he wanted to make before he returned to his family.

BAEL REAPPEARED outside the Scorpion stronghold, high in the mountains. His arrival inspired a wide range of reactions from the guards walking the walls, from deep bows to shouts of welcome to a few cold glares. He bowed toward the walls, then walked to the gate, which opened for him without challenge. One of the adanists standing guard met him on the other side of the wall. "We've been wondering when you would show."

It wasn't intended as a challenge, and Bael dipped his head toward the adanist. "I wanted to ensure Erhart and Amelyn heard from their own adanists before I arrived."

"They're in the castle and will be eager to see you. Amelyn, in particular, has many questions."

Bael made his way down the narrow streets of the Scorpion stronghold, smiling to himself at the twist of fate the Scorpions now faced. For generations they had held fast to their mountains, largely separated from the battles and conflicts that had raged among the other wandering clans. It wasn't until Elian had recruited them to fight the Debru that they'd come down from the mountains and spoken up around the council fires.

Now it sounded as though Amelyn and Erhart had become the leaders that all the other clans looked to for guidance. Amelyn had assumed the role back when the head emissary had issued her ultimatum, and no one was interested in challenging her for the position.

Bael didn't blame them for not seeking the responsibility. Amelyn had no easy task before her.

He found the Scorpion elder and leader inside the castle, waiting for him inside their receiving room. He bowed down deeply to them, and the gesture was returned in smaller measure.

Erhart spoke first, as befitted the leader of the Scorpions. "We have heard the stories of the adanists that have returned to us, difficult as they are to believe. We'd hear, now, your account of the story."

Bael obliged, holding nothing back, for there was no need for secrets. Erhart and Amelyn listened without interruption, and when he was finished, silence settled over the room for a good while. Eventually, Amelyn asked, "So it's over, then? Void is gone?"

"She is, and yes, as far as I can tell, the threat of Void is over."

"There's no trace in Elyn?"

"None."

Erhart and Amelyn shared a look, and Erhart said. "The fact that Void was contained by a weaving so far beyond our skill concerns us. Have either you or Elyn learned the source of the weaving?"

"No, sir. Elyn speculates that because the weave was slowly unraveling, whoever created it is likely gone. Dead, maybe, but there's no telling. What Elyn did learn as she was upon the Void's home planet was that life has arisen time and time again throughout the stars. She saw many visions of societies stronger than ours, and it's possible the weaving came from one of them. We are not alone."

"Does that knowledge worry you?" Erhart asked.

"A little. Only because it means there may be threats out there we don't know about. But it might also mean we have allies on different worlds. Whoever caged Void certainly seems to qualify. Ultimately, I don't think it matters in the immediate future. Whether we are alone or not, our only goal needs to be rebuilding our world. We need to recover regardless."

The answer didn't satisfy the Scorpions, but Bael didn't have a better one to offer. His comment led naturally, though, into the daunting task facing the clans, which was to restore life to an injured world.

They danced around the subject for a bit, speaking of herds, fields, and the needs of the cities before Amelyn addressed the root cause directly.

"Did you kill the Great Heart?" she asked.

"No, but there's no denying that it's wounded."

"Can it be healed?"

"Not through any act I'm capable of. Healing the Great Heart will likely require generations of consistent effort."

"Of what nature?" Erhart asked.

"I'm not entirely sure. My best suggestion would be for the wandering clans to all take up the work my grandmother began after the defeat of the Debru. You should continue to wander, planting new hearts wherever you go, and you must be careful about how they are used. I do not think it is wise for the clans to forget how to ascend using the hearts, but I question whether the practice needs to be as common as it has been for my generation. And no one, I think, should complete the transformation I underwent. Not until you better understand what it means."

"You talk of 'you,' instead of 'we.'" Amelyn observed.

"The wandering clans are as safe as I can make them, and I do not intend to make use of my connection to the Great Heart unless in the most dire of needs. I plan on asking my father if I may rejoin his clan, but I seek no leadership."

"You are still the most sensitive being on this continent," Amelyn said.

"And if that skill is useful, I'm at your service. My eyes will remain open, and I will watch and help how I can, but I hope it will be in the role of a mere adanist and nothing more."

"It's a shame you only learn humility after nearly destroying our world," Erhart said.

The comment slid off Bael without touching him. "Is there anything else?"

Erhart looked ready to throw him out the door, but Amelyn held up a hand. "We've sent our healers to the town destroyed by the head emissary, and they're disturbed by the perfect lack of adani within the circles of the void's destruction. Can they be healed?"

"With time, perhaps. You can't force adani through what has been destroyed, but adani is life itself. It spreads. Hopefully, one day it figures a way to grow where the void struck, but I fear it will not be for some time."

Amelyn nodded. "Then go in peace. Hopefully for a very long time."

Bael was only too happy to obey. He'd been gone for too long, and he feared Shayna would have need of him soon.

FORTUNATELY, when he returned, Juula was just beginning to stir from her slumber. He picked her up and carried her outside. She yawned and stretched in the late afternoon sun, and of all the wonders he had seen, none compared to her smile when she saw him there. Amelyn, Erhart, and the Scorpions would lead the rebuilding of the land and the healing of the Great Heart. Elyn, he hoped, would find the peace she sought as she became a farmer once again. And as for him?

Juula laughed and tickled his beard, and Shayna came beside him and wrapped her arm around his waist, snuggling in close. He knew what he wanted to build, too, and it was right here.

Blades of the Fallen

Nightblade's Vengeance

Nightblade's Honor

Nightblade's End

Saga of the Broken Gods

Band of Broken Gods

Fall of Forgotten Gods

Rise of the Resurrected God

Oblivion's Gate

The Gate Beyond Oblivion

The Gates of Memory

The Gate to Redemption

Relentless

Relentless Souls

Heart of Defiance

Their Spirit Unbroken

The Sentinels Saga (with Taylor Crook)

Path of the Eternal Sun

A Path Divided

A Path Reforged

Primal

Primal Dawn

Primal Darkness

Primal Destiny

Song of the Fallen Swords

These Fallen Swords

Standalone Novels

The Last Fang of God

Blades of Shadow: A Nightblade Story

ABOUT THE AUTHOR

Ryan Kirk is the award-winning and internationally bestselling author of over thirty fantasy novels spanning nearly a dozen worlds. He lives in Minnesota with his family, where he enjoys long, meandering walks outside even when the snow is high enough to cover his legs. When he isn't glued to his keyboard, he's usually in the woods, either on foot or on bike.

facebook.com/waterstonemedia
instagram.com/authorryankirk
bookbub.com/authors/ryan-kirk